40 Fights Between
Husbands and Wives

40 Fights Between Husbands and Wives

COLM LIDDY

PENGUIN
IRELAND

PENGUIN IRELAND

Published by the Penguin Group
Penguin Ireland, 25 St Stephen's Green, Dublin 2, Ireland
(a division of Penguin Books Ltd)
Penguin Books Ltd, 80 Strand, London WC2R 0RL, England
Penguin Group (USA) Inc., 375 Hudson Street, New York, New York 10014, USA
Penguin Group (Australia), 250 Camberwell Road, Camberwell, Victoria 3124, Australia
(a division of Pearson Australia Group Pty Ltd)
Penguin Group (Canada), 90 Eglinton Avenue East, Suite 700, Toronto, Ontario, Canada M4P 2Y3
(a division of Pearson Penguin Canada Inc.)
Penguin Books India Pvt Ltd, 11 Community Centre,
Panchsheel Park, New Delhi – 110 017, India
Penguin Group (NZ), 67 Apollo Drive, Rosedale, North Shore 0632, New Zealand
(a division of Pearson New Zealand Ltd)
Penguin Books (South Africa) (Pty) Ltd, 24 Sturdee Avenue,
Rosebank, Johannesburg 2196, South Africa

Penguin Books Ltd, Registered Offices: 80 Strand, London WC2R 0RL, England

www.penguin.com

First published 2009
1

Copyright © Colm Liddy, 2009

Set in Imprint MT
Typeset by Palimpsest Book Production Limited, Grangemouth, Stirlingshire
Printed in Great Britain by Clays Ltd, St Ives plc

A CIP catalogue record for this book is available from the British Library

ISBN: 978-1-844-88191-8

www.greenpenguin.co.uk

For my own darling wife, Niamh
*So there! All my messing on the computer was not
a complete waste of time . . .*

'I do'

You take for better or worse, for richer or poorer, in sickness and in health, all the days of your life . . .

Because you are deeply in love with your perfect soul-mate, in union for all eternity.

Or because you've been going out together for seven years and, though the passion is long since dead, you couldn't contemplate splitting because then it would all seem like such a waste. Anyway, it's too late to back out, not without making a massive scene. It would absolutely kill your mother. His mother too, for that matter. Like everyone else, they think you make such a cute couple. They think you're perfect for each other. And in a way they're right. This past year, living together, has proved that: though not great lovers, you two are perfect flatmates.

Or because your bride has missed three periods already and she didn't want a bump to spoil the photos. Jesus' sake, my boy! In less than six months you're going to be a daddy. And whose fault is that?

Hers, for not being on the pill? Or yours, for not wanting to spoil the moment by getting back out of bed, finding a condom in the sock drawer, tearing the foil, putting it in place and rolling it down while carefully squeezing out any pockets of air?

Or because the harvest was poor, the pig died, the tax is due, the local priest laid a curse and the hens are staying in their shed, looking decidedly unwell? Or your parents have sold you in exchange for some goats?

Because.

Because.

Because.

Whatever the reason for marrying, though, even starting with the best of love, the time will come when something is wrong in the marriage.

Which can no longer be ignored and simply must be fixed . . .

When the other person needs to do something or say something differently . . .

But they don't do and they don't say. Well, maybe once or twice, they make a half-hearted attempt to shape up, but it doesn't last long. And then you just have to face it: the other person will never really be fixed.

You may accept this and focus instead on all the good things. Or you may not. Either way, the thought must sometimes flicker through your mind that you were once asked a question, and that you could have taken the other option and said . . .

'I don't'

1

The bride is crying in a toilet cubicle

Roscommon, Ireland, 2006

The bride is crying in a toilet cubicle. She is crying for two reasons, the second of which is she desperately needs to pee and can't. The problem is her wedding dress is so large that it takes up the entire space. One minute ago, she bolted into the cubicle as voices approached, girls from work looking for a mirror to reapply lipstick and check hairdos. Once in, the bride managed to twist around sufficiently to close and bolt the door but then found herself stuck.

Stitched deep within the fabric of the dress is a series of three wooden hoops that maintain its magnificent volume. Somehow, somewhere behind her, one of these hoops has got caught on the toilet-roll holder. She has tried several times and found that she cannot take a step back, or a step forward. She has tried shaking it loose, but the problem is directly behind her so she can't see how.

She closes her eyes and leans her head against the wall for support. She is not at all noisy but her chest makes jerky little spasms. Her make-up, which had been so lovely, is being ruined. She thinks back to this morning, when the lady from the beauty salon came out to the house and did up herself and the two bridesmaids in the front room. They all had a glass of champagne. Well, it was supposed to be champagne but the second bridesmaid forgot and could find only sparkling wine in the local Londis.

In a moment of inspiration the bride tries to wriggle out from under the dress, but the back is a lattice of pearl buttons and knots that only a bridesmaid could open.

In the neighbouring toilet cubicle sits her first bridesmaid and best friend since they met in the Gaeltacht, summer '93. In normal circumstances she would have heard something of the bride's distress and rushed to her aid. Hers, however, are not normal circumstances. She is sitting on a closed toilet seat with her left breast exposed. Clamped upon it is an electric breast pump, and it is making a loud rhythmic humming noise as it extracts the milk. Loud enough so that she hears nothing of the goings-on around her.

She has recently had a baby boy. At the moment he's being minded in the hotel room above by a babysitter. The first bridesmaid has left a bottle of boiled cooled water and a plastic canister containing six scoops of formula, so the sitter can feed him if he wakes up starving and it's absolutely necessary. But, all the same, she'd really rather he was fed exclusively on breast milk. There is an absolute ton of research about the benefits in terms of intelligence, physical development and especially susceptibility to disease and disorder. It's simply not worth it. Once the other breast is emptied she'll drop the contents up to the room and be back on the dance floor before anyone knows she was gone. She looks down along her cerise gown and notices that her belly looks bloated again. Jesus! But then it's been only five weeks since the birth and also the meal portions were gi-normous! That girl taking the orders was spot on when she recommended the braised lamb.

In the third cubicle sits a member of the hotel staff, again on a closed toilet seat. At this exact moment she should be working, clearing tables, but instead she is reading a copy of *OK!* magazine. Between scanning articles about Posh and Becks she breaks off to just stare into space. She is seriously considering a one-way ticket back to Warsaw.

The waitress arrived in Ireland just seven months ago. She was hoping for a new life of opportunity and a higher standard of living. The reality, so far, has fallen short. She is living in accommodation that she shares with three Latvians, none of whom she particularly likes. They made her take the box room. They never trouble themselves to wash the grill after cooking meat. She has two jobs: this one as a casual waitress at weddings on the weekends and another stacking shelves in a supermarket by night. Both for the minimum wage.

Back in Warsaw she qualified as a pharmacist. However, her degree counts for nothing over here. She applies for all sorts of pharmacy jobs but they simply throw her CV in the bin. The problem, as an official from the HSE told her, is that as yet 'the EU does not recognize professional qualifications from the newer accession states'.

In both her jobs, she meets many other Poles. The new duty manager is from the same street as hers in Warsaw. They were in the same school, even the same class together. The waitress was quiet and studious; this other girl, disruptive and bold. Back in Poland, it was always clear which girl would come to something. But here in Ireland? Here, she must take orders from a fucking *prostytutka*!

In the fourth toilet cubicle sits an elderly lady. She is a dear neighbour of the groom's family. She is partly thinking what a nice surprise it was to find Father Pat Murnane seated at her table – using two walking sticks but mentally still perfectly agile. He must be – what? Ninety-four or ninety-five at least. She assumed he was dead long since. God knows, nearly everyone else is, at this stage! But mostly she is thinking about her task in hand, that for which the toilet was intended. As she waits impatiently for the second instalment another thought occurs. 'When I get back to the table, I really must ask Father Pat whatever became of Father Michael?'

In the fifth and last cubicle there is a man sitting on a closed toilet seat. He is the groom and he is not wearing his trousers. They have been pulled off and thrown on the floor towards the front of the cubicle. Straddling him is a woman with a cerise dress hitched above her hips. Their nether regions are conjoined, and his face is buried between her bosoms. They are rocking very slightly and trying to be Oh So Very Quiet.

They were discovered by the bride, one minute ago, when she was desperately seeking a free cubicle in the ladies and noticed something very odd. On the tiles, just inside one of the doors, was a gleaming and distinctive belt buckle. Tilting her head sideways and crouching down (as much as her dress would allow), the bride saw the crumpled pair of trousers to which the belt was attached. She recognized the label inside the waistband and the design all too well. Hadn't she gone for the fitting months ago, when choosing which suit he would hire? Hadn't she picked up the outfit herself in Fitzpatrick's when her husband-to-be could not find the time?

As to what he was doing? She pressed her ear to the door and detected just enough rhythm to know that his 'mistake' with the stripper on his stag night was being repeated only inches away from her.

As to with whom? She didn't have to see to know it was her second bridesmaid. The one with the big tits and nothing else to recommend her. The one who was a total bitch. The one who was her cousin. The one that she never wanted as a bridesmaid in the first place, only her mother guilt-tripped her into it. Since they were born on the same day twenty-nine years ago, their mothers have maintained the fantasy that they're the best of friends. They're not.

The bride's first instinct was to pound the door, to scream at her husband and scrape her fingernails across the second bridesmaid's face. But she didn't. Somehow she was not one hundred per cent surprised and had already half rehearsed such a situation in her mind. She realized that to face them down here, in public, would only invite pity and bring mortification upon herself. Everyone would see. And those who didn't see would be told by those who had. And then they'd all stand around in huddles whispering. Saying what an awful man he was. *Awful! And the bride? Poor thing.*

Imagine – on what should have been the best day of her life. Yes, a pathetic poor thing. As if they were really sorry. When, in fact, they'd be delighted to have something so juicy to gossip about.

Then the bride heard the girls from work coming into the ladies and bolted into the first cubicle.

In the fifth cubicle they begin to rock a little faster. Then faster still. They allow themselves the odd gasp and moan, moving now in a determined fashion towards the finish line.

But all is not well. The second bridesmaid is a substantial girl, and, as her feet leave the floor, her weight falls fully on the groom. His body slips slightly sideways, and as a consequence he feels the flushing lever pressing into one of his back ribs. It's uncomfortable, and as their combined weight shifts further it feels downright painful. In an attempt to straighten up, he removes a hand from her buttock and pushes against the cubicle wall. But he can't manage it. Now the toilet lever is boring a hole in his back. He stops rocking. It matters not: the second bridesmaid continues heedlessly. As his potential orgasm drains away, it does sound very like she is coming.

The bride is still crying in a toilet cubicle but not as intensely as before. She is sitting down on the toilet, and one of her reasons for crying has disappeared: the wooden hoop in her dress is now broken.

She tears off two squares of toilet tissue and blows her nose. Then she flushes the toilet. At the same moment, the four neighbouring toilets also flush. It's time for the bride – it's time for all of them – to go back out to the wedding party.

2

Always and everywhere, until the end of time

Kinshasa, Belgian Congo, 1881

'I love you,' he whispered, one romantic evening before they were married.
'Perhaps,' she replied. 'But for how long?'

During his time in the Congo, the linguist Ferdinand de Saussure conducted a remarkable experiment. Being something of a genius, he was bored and unfulfilled by his job translating Swahili into German. So he employed a gang of local coolies to round up twenty-seven mangabey monkeys from the surrounding jungle and bring them to his home on the outskirts of Kinshasa. A three-storey mansion, it had a large open-plan basement that proved a perfect holding pen. He furnished the chamber with climbing frames, leafy branches and an abundance of tropical foods. The only incongruous articles were a carved rosewood desk in the centre, a thick ledger upon it, beneath it a chair. His plan was to study the monkeys at close quarters and perhaps learn the basics of their language.

*

Ferdinand had married his wife, Madeline, just before leaving Zurich. Theirs had been a whirlwind romance.

'I love you,' he had whispered as the sun set behind Walche Bridge.

'Perhaps,' Madeline said. 'But for how long?'

'Always and everywhere,' said Ferdinand, pulling her close, 'until the end of time.'

That seemed to satisfy her. She accepted his proposal, and once they arrived in Africa she proved an excellent wife. Unfazed by the tropical heat, or by the alien habits of a strange people, the feisty French girl was a capable mistress of the house. While her husband spent more time on his monkey project in the basement, Madeline organized her servants into a thorough refurbishment of the mansion. She was also attentive to her new husband in many small ways. Worried, for instance, by the effect on his posture of sitting for long hours on a hard chair, she insisted he place a cushion behind the small of his back. When Ferdinand's dedication kept him below at lunchtime, she hurried down the staircase with a cold salad. If he remained at his desk burning midnight oil, she invariably popped down with some biscuits and milk.

Ferdinand was blessed with intuitions about the underlying structure of communication. In later years he became a world-renowned language expert. As a young man in Africa, however, this raw talent meant that he made speedy work of distinguishing the mangabey monkey's four methods of conversing: facial expressions, hand signals, shoulder shrugs and verbal sounds from a whisper to a screech.

Within a week he entered in his ledger the entire

set of signs for hunger and thirst; in a fortnight, anger and happiness. He progressed, and realized that more complex pieces of monkey communication involved two or more modes of expression simultaneously. To record the combinations in his ledger, he devised an elaborate form of notation.

After every observation session Ferdinand ticked off the date in the calendar at the back of his ledger. The ticks soon stretched across weeks and then months, as his initial enthusiasm deepened into obsession. Slowly, painstakingly, his empty ledger was transformed into a comprehensive monkey dictionary.

Around his hundredth session watching the monkeys, Ferdinand felt himself on the threshold of an important breakthrough. He had been puzzled by seemingly random variations in the signals used by monkeys when complex matters were at issue. He finally understood that the monkeys, while they all seemed perfectly similar, should in fact be divided into two distinct sub-groupings. For certain topics, half the monkeys used one set of signals and half used quite another.

After a long and gruelling day he emerged from the basement, exhausted but exhilarated, to find Madeline already in bed. As he unbuttoned his shirt, he thought she seemed a little peevish. While discreetly lowering his trousers, he asked her how was her day?

'Wonderful!' she said.

'That's good.'

'Absolutely magnificent!' she said.

Had her day really been that good? Ferdinand was suspicious.

'Darling, is there anything the matter?'

'No,' she said.

'I'm sorry I'm so late. The monkeys were particularly fascinating and infuriating today. Are you quite sure you're all right?'

'Yes,' she said.

'So nothing's the matter, then, definitely?'

'No!'

Reassured, Ferdinand fell into bed beside her and quickly passed out.

When he awoke next morning, he found Madeline already dressed and no longer in a fretful mood. In fact she seemed positively exuberant as she announced she was going into town.

'To buy a dress,' she said, as she left the bedroom. A few moments later, she stuck her head back in and declared, 'A red dress!'

After a plain breakfast Ferdinand went down into his basement and was struck by an ominous silence. The monkeys were gone. High up near the ceiling, a grating that led out into the daylight was unlocked and swinging open. In a frenzy, he scaled the climbing frame and looked out through the opening. He couldn't see a single monkey on the lawn; they had scattered into the surrounding jungle.

Shivering and wild-eyed with shock, Ferdinand climbed back down and stumbled over to his desk. His hands were shaking as he took his monkey dictionary from the drawer. When he tried to open it, however, he found that the pages were stuck together. He prised it open more forcefully and found that every single sheet was now sodden with ink. It had been poured on in thick layers, making the dictionary completely illegible. Ferdinand could hardly breathe, such was his bewilderment and dismay.

He turned to the calendar at the back of the ledger. The ink hadn't yet soaked that far, so it was still perfectly readable. There were the ticks marking the date of every observation session. One hundred ticks, one hundred days. Wasted. Ferdinand noticed, though, that he had forgotten to tick off the date of the previous day's session. He stared at the number intensely for a few seconds and began to groan. He banged his forehead on his desk. It was the date of his wife's birthday.

3

Our last night alone, lying in bed together

Clare, Ireland, December 2008

He tries to be gentle, but I still plop onto the bed like a sack of potatoes.

'Sorry, pet,' he says, 'I banged my shin off your wheelchair and dropped you with the shock.'

It's 10 p.m. and my husband has just wheeled me back from a trip to the toilet. I have enough strength to pull myself towards the headboard as he goes around to the other side and gets in beside me.

'All right now, pet?' he says, and proceeds to prop me up comfortably with pillows all around. 'Anything else I can do for you?'

I turn to answer, but he already has his glasses on and the lamp extended, engrossed in the glossy brochure on his knee. I pick up the TV remote and search for a good channel.

It is 29 December, one of those muted days after Christmas. Earlier we said goodbye to our youngest, Paul, who had been home since Christmas Eve but had to get back to Manchester for an important business meeting. Tomorrow morning promises the arrival of our eldest, Monica, with her husband and our boisterous but gorgeous grandchildren. They'll stay until 2 January. Their departing flight isn't due out until 3 p.m. so they'll have just enough time on the final morning to leave me in Limerick city. Well, Limerick Hospice to be precise. Or, to put it more bluntly, they'll be dropping me off at the place where I expect my 'long courageous battle' with leukaemia to end. Where I will die.

Monica is a dote and I can already guess that she'll be like a woman possessed, cooking, laundering, vacuuming like mad, trying to do everything she can. But, by the same token, she won't give us a moment's privacy. The toddler, Daniel, will be allowed to wreak havoc in every room, and she'll insist we leave our bedroom door open all night lest I have a bad turn. That's why I think of tonight as effectively my last with my husband. Our last night alone, lying in bed together.

'I think,' he says, nodding solemnly, 'that we'd be as well off to go with the PowerTec F45. For the extra few hundred euro you get an awful lot of accessories.'

For a moment I haven't a clue what he's on about. Then he shows me the brochure. The PowerTec F45 is a type of expensive electric wheelchair. He wants to buy one to replace the manual model I was given free, last week, by the hospital. This is all because some nurse said I'd probably be in the hospice for a month or two. Yes! And then I will leave it in a wooden box. But my husband does not seem to grasp that soon I won't be needing any kind of wheelchair. He is in denial and likes to think I'll be coming out feeling much better.

'Y'see, it comes with its own six-amp charger,' he says, 'and look, it says here that it "collapses down easily into this small carry-case that will fit in the boot of even the smallest car".'

'That's all very fine, but I don't like that shade of grey,' I say, meaning to be sarcastic. But he is oblivious.

'No problem there, pet. It comes in a choice of five colours!'

I close my eyes and think back six years, before the diagnosis, when death seemed so distant. Ask me then how I'd spend the night I knew to be my last alone with my husband. I'm sure I'd have been teeming with excellent ideas; about what wine we'd drink, the flavour of ice cream we'd devour and the final feel-good film we'd cuddle up together to watch. I'd have made lists of long-burning questions that I must ask him and a few unpleasant secrets that I should finally reveal. But that's not how it actually is.

Wine of any description is a no-no unless I want to be up and down all night to the toilet; having to be lifted on and off the wheelchair each time. Ditto the ice cream, only in that case my trips to the bathroom would be for the purpose of throwing up. Several hundred pills have made bits of my stomach, I can't tolerate any dairy.

Regarding the exposure of secrets, well, what really would be the point in upsetting ourselves at this stage? In any dictionary, happiness comes before honesty. As for the feel-good film? I have scanned across twenty television channels and my overwhelming emotion is annoyance. On every station there is some boy or some girl getting extremely worked up about something or other. But their concerns are foolish. None of them will be dead in a month's time.

I realize clearly that there is just one element of the 'ideal last night' that I would like: a cuddle with my husband. I turn to him but his chin has fallen onto his chest and his brochure to the carpet. I reach out to take off his reading glasses and he burrows down further into the quilt. Between snores I can hear him murmur, 'A top speed of four miles per hour!'

I lie back on the pillow and consider for a moment whether to wake him. But then what? Just a load of fussing. 'Pet, what's wrong, did I forget your painkillers?'

How to say to him what I'm really feeling?

How to make him see this really is the end?

'Not at all, pet. Don't be silly. You'll live to a hundred yet! Wait'll we get you in and out of that hospice!'

And so on. Words meant to contradict and console me. Logical reasons why I shouldn't be feeling what I am nevertheless feeling. My impending death will once again be disproved by a few selective quotes. The consultant oncologist who said I'd a thirty per cent chance. The radiographer who saw signs of slight remission.

Then my devoted husband will drift back to sleep.

I decide not to bother. I switch off the reading lamp and listen hard. From outside there's not a whisper of breeze. It somehow sounds cold, though.

I awake to the peals of a screaming radio alarm clock. It's 1 a.m. My husband shuts it off quickly and levers himself onto the floor. He dresses with a thick vest and an extra jumper. Then I receive a soft peck on the cheek and he's away out the door.

That peck is an irritation, another reminder of something that I can't seem to convey to him. I am not a china doll. If he were to press a little harder I would not break. But ever since the diagnosis, he's got more reticent about pressing, about squeezing. Admittedly, once the treatment started, my body gradually shrivelled up. One day during chemo he swept his fingers through my hair. A clump came loose and he ended up with a handful of hair. Pathetic scenes followed as he tried to put it back in place. With a lick of spit he managed to pat it into position up against my skull but I couldn't help crying. Nowadays he says, 'I might hurt you again,' as our physical relationship drains away to nought. All that remains is those soft pecks on the cheek. Occasionally we hold hands.

He's gone out to look at the cows. He has several that are near calving and they have to be checked in case they need help. The big event often takes place during the night, so he sets out across the dark field armed with a gammy old torch and a calving jack. He finds most of them standing chewing cud down by the far hedge. The one that's calving, though, will have gone off on her own. She could be anywhere. At nine acres the field is a big stony crag. Never properly reclaimed, it's pockmarked with humps, hollows, bushes and small trees. The one who is in distress will be crouched down, silent, trying to look inconspicuous. When he finds her he will get close and assess the situation. Any sign of a small hoof sticking out? Or two? That's the way the calves are supposed to come out, like a diver, first the two front legs, then the head, then the rest. If it's turned upside down or back to front, the contractions will never get anywhere. He must intervene.

My husband is supposed to be retired. There is no way that he should be out at 1.52 a.m. on a cold winter's night searching that big field. We had an agreement that he would retire at sixty-five and there's certainly no financial need for him to keep on slogging. Somehow that deal was forgotten with all the hulla-baloo about my cancer. Maybe he was still hoping that Paul would miraculously change his mind, come home and take over. Or one of the girls. Anyway he was nearly sixty-eight by the time I persuaded him to rent out the farm, including milking parlour, to the Mc-Namara lad. Even still he held onto the twenty acres immediately surrounding the house. 'Just,' he said, 'so I could still have a few sucklers to play with.'

He's been out there playing for nearly an hour now.

'Here you go, pet,' he says at 2.19 a.m. In his fists he holds two mugs of coffee, mine decaf and neces-sarily without milk. I am too annoyed by his long absence (on this our last night, effectively!) to thank him with more than a grunt. He undresses and gets back into bed. His legs are freezing and will take ages to warm up.

'Bit of worry with the black cow,' he says by way of explanation, 'still not really sure, bit of worry with her, could go either way.'

I stare straight ahead and do not respond.

After a silent gap I was supposed to fill, he says, 'Pet, did I disturb you, is it that you want to go back to sleep?'

'No, I do not want to go to sleep!' I say.

'Well, what, then?'

Now obviously if I was in some sort of communicative marriage I would just say nonchalantly, 'I want a cuddle.' But no, that is not my style. If the only way I can have one is by asking for it, then really I'd just as soon go without.

He pauses for a ponder before trying to move things forward again. 'Well, then, why don't we have a nice chat about your trip into Limerick next Friday?'

'Yes?'

'Out in the field I'd plenty of time to think, and I figured that the average quote from the nurses is you'll be in the hospice for about six weeks. Therefore I have about six weeks in which to renovate this house and make it more wheelchair friendly before you come back out.'

Oh, no. Here we go again.

He continues, 'I got a book from the library yesterday that is full of advice. Like when you're building ramps, for instance, did you know that the maximum slope that can be climbed easily is only one to twelve? I reckon if I'd gone off half-cocked I'd have built one a lot steeper than that. Did you know about the one-to-twelve rule, pet?'

No, I did not. I do not reply. I stare into space. I sip coffee without caffeine, without milk. It tastes horrible.

'And the ramp must be thirty-six inches wide. Where there's a landing you'll need fully sixty inches to turn . . .' And on and on he goes. '*Blah blah . . .* slip resistant . . . *Blah blah . . .* widen doorways . . . *Blah blah . . .* lever-handles instead of knobs . . . *Blah blah bloody blah.*'

'I think I will go to sleep, actually,' I finally inter-rupt. I curl up sideways, looking away from him.

'That's grand so, pet,' he says, already up and onto

his feet. 'I'll just take another quick stroll to see how that auld black cow is doing.'

I am not asleep. It's well after 3 a.m. now and I lie with the lights off, listening. It is no longer silent outside; the freezing has given way to a storm. A western wind howls around our window and the branches from the two big sycamores are clattering together. I begin to feel very hot. There's a throbbing pain in my side just below the ribs. Probably some as yet undiscovered secondary on my spleen. I take one of my MST tablets and swallow it back with the dregs of horrible coffee. Within minutes I get a dreadful feeling of nausea.

Usually I get my husband to bring me to the toilet, so I'm quite proud of myself for mustering the strength to slide out of bed and into the wheelchair. I roll into the en suite bathroom. I'm not so proud about my clumsy attempt to get off. I lean forward and grab the toilet seat in both hands. I forget, though, to apply the brake, so the chair shifts backwards and I fall forward, banging my chin down on the toilet. Anyway it turns out to be a quick dry retch; I produce nothing. I allow myself to slide down sideways to the floor. It is tiled. The cool smooth surface feels good against my hot cheek. Somehow I find the cold makes the nausea fade away and I am overcome with a wave of tiredness.

I welcome the thought of sleep but am just too lazy to try to get back into the chair. I wriggle out of the door to the bedroom and pull a big beach towel down from the radiator. This will do fine as my blanket.

I am about to close my eyes when the back door opens and my husband returns. The storm noises are tremendous before he slams it closed. While he takes off his wellies in the hall, I sleepily put out my arms like a damsel reaching for her saviour.

But he does not come.

I hear his clumping footfalls going up the staircase and know what's gone wrong. It's happened twice before and he was all apologies in the morning. Not surprisingly the man is exhausted from his exertions. He may be awake but he's on autopilot. Consequently, he is headed, from force of a lifetime's habit, for the master bedroom, which is upstairs. There he will throw himself down on the bed and pass out immediately, only realizing his mistake in the morning. The master bedroom is not wheelchair accessible. We sleep in the guest room now because it's on the ground floor.

'This is where I am!' I suppose I should shout out. But I don't. I sob quietly for a few minutes before exhaustion sweeps me away into slumber.

When I awake the storm is gone and the room is bright, early morning light leaking in despite the curtains. I get onto all fours, crawl to the wheelchair and pull myself aboard. Then I wheel over to the window and lift a corner of the drape. It seems the storm left something behind: a heavy fall of snow. Despite myself I smile. I decide that I'm going out.

I manage to pull a sweater over my nightie and tuck the beach towel around my legs. Unfortunately I'm just too weak to put on socks and shoes. In the hall I park near my husband's big wellies and pull them on easily enough. I'm ready.

I open the front door to a blast of cold air.

I go back to get gloves and a hat.

Outside my progress is slow but there's no hurry

and the scene is magical. There's a pristine two-inch blanket on everything; no living creature has yet left a paw or footprint. The world is silent, the only sound my wheels crunching snow and my lungs labouring. I wheel around to the backyard and start along the gravel path, which slopes gently towards the river. I meet my first pothole and am about to steer around when I think better of it. Just like my boy Paul, on his tricycle twenty-eight years ago, I crunch straight across the frozen puddle, breaking ice to splinters, churning up the muddy water beneath.

There's no need to go to the end of the path; the river has come out to meet me. It's flooded a good twenty yards this year judging by the distant rushes, their forlorn tips far from the bank.

From back up at the house, I hear movement, a door being closed. Without really thinking it through, I try to hide. Frantically, I wheel over behind a hay-feeder. It's a large metal contraption that my husband uses for feeding the cows when they're in this field. It will, I think, provide perfect cover as long as I sit still. But through the rusted metal bars I see him heading straight for me. Oh, yes, I forgot. The tracks of my wheelchair.

When he gets within range I throw my first snow-ball at him. I miss. Not to worry – I've prepared ten from the snow that had lodged along the metal bars. He continues his approach and my second missile connects with his shoulder.

'For Jaysus' sake, pet,' he yelps, but I maintain the assault and swing over another three. All go close; all miss. 'Pet, go easy, go easy,' he says. 'You're going to make me spill!'

For the first time I notice that he's carrying a mug

in each hand. I relent. It turns out they're two steaming hot whiskies complete with lemon and clove. In mugs!

'Typical man,' I say, pretending to grouse as I take the first sip. But, God, does it hit the spot!

'Well, pet!' he says. 'I see you've no trouble when you're aiming at your mouth.'

I laugh, and our hot breaths mingle, condensing in the frozen air.

'Sorry, anyway, pet,' he says after a minute.

I acknowledge him with a nod. 'So did the black cow calve or what?'

'She did not!' he says, feigning wrath. 'The fucking bitch kept me up all night and all she had was indigestion! She'll not calve for another month!'

We both laugh again. For a minute, there is no more talk, only delicious sips and swallows. An occasional chuckle. Then my wheelchair starts to move. Backwards. I have forgotten to apply the brake. Slipping back the first inch, I giggle until I realize that the river is somewhere behind me. My husband is in a better position to see the danger and bounds after me. His hand reaches to grab the wheelchair but slides off the plastic armrest. Having stretched so desperately, he loses balance and falls face down in the snow while I continue to careen backwards towards I know not exactly what. I scrunch up my body and my face, expecting to hit ice, then freezing water. But the chair slows and I look down to see thicker snow. The drift comes up around my wellies and stops me just before the river. My husband picks himself up. His face and the whole front of his body are caked in snow. I laugh. He replies with a snowball thrown right into my belly.

*

He drops me onto the bed like a sack of potatoes. Once again.

'Sorry,' he grunts, 'I banged my shin off your wheelchair.'

Sopping wet, he has stripped to his socks and underpants. Now, as tenderly as he can, he begins to undress me. Off come the wet gloves and beach towel, the sweater and even the nightie that was drenched in sweat. There is a large unhealed abscess below my left knee. He turns to the task of replacing the dressing, and as he works I find my head directly beside his underpants. It's the faded navy one that I have laundered several hundred times. It has a button missing that I should've sewn back, but it's too late now.

'Y'know Monica should be here within the hour?' he says.

But I do not answer. I stare into space and my thoughts drift onto the subject of – God forgive me – my husband's penis. Obviously it's played an important role in my soon-to-be-over life. It's the only one that's ever been inside me. It's the one that's given me my precious children. And yet I've no clear picture of it. I am not that kind of woman; my husband is not that kind of man. We have sex, proper natural sex, at night, with the lights off. We don't go in for this lark of one spouse brushing their teeth while the other has a piddle. God, no.

My eyes refocus and I find my hand has strayed upwards to the fabric of my husband's underpants. It is holding open the flap where the button is missing. I look inside and see a small squashed twist of hairy flesh. For a moment my husband does not react. He keeps working on dressing my abscess, first the cream, then the powder. His breathing, though, is a shade heavier. Inside the underpants there are faint stirrings as the twist begins to straighten. I close my eyes.

A moment later I open my eyes, but just a fraction. This way I can watch my husband's actions in broad daylight. If I opened them properly and we made eye contact, the spell would be broken. Having finished the dressing, he turns and kisses me on the mouth. It's a proper kiss, not a peck. His fingers run through the light stubby tufts of hair on my head. I continue to watch through slits as he plants a line of light kisses down my neck and in a circle around each breast. What's left of them. The radiation, the chemo, the disease, I don't know which, has punctured them like balloons. My husband kisses me three times on each nipple. Standing back for a moment he slides down the navy underpants. 'It' is not as big as I imagined, but it's probably big enough.

He gets onto the bed. He gently moves my thighs apart and kneels between them. I deduce that he is not going to bother removing his socks.

This is more than I hoped for. God, this is good. I will take this image, this sensation, and store it carefully, to have in the hospice, to recall and rekindle. God, yes, it is good.

Ooooooooooooooooooooooooooooooooooooooooo . . .

Every cell in my body thrills to the rhythm of him in and out. Or nearly every cell. There is one dissenter chattering in the back of my skull . . .

But why oh why oh why . . .

In this, our last hour alone together . . .

Couldn't I have had what I actually wanted?

A cuddle.

4

The case of the woman
surrounded by shoes

'Inspector,' I said, 'I think you'd better come and have a look at this.'

In my gloved hand I held a bank statement that I'd retrieved from under the bed.

Inspector Reed gave it the merest glance and nodded grimly. 'Well, Turner, I rather think that puts the tin hat on it, what?'

I murmured my agreement and waited respectfully while he rummaged in his pocket and produced a chocolate-coated bar of Turkish delight. I had been in Reed's squad barely a week but already understood that this was part of his silent celebration when a case was solved. He slid off the wrapping and, as I knew he would, asked me to give my impressions of the crime scene.

'Well,' I began carefully, 'a murder has taken place in this bedroom. Before us lies a young woman, of Vietnamese extraction, I'd guess. A neighbour has identified her as Suki Mason. She is clad in her pyjamas and has been beaten to death. The blows were primarily to a point on her skull just above the right ear and, it's reasonable to speculate, were inflicted with the heel of a stiletto shoe. Such a shoe lies bloodied and broken on the carpet.'

'Good so far, Turner, now go on,' said Inspector Reed, carefully unfolding the foil from the top squares of his bar.

'Also in this room,' I continued with more confidence, 'is a dressing table upon which sit two empty bottles of red wine and a single used glass. Under the bed I have just found a recent bank statement issued from a joint account in the name of Tyrone and Suki Mason, presumably that of the deceased woman and her husband. The bottom line on the monthly statement is a substantial over-draft of £4,000 and numerous entries therein have been underlined in red pen. They are debits run up on a charge card and are for considerable amounts ranging from £100 to £300. The charges are all credited to Harvey's Shoe Emporium, Oxford Street.

'This leads on to one final telling piece of evidence: namely, the enormous number of shoes in this bedroom. There are shoes strewn all over the carpet, in the drawers, in the wardrobe and under the bed. Every kind of court shoe, boot, platform, sandal, slipper and runner.'

I gestured at the room's most notable piece of furniture. 'And then there's this giant shoe rack. It's filled with high heels, many of which look very expensive and are presumably desirable brand names, but in quantity alone there must be a hundred.'

'Excellent,' said Inspector Reed as he finally broke off two squares of his Turkish delight and put them in his mouth. 'So much for the evidence. Now, Turner, tell me exactly what happened.'

I took a deep breath and threw out my theory. 'Okay, the murderer was clearly the husband. It was probably not premeditated, but the result of a domestic squabble. Plainly this man had a wife who refused to live within their means and spent ridiculous sums of money on shoes. Last night, I imagine, he came home late from a bad day at work to find another depressing bank statement and a wife who had drunk two bottles of wine on her own. He decided to go over the details of the statement with her and ask for explanations about the charges at Harvey's. Things did not go well. Perhaps she even denied going to the shoe shop, or maybe she hissed that she was perfectly entitled to the occasional little luxury. In any case, the drink had made her particularly cantankerous, and she hurled abuse back at him and needled him. She pushed all the buttons that years of marriage had taught her were particularly effective and riled him mightily. Perhaps she calculated that his annoyance would drive him to say something terrible or maybe give her a smack. Either way, their argument would then be about something different: the necessity for him to apologize. She'd claim the moral high ground. As so often before, he'd actually wind up being the one to say sorry.'

I was carried away by the picture I had conjured up; I had to swallow before finishing.

'This time, though, she went too far. This time, he went too far. The husband killed his wife with one of her precious shoes and then fled the scene.'

Inspector Reed broke off some more Turkish

37

delight while shaking his head and sighing slowly. 'Well, you got the murderer right, but not a whole lot else.'

I was surprised. I was sure I'd nailed it.

'The first thing you failed to notice,' said Reed, 'was the single credit item on the bank account. It's manifestly a monthly payment of salary by standing order. The entry reads "ChildCaAgenc." – in other words, one of the couple worked for a child care agency. We can easily confirm this later, but I'm confident it was the wife. The absence of any other credit entry suggests it was the husband who' – and here Reed winced slightly, obviously uncomfortable with the concept – 'worked in the home.

'Also,' he said, 'I'm convinced that forensics will find that the fingerprints on the wine glass are his.'

'Okay, I did overlook that,' I admitted, 'but the row was still basically about –'

'No, Turner. The row was quite different.' He walked over to the enormous shoe rack and plucked off five high heels at random. 'Here,' he said, handing them to me, 'put these on Cinderella.'

I tried each in turn on the feet of the corpse. Not one fit.

Thoroughly stumped, I turned to Reed for inspiration, but he had moved to the window and was gazing down the street, eating up the last of his Turkish delight and smiling contentedly.

The poor woman's feet were tiny, far too small for these sequined designer shoes. I turned one over to check the size and the penny finally dropped.

It was the husband who wore size 8.

5

Eleven ex-boyfriends have yet to be identified

I was not my wife's first love. In fact I was her thirteenth boyfriend. Before we met she had managed to get through a dozen other fellows, all from this city. Thus, as I walked daily through crowds on Grafton Street, I was intensely aware that any man among them might once have held her hand. Might have brought her a bunch of flowers and whispered sweet nothings in her ear. More disturbingly, any of these men might several times have had sex with my gorgeous wife.

A few days earlier I had seen, from a distance, one of these ex-boyfriends – not just once but twice. The rest were a list of first names, occasional odd details – a job here, a hobby there – and little more. I did not know them but it was possible that some of them knew me. Perhaps as I stood here in the taxi queue on Stephen's Green her first ex was the man half smiling in my direction. Maybe he was looking over, thinking to himself, 'I have had sex with your wife! Before you! Your entire sex life is now spent retracing my steps over skin I mapped fifteen years ago. There is nowhere that you can place your hands or your tongue that I haven't already been.'

Plainly this notion was preposterous. My wife, Christine, had better taste. The man was podgy, with sticky-out ears, and he was a bit too old. Nevertheless, and despite the first spatters of rain, I decided to walk home. Up along Harcourt Street, I glared at passing strangers.

This uneasiness had started a few days before. Christine and I were at the Gate Theatre on the opening night of some Beckett thing. At the interval Christine went out to the ladies while I remained in my seat. I turned around to survey the rows behind. A man sitting near the aisle winked at me. I looked away. Then I wondered whether he had really been winking at someone else and looked at him again. He winked once more. This time there could be no doubt. Although a total stranger to me, he was smiling directly at me and had one eyebrow raised quizzically. Astonished, I turned away. An announcer told everyone to return to their seats, Christine sat down, and the play recommenced.

Later, when the lights were up and we were getting up to leave, I pointed out the guy to Christine and asked if she recognized him.

'Oh, him,' she said. 'That's Eric. I knew him years ago when he was doing the Masters in Journalism at DCU. He's an old boyfriend of mine.'

It was quite a shock. I had figured that perhaps he was some kind of simpleton and his winking a harmless foible. This news cast things in an altogether different light. Plainly he had recognized my wife and guessed that I was now her husband.

'And when you say boyfriend,' I asked Christine, 'you mean, don't you, that he is someone you had sex with?'

'Well . . . yes,' she said, wrinkling her forehead the way she does when she thinks I'm being a plonker.

'How many times?'

'Oh, come now,' she said, 'I don't know. A few, I suppose.'

'A few?' I said. 'How many times is a few?'

'You are being ridiculous,' she said. 'I don't know! It was years ago. Maybe eight or nine times. Ten maximum.'

'Feck,' I thought. You could fit a lot into ten times. You'd be way past the missionary position. This Eric guy had probably had my wife every which way. And now, years later, he was winking at me. Feck!

We shuffled along the row and made our way out onto the street. There was no further sign of Eric but still I was troubled. As we headed to the car park, Christine noticed. 'So now you've gone into one of your sulks,' she said.

'I'm not sulking!'

'Well, what are you, then?'

'I'm just thinking, that's all.'

'Thinking? Right, so what are you thinking?'

'I'm thinking, to be honest, that I do not like the thought of that smirking idiot Eric ever having been intimate with my gorgeous wife.'

'Oh, come on, I can't believe your immaturity,' she said. 'That was years ago. You're being silly.'

I did not reply.

'Look,' she said as she hit the central locking, 'the last

I heard he'd got a job with one of the newspapers doing reviews. Presumably that's why he was here tonight. If you're going to throw a big sulk, though, over seeing a guy I dated briefly years ago, then maybe we should just avoid going to any further opening nights.'

She was being sarcastic.

'I wholeheartedly agree,' I replied, not sarcastically at all.

So we would never again go to any kind of first night, that much was settled in my mind. Precious little else was, though. As I lay awake at 1 a.m., unwanted visions of Eric floated into my mind. Beside me, Christine was sleeping soundly.

'Goddamn this filthy cockroach Eric,' I murmured, 'who has trespassed so grievously upon MY WOMAN.'

Yes, I was being irrational. Eric was nothing new. He had long since existed and I had long since been told about him. He was one of a list of names that Christine had gradually revealed, years ago when we were courting. When we were in the 'getting to know everything about each other' phase. But . . .

But back then my wife was not yet mine. Whom she had slept with before was of no relevance. What was relevant was that she was gorgeous. What was relevant was: would she sleep with ME? And then how often.

'But now she is mine,' I murmured, 'and the theoretical name gets a face.'

And this face had made love to my wife on at least ten occasions. That was a substantial number. It raised questions, terrible tormenting questions.

Did Christine enjoy sex with this Eric?

I suppose . . . yes, obviously. She'd hardly just lay there letting him do stuff to her.

Did she have huge, piercing orgasms? Which rolled and tumbled onwards and inwards for several minutes? Did the fabulously rhythmic Eric always hit the spot?

Ahmmmm . . .

And, in the bucolic bliss of her sweaty aftershocks, did she, despite herself, let slip a tiny whisper of 'I love you'?

Stop.

And now, years later, while doing 'conjugal duty' with her husband, when she's bored, not particularly turned on, does her mind drift back to thoughts of Eric?

I said stop!

Or, worse, when she IS turned on, IS about to orgasm, is it because she's just visualized Eric's massive throbbing . . .

Stop. Stop. STOP!

To break the train of thought I went for a piss. I was too agitated to hit a target so I had to do it sitting down. Another irritating detail from earlier came back to me.

'Who broke up with whom?' I had asked her in the car on the way home.

'When are you going to cop on?' she said with a sigh. 'I don't know, it was all a long time ago. I think he dumped me because he was taking a year out to work in America and wanted no ties.'

So this idiot had sampled my wife, taken her for a test drive and found her wanting. How dare he? The fecking fecker. Jesus! I wanted to kill him. Or at the very least find him tomorrow and punch his lights out.

1. For his bloody nerve in winking at me.
2. For his bloody nerve in having shagged my wife, even if it was in the distant past.
3. For his bloody nerve in making me lose sleep thinking about the possible dimensions of his penis.

Yes, tomorrow I must make it a priority; surf the internet, scour the telephone directory, ring every newspaper, whatever it took. Tomorrow I would systematically search this city of one million souls until I found Eric.

Or not, as it transpired.

I came across him again by accident, first thing in the morning, before I was even fully awake. Bleary-eyed after a sleepless night, I took the Luas to Sandyford for a meeting. When it stopped at Kilmacud, I glanced over at the far platform. There stood Eric. Fidgeting with his mobile, texting someone, he was too engrossed to notice me as I leaped out of my seat and went to disembark. In a matter of seconds I would circle around the last carriage and cross the tracks over onto his side. Then, before he knew what was happening, he'd be getting his jaw broken.

But then what will happen? I asked myself.

Maybe he'll hit you back. Are you ready for that?

Yes. Feck him! Let him have a go. I'll repay every blow with interest.

Okay, so you win the fight, what then? Do you really think that'll be the end of the story?

Huh?

No doubt with so many witnesses the cops will nab you. 'A totally unprovoked attack, guard! I saw everything!'

So I have to pay a fine, spend a day or two in custody. It'd be worth it.

While your wife finds out what you did? Says 'I can't believe his immaturity!' Feels duty bound to visit poor injured Eric in the hospital with grapes and a bunch of flowers. He says, 'Wow, you look fabulous, babe . . . what a fool I was to let you go . . .'

Stop.

All along the train, the doors slid shut with a hiss. I was still aboard.

Many times over the next few miserable days I repented of my reasonableness, my prudence, my cowardice. Rattled by two sightings of an ex-boyfriend in as many days, I began to imagine such creatures everywhere. In the queue at the ATM, busking down King Street, smiling at me slyly in the taxi queue on Stephen's Green.

Later that evening, after eating only half my dinner, I lay soaking in the bath. Christine came upstairs.

'Are you still moping about seeing Eric, four days later?' she asked.

'Yes,' I said. 'But I also saw him again the next day on the Luas. That was only three days ago.'

'And what did you do?' she said, looking alarmed. 'Abuse him? Attack him?'

'No, I did nothing, said nothing.'

'Thank God,' she said. 'That was surprisingly mature of you.'

She turned to straighten one of the guest towels, which was an inch askew. Seeing her from behind gave me an idea.

'Hey,' I said, laughing mischievously, 'since I've been so mature maybe you'd like to demonstrate your approval. By joining me in here.'

'You want me to have a bath?' she chuckled. 'That's a very strange way of showing your approval. Perhaps you'd prefer a cup of tea.'

'No, no tea.'

'Not even with a chocolate biscuit?'

'No, none of the above, just you, right now, in this bath.'

'Well, all right, then,' she said, and began to peel off her top. 'In honour of the fact that you now accept my past, that it did occur. But is over.'

She undid the zip in her skirt and that too fell to the floor while she continued talking. 'In honour of the fact that you refuse to allow your mental state to be dictated by some random guy whom I dated years ago.

'In honour of the fact . . .' Christine kept on talking, but, as her underwear was cast aside, I was too busy lusting to listen. I was, though, fervently believing her. From now on, I would indeed be a better, more mature person.

Two minutes into our post-coital bliss I began to backslide.

'But twelve! How did you manage to get through twelve boyfriends?'

'Look,' she said. 'I first had sex when I was sixteen. I met you when I was twenty-nine. Is one a year really so many? Is it really so sluttish? Some were one-night stands; some relationships that didn't last;

48

the longest was six months. Believe me, there were long periods of having no sex at all.'

'Okay,' I said. 'Next question: now that I'm taking a mature outlook, could you explain specifically why you went out with Eric?'

I wanted her to tell me he was an unfortunate mistake. That he turned out to be useless in bed. That she never loved him.

'Well, Eric could be very charming when he wanted to be.'

'Mmm.' *My heart is prodded by a particularly sharp dagger.*

'He had a great sense of humour, fairly good-looking. A lot like you, really.'

'Mmm.' *The dagger starts to make slices diagonally.*

'Yes. But obviously I prefer you.'

'Mmm. Why exactly?' *I have no heart. Only strips of meat remain.*

'Well, you're much more sincere, more considerate. Usually anyway. Kinder.'

Feck that! I don't want to be picked for being sincere. For being kinder.

What would you like to be picked for?

For having a longer penis. Or wider, that would be good too.

I did not share these thoughts with Christine.

'It's just what unsettled me about Eric is he makes our love seem contingent on time and place, the age we were when we met. Nothing to do with some sort of special connection. You could just as easily have married him.'

'Well,' she said, 'what about that girl Audrey you went out with for seven years? Don't you think that's a bit intimidating for me?'

'She was just a mistake. I've always made that clear,' I said.

'Oh, come on! How did ye stay together for seven years if the relationship was so bad? You must have loved her. You must have had quite a bit of sex with her too. Well?'

I did not answer. I grabbed a towel because the bathwater suddenly seemed quite cold. But yes. While Christine spent her twenties flitting from short-term relationships to one-night stands, I used up 6¾ years with just one woman. And admittedly, yes, I had loved her, and we'd had lots of sex, for the first five years at least. As Christine stood up and dripped across the tiles towards her dressing-gown, I closed my eyes and pondered Audrey for the first time in an age.

We had probably had sex about a thousand times. Jesus! It sounds massive, doesn't it? But six years and nine months is 2,463 days. At the start we did it at least daily (once we managed four times in twenty-four hours!). Then by year three it was down to every second day, then twice weekly, then weekly and then for that last sad period almost never. By then we were living together, hoping that would fix our problems. By then we were good flatmates, no longer really lovers.

Another thing about Audrey. Like me, she was a virgin when we began going out. And she was never unfaithful to me, as far as I could tell. The last I'd heard of her was two years ago, when she was still single according to some mutual friends. I wondered if she was attached now, four years after our split. Surely, yes. Yet, if she'd not met another man, then . . . I would be the only man she'd ever slept with.

*

50

The next day I ran into Eric yet again, while having lunch at my favourite restaurant, T. P. Smiths. I was at the side counter, choosing between Confit of Salmon with Smoked Garlic Cream or Gratin of Prawn Tails and Tortellini. Not only did Eric walk in, but he strolled up and sat on the high stool right alongside me. Admittedly the place was packed; admittedly seats were few and far between. Still, I could not credit his cheek.

'I'll have the Steamed Cod,' he shouted to my waitress and proceeded to make himself comfortable, hanging his jacket on a knob. Then he turned in my direction, acted as though he'd just noticed me for the first time and nodded. I braced myself, waiting for some smart comment, but none came. Instead he fished out his mobile and got down to texting.

Our orders arrived. The lunch, though mercifully free from any attempt at conversation, was an uncomfortable business. While I tried to eat, Eric's elbows were at an angle clicking off mine, as his thumbs twiddled on the tiny console. While I tried to eat, his phone bleeped constantly, signalling incoming messages. While I tried to eat, I was inches away from a moronic jackass who had sampled the pleasure of sex with my wife.

Finally, having gobbled his rations, Eric got up to leave. He put his jacket on before leaning over to whisper in my ear, 'Please give my regards to the lovely Christine, won't you?'

Feck it! How dare he call my wife lovely? She was, of course, but how dare he? The syrupy way he said her name, he might as well have said he remembered her as quite a goer beneath the sheets.

'WHAT!' I shouted, but Eric had already started

moving towards the door. I stumbled off my stool to pursue him but became entangled with a waitress carrying three plates of potato wedges. By the time I got to the street he was out of sight. I tried running towards the Jervis Centre but there was no sign. I jogged left to Capel and all the way down. Nothing either. 'Feck him!' I shouted at the river. 'FECK HIM!'

I was still murmuring those two words to myself, over and over, later that night in bed. In a vicious mood demanding decisive action, I considered the position. Plan A for dealing with this situation had been the simple expedient of avoiding first nights. Plan A, it was fair to say, had failed utterly. Time for Plan B.

It was not, I'll readily admit, a nice plan. Which is why I had kept it in reserve, hoping never to have to implement it. Simply put, the time had arrived for me to have sex with another woman. Only in this way could I restore some balance to the situation between me and Christine. The absolutely ideal scenario for poetic justice would be if I could go out to Kilmacud, seeking and seducing Eric's current girlfriend or wife.

Or alternatively it could just be any woman I managed to pick up at a nightclub. (I'd tell Christine I was going to drinks for a guy leaving work. When I'd got a woman, we could use a hotel room and I'd be home by 2 a.m., 3 tops.)

Or, and this seemed the easiest, cleanest option, I could just go around to my ex-girlfriend Audrey's last-known address . . .

*

At eight o'clock in the evening, the traffic across town should've been non-existent. Instead I drove quickly as far as the quays before getting stuck behind a collision between a car and a bus. There was no way around so I had to sit and stew while the emergency services were called. I turned on the car radio, then turned it off again in agitation. I closed my eyes and tried instead to rehearse what might happen if, as I hoped, Audrey still lived on Whitworth Road.

'Hello. I don't suppose you remember me?' I would begin. Despite herself Audrey would smile.

'Nice place you have,' I would say when she invited me in but I would be lying. I'd never visited, but a mutual friend had. He told me it was a dimly lit basement flat, with a tiny kitchenette and tinier toilet. The carpet would be hideous. There'd be greyish-white underwear tumbling out of the laundry basket, and the only table would be home to a laptop swamped by piles of folders and loose pages.

'My thesis for the MA,' Audrey would tell me apologetically. 'Sometimes I wonder if I'll ever be finished.'

I imagined big box files piled precariously on the two chairs in the flat. I would perch instead on the edge of her locker while Audrey put on the kettle for tea. I'd then have a moment to confirm another detail I learned from our mutual friend. He has a poor sense of smell but he detected the whiff of cat. Or cats. There were none visible, he told me, but her window was open and out on the sill were an assortment of feeding bowls and a tray of sand. That, no doubt, was supposed to be their toilet. He suspected the cats did not always do as they were supposed to.

Audrey would then bring me my tea, correctly two-sugared without my having asked, and sit on the bed. And then . . . hopefully . . . I would notice that the top two buttons of her blouse had somehow come undone. While I was looking down into her ample cleavage she would bounce up off the bed and suddenly be in my face with two pouting lips. I would kiss her. I'd grab a hold of her bottom, pull her close and we'd kiss again with tongues twisting slowly.

'Oh, God,' I imagined she'd say. 'That is so good. Give me more.'

I would reply . . . 'But what about Christine?'

I opened my eyes abruptly and saw that the bus was now only blocking one lane. The traffic would be allowed to move soon. And, yes, what about Christine? Her other lovers were before our marriage. I was about to have one during it.

Fiddlesticks! I closed my eyes again and tried to return to my enjoyable little fantasy. I pictured myself back in Audrey's flat, back in her embrace. I couldn't muster as much enthusiasm, though. I looked over her shoulder and saw a brown cat appear at the windowsill. It came inside and then straight over towards me. I felt it wrapping its tail around my leg. I didn't like the sensation. I opened my eyes.

The actual attempt to implement Plan B took place fifteen minutes later. I arrived at the address on Whitworth Road, which did look as I'd imagined. I pressed the doorbell for Flat 8 several times but there was no reply. Then I rang Flat 7 and a Polish guy came out to the door.

'Yes,' he answered me, 'there is a dark-haired woman living in Flat 8 but I don't know her name.'

I questioned further.

'I don't know,' he said. 'It's not my business whether she has a boyfriend.'

So I came away knowing neither if Audrey still lived there, nor if she had a partner. As I closed the front garden gate, I noticed two cats lying in their cubby-hole in a corner. They stared at me coolly. This may or may not have had any significance.

Maybe I should have pursued it, but I lost enthusiasm for Plan B. I went back to Plan A, in a new and improved version. It demands that I avoid not only the opening night of all theatre, but also the Luas (Red Line – as far as I know the Green is okay) and Smiths restaurant. Initially, I'll admit, these strictures seemed cumbersome but in no time I discovered perfectly adequate alternatives for each: another restaurant; a new impetus to take the healthy option and walk into town.

It has been four months now without a single sighting of Eric. My reward has been a gradual reduction in sulking with my wife and scowling at strangers. In short, a less distracted mental state. I am optimistic that I can keep a lid on my jealousy but there's a threat hovering on my horizon. Eleven more of Christine's ex-boyfriends are still out there, each with his own workplace, his own favourite bar, his own daily pathway through this city.

To the men I know only as David, Michael, Brian, Frank, Liam, Sean, Ger L., Anthony, James, Ollie and Ger O. – my silent prayer, indeed my violent prayer, is this: That You. All. Stay Out. Of My. Life.

6

A lifetime of coming second

'Oh, Xylon, please, please, please,' she wailed.

'Stop your sobbing, my foolish wife!' he said. 'It would be more constructive if you put forward even one good reason why I shouldn't throw this cat of yours over the cliff.'

She kept on weeping. Xylon took the cat by the scruff of its neck and began his backswing.

The problem dated back to Xylon's schooldays. He was very clever and in any other schoolroom he'd have been considered the class genius. Unfortunately the boy in the desk next to him, Socrates, won every quiz, scored a hundred per cent in every spelling test and would later lay the foundations of Western philosophy. Xylon amassed a fine collection of blue rosettes but grew steadily more embittered about never once claiming the red.

After school their paths diverged, Xylon taking a position in the Academy, Socrates becoming something of a wandering intellectual. Over the next three decades, Xylon progressed steadily up through the ranks of academia until he made vice-provost. On his hefty salary he had wealth enough to upgrade his chariot every year and to buy a pretty villa on the coastal road to Attica. Meanwhile Socrates lived on the scraps of money he made tutoring students privately. Having no chariot, he walked everywhere and his possessions amounted to what he stood up in. He lived nomadically and slept on spare beds and behind sofas in the living rooms of his admirers.

Late in their fifties, the old rivalry between Xylon and Socrates was reignited at the Symposium of Athene. This was an annual event to celebrate the Goddess of Wisdom and involved several hundred scholars gathering at the Parthenon to get very drunk. The serious business happened only on the third and last day, when the debating contest took place. A series of knockout rounds weeded out the contenders. By seven o'clock they'd be down to two men and one final debate. For nine years in a row the finalists were the same and so was the result: first, Socrates; second, Xylon.

Frustrated in his public life, Xylon found some respite in his own home. No matter what happened outside, he was Lord and Master back in the villa. To put it bluntly, he bullied his wife, Demtres, relentlessly. When her attire was inappropriate or her laundering imperfect, he spent thirty-five years letting her know.

His persecution of the poor woman was true to his profession and took the form of debates. Instead of simply criticizing her cooking, he would open with a question.

'Can the slop on this plate rightly be described as "food"?'

Demtres had to respond. If she chose not to, if she walked away into another room, he would follow her reiterating the question. Eventually she'd be prodded into some sort of response, but her case was hopeless. Although she was an able woman in many respects (and indeed an excellent cook), she was powerless against the disputation skills of the second-best debater in Greece. Inevitably she would quietly concede that the 'slop' was not 'food' and utter some words of contrition. Having scored victory, Xylon would brighten and return to the table, telling Demtres of his day's work. Between anecdotes he would shovel down the food. Demtres would remain standing by the sink, half listening to her husband. While her cat flexed and wound itself around her swollen varicose legs, she would stare out of the window at the sparkling blue waters of the Aegean.

The year after Xylon had come second for the ninth time, Socrates made an announcement that stunned the intellectual community. A month before the Symposium he let it be known that he would not be entering the debating contest. The bookies immediately installed Xylon as favourite. The man himself calmly told his colleagues that he would take nothing for granted and that there were many other talented debaters capable of a big performance on a given day. Secretly, he punched the air: his moment of triumph was at hand.

Xylon took the final week off work to focus solely on the contest. He spent it locked in his study, poring over books, leaving nothing to chance. On the morning of the contest, he was in a buoyant mood, even pausing at the door to give Demtres a peck on the cheek. She waved him goodbye. Hopefully. Anxiously.

By the reckless clatter of his chariot up the avenue that evening, Demtres guessed he had not won. When he came in, Xylon was in his foulest mood ever.

'Everything went wrong from the very start,' he shouted. 'I couldn't find parking anywhere near the Parthenon. I circled it three times before eventually abandoning the rig a quarter of a mile away!'

'Oh, dear,' said Demtres.

'And as for the contest? Second yet again! But not to Socrates. No! This time, son of Socrates! It was a star pupil of his by the name of Plato. A mere lad of nineteen! And yet he beat me! Do you see what this means?'

Yes, Demtres saw. The young Plato had already absorbed everything Socrates knew. Potentially he would be even stronger next year and the year after too. Her husband had spent years coming second to Socrates, and now all that lay ahead for him was to come second to the new young buck.

'Why not sit down to supper, darling? It's your favourite,' she said. Xylon was in no mood to be placated. He wanted a fight, a winnable fight. His eyes were fiery like a cornered rat's. His stubby head was like an owl's, swivelling slowly, scanning the room for something out of place. There seemed to be nothing. Then he spied that the door to his study was slightly ajar.

'A-ha!' he shouted and went inside. After a few minutes, he emerged and marched up to Demtres with his hand held out towards her and his fingers pinched together. When he got closer Demtres could see that he was holding a cat hair.

'Is it not the case that your cat is expressly not allowed in my study? And haven't I given fair warning that his next incursion would be his last, foolish wife?'

Xylon grabbed a spoonful of his dinner and bent down on one knee. With a grim smile and a *ss-spss-spss* he called the cat over. Like Xylon himself, it was a fat little creature, accustomed to a steady diet of treats. As it licked the spoon, he gently scooped a hand underneath. He was devious enough not to be rough with it yet.

'No, Xylon, please, no, no, no,' shrieked Demtres, as she realized what he was about.

'No, no, no,' she cried, as she scampered after him out onto the lawn, towards the low back fence on the brow of the cliffs.

'Stop your sobbing, my foolish wife!' said Xylon. 'It would be more constructive if you put forward even one good reason why I shouldn't throw this cat of yours over the cliff to be dashed against the jagged rocks below.'

Demtres kept weeping. Xylon took the cat by the scruff of its neck and began his backswing. Finally realizing the situation, the cat's claws shot out and its paws flailed wildly as it tried to find something to cling to. Its neck twisted and its sharp little teeth tried to bite Xylon. But it was too fat to be a fighter.

'The basic premise for your allegation remains unproved!' Demtres suddenly exclaimed.

'What do you mean?' Xylon said, shocked by both her claim and the technical jargon in which she'd expressed it.

'Just stop for a moment and look at that cat carefully,' said Demtres.

Halfway through his upswing, Xylon stopped while Demtres continued with a question. 'I don't really know much about these things, darling, but can you tell me how many hairs he has on his body?'

'Thousands, millions, billions, perhaps. Obviously beyond count. Why do you ask?' said Xylon, his eyes narrowing. The cat struggled again; this time Xylon dropped him to the grass.

'And how many hairs, darling,' continued Demtres, 'do you think he had on his body this morning?'

'The same obviously,' said Xylon, still not grasping it. 'Millions, billions.'

'Then how can you prove that there's one missing? How can you establish that he has lost one and deposited it in your study?'

Xylon's mouth opened to answer her, but found his brain unable to formulate a response. Momentarily, he was stumped. Momentarily, his wife had won. She smiled demurely while driving the logic home one more time.

'I don't really know much about these things, darling! But I suppose that only by exactly counting every hair, before and after, could you prove your point definitively.'

Faraway, on the other side of the garden, the cat meowed.

Momentarily, Xylon was floored by his wife's argument. Defeat at the hands of Socrates and Plato was one thing, losing to her quite another. It just could not be allowed to happen. While his mind pondered, his face reddened and his teeth gritted.

Momentarily, Demtres had won, and it was a

wonderful state of affairs. Though usually in the right, she'd spent a lifetime being the one to say sorry. Just this once, provoked by an emergency, she had conjured Xylon's own type of specious argument against him. It was, she thought, tremendously satisfying.

'Hold on. Hold on!' shouted Xylon with pouting lips. 'I need just one more second to consider.'

Seeing his expression, Demtres could not help laughing out loud. Which made him madder. Which made his nostrils open wider. Which made Demtres laugh even harder. All the tension she'd built up in thirty-five years of doormat diplomacy poured forth in an ecstatic, hysterical cackle.

Her reaction was understandable, but it had tragic consequences. Eyes closed and body bent over lest her ribs would break, she backed away blindly. Still laughing, she tripped on the low garden fence and toppled over the edge of the cliff.

To his credit, Xylon was not frozen to the spot. Nor did he have to think twice; instinct took over. Calmly he stepped out over the cliff edge and followed her into the abyss, lunging to try to catch up. As the moment of destruction on the rocks came closer, he shouted at his wife the scathing rebuttal he had finally composed. There was not enough time for Demtres to get in a reply.

7

There must be fifty ways to annoy my husband

My husband is very sensitive. There must be at least fifty ways to annoy him. Mostly I do it by accident, like forgetting to buy his cigarettes, or serving the same dinner two nights in a row, or asking him a question while he's watching soccer on TV. Last night, though, on his thirty-fourth birthday, I discovered a new way of annoying him.

After midnight, we were out on our balcony. The city below was aglow, so you could easily trace the slash of darkness, a brutally straight line, halfway out towards the horizon. My husband was not looking at the Wall, however. He was 'making love to me' and his eyes were closed tight. I say 'making love to me' wryly because he wasn't really. He was (please don't choke yourself laughing) making love to Marilyn Monroe.

He has always been in the habit of closing his eyes from the moment foreplay begins. I've had my suspicions about what was going on inside those eyelids, but never been sure until yesterday. Because it was his special day, I asked what he would like.

'Really like?'

'Yes. What would you really really like?'

'Why don't we,' he said, 'try a little bit of role play? To spice things up.'

'What do you mean exactly?'

He launched into a detailed outline of his fantasy. I should pretend to be Marilyn Monroe and he'd act like Joe DiMaggio. Who he, I wondered? A famous American baseball star, I was told. Also we must pretend it was 1961. Why? Because my husband had researched the matter and found that was the only year these Americans could both plausibly have visited our city: Marilyn to shoot some scenes for a film, DiMaggio to play an exhibition ballgame for the Allied occupying troops. Also, that was the year the Wall was actually built by Khrushchev's soldiers. My husband asked me to imagine we were in the penthouse suite at the Askanischer Hotel and that we could smell the cement still drying.

I didn't agree to any of this but I felt I couldn't reject it either. Not on his birthday. So off came our clothes and he lay on top of me. He closed his eyes but I kept mine open. Far from arousing me, the idea of having sex with an ancient baseball star was a complete turn-off. I accepted that this was going to be one of those sessions (surely every woman knows the feeling) during which I just lie there, let it happen and ponder what I'll wear to work tomorrow. Then my husband opened his mouth.

'Ooooooooh,' he murmured and continued in an American accent while kneading my breasts. 'Shucks, Marilyn, you sure are swell.'

Yikes. That was just too creepy. I know, I know, it was my own fault for having asked him what he'd like. But this was too much – to have it rubbed in my face that I may as well be a blow-up doll, that I was just a woman-shaped piece of meat on which he could project the image of Marilyn.

'Don't you "Shucks, Marilyn" me,' I hissed. 'Those are not her breasts, but mine. Elena's!'

He shrugged (in an American accent, I swear) and, with eyes closed, resumed thrusting inside me.

'And,' I continued, mouth right up to his ear, 'you are not Joe DiMaggio, legend of the New York Yankees. You are Helmut Milch, a forklift operator at the District Fabrik on Münzstrasse.'

He scrunched his eyes tighter together and his plunging grew faster, desperate for the finish line.

'And one last thing,' I said, poking his ribs with my fingernail, 'we are not in the Askanischer. We couldn't possibly go there as we live east of the Wall!'

'Blast you anyway, Elena!' he said as he disconnected from me abruptly. 'You're ruining the whole thing.'

Then he staggered down the dark corridor to the communal toilet, one hand out to guide him, his eyes still closed.

8

My ex-wife:
a user's manual (excerpt)

Section 7: Troubleshooting

Problem	Likely cause	Solution
She seems quiet … *When you place a comforting hand on her shoulder, she looks up and smiles weakly. Removes your hand gently. Face resumes grim expression.*	**… is other people** — is thinking that today was definitely the day that her mother was due to go for her endoscopy appointment at the clinic; — is replaying an encounter at work in which she let that bitch Emma undermine her once again – it's enough to make her consider going back to working part-time; — has just discovered a voice message from the school asking that we come in for 'an informal chat' about Jack's 'attention-seeking antics' – what has he done now?	**Ask what's wrong.** Listen. Nod. Offer a (tentative!) opinion to show you've understood properly.
She seems quiet … *When you place a comforting hand on her shoulder, she doesn't react,*	**…is herself** — is guilt-tripping over not going to the gym for nearly three weeks now. Thinking, *if we were to buy our own treadmill, which room would it fit in?*	**Ask what's wrong.** Several times if necessary. Listen. Nod.

doesn't notice. Too deep in reflection.

- is dismayed at being nearly forty; mulling over (yet again) whether to have another baby before it's too late;

- has remembered that next week is the application deadline for that Masters in Creative Writing she'd really love to do. But, even if done by correspondence, it could be quite a burden on all of us. Yet how else is she ever going to break free from the grind and do something actually meaningful with her life?

DO NOT OFFER ANY REPLY WHICH MIGHT BE CONSTRUED AS ADVICE, OR A SOLUTION, OR TELLING HER WHAT TO DO.

She seems quiet ...
When you place a comforting hand on her shoulder, she shrugs it off. Violently.

...is you

- is peeved that you did not consult her before agreeing to dinner with the Taylors on Friday week – as usual, you just assumed;

- is angry because yet again you did not clean the grill or wipe down the work surfaces after cooking – it seems as if she's the only one around here who notices the filth;

- is outraged not so much by what you said last night as by the way you said it.

DO NOT ASK WHAT'S WRONG.

Ignore the situation for an hour, a day, a week. It WILL go away.

9

Two in the bed and the little one said

Waterford, Ireland, September 2008

I walked through my bedroom door and was shocked to find a young woman I recognized from McCarthy's Insurance Brokers. She was not, however, in her work uniform, which is a navy skirt and white blouse with name badge. No. In fact she was entirely naked and straddling my husband, who was also naked. My immediate reaction was to shout and hurl a hairbrush. It served to clear them both from my sight.

'I'll come back and get my things when you've cooled off,' my husband shouted as he limped away, rubbing a bump on his thigh.

My rage lasted only a few hours and in its place . . . nothing. I did not cry, but I did mope. I lay on the sofa watching *Oprah Winfrey* and *Dr Phil* and *Judge Judy*. I contemplated going upstairs and taking a scissors to the contents of my husband's wardrobe. But, except for toilet breaks and making cups of tea, I remained on the sofa. I stared at the ceiling and listened to the faint sound of waves breaking on Tramore beach, through night and day and night once more.

There were no interruptions, not even a phone call from my son, Tony. Finally I heard a jangle of keys at the back door. My husband had come back for his things. There was a curt 'hello' as he jogged up the stairs. I lay listening to his heavy footsteps through the ceiling overhead. The packing took just twenty minutes. He lobbed the whole lot out to his car in three suitcases. He returned for an equally curt 'bye'. There was no attempt at an apology or explanation for what he had done. There was no begging for forgiveness or to be allowed to stay. I remained where I was for a further hour, lying in total silence.

Eventually, I got up from the sofa. I put on a pair of gardening gloves and went out to do some work in the flowerbeds. It was the time of year when weeds get ahead of you in a matter of days.

That evening my spine was quite stiff from hours spent kneeling and reaching. Without thinking, I went up to my bedroom for the first time since discovering the girl from McCarthy's Insurance. The scene was just as it had been: my husband hadn't bothered to tidy it. The bed was unmade, prompting easy remembrance of the position in which their bodies had been. Joined together. Half concealed under the quilt lay the young woman's bra. With the point of my shoe, I poked it further into view – 38D! A big girl, evidently. Also, judging by the stuffy lingering scent, she was partial to Tommy Girl perfume. I threw open the window and went to sleep in Tony's room.

Over the following days, I became determined that I would never sleep in that bed again. It was where

I'd slept for the twenty-nine years of my marriage; it was where I'd given birth to Tony when he popped out ahead of schedule. But it had been desecrated. Wearing a pair of yellow gloves, I rolled the sheet, pillow and quilt into a ball and binned them. I drove into the city to Oakland Furniture Warehouse and bought a new bed, paying extra for delivery and assembly on site.

'To be honest, ma'am,' said the grey-haired half of the delivery team as they sipped the tea I'd made them, 'the new yoke we've delivered you hasn't half the quality of the old one. You'd know it by the weight, if nothing else.'

'That's a fact, ma'am,' chipped in his bald-headed colleague. 'Jaysus, the old one must be pure mahogany or ebony or some such. And tough: there's not a scratch on either head or footboard!'

Which is more than could be said for my good wallpaper down along the staircase. The men had wrestled and rotated the old bed for half an hour to get it to the bottom.

'What are you planning to do with it anyway, ma'am?' asked grey hair, gesturing to where it now stood, by the street, on the path outside my house.

'What am I . . . planning to do?' I said.

'Yes, ma'am?'

'But I thought that you'd take the old bed away.'

'Jaysus, no, ma'am,' said baldy, shaking his head. 'We tried to help you as best we could by bringing it downstairs, but as to taking it away? No can do. We'd never fit it in that wee van we have. The new beds, see, do come in flat-pack. But the old 'uns, God, you'd need a fair-sized truck.'

'Well, the fact is that I don't have any plans for it,'
I said, annoyed at the perfect reasonableness of his
excuse. 'I just want it to go. To disappear. To be out
of my sight. To just be not here.'

'Oh,' said baldy, and took a bite of his biscuit.

'Oh,' said grey hair, before breaking into a smile.
'But getting rid of a bed of that quality'll be no
bother. If you just leave it where it is, out there on
the street where passers-by will notice, 'twill soon be
gone. Isn't the whole of Tramore chock-a-block with
young couples looking to furnish their new homes?
Mark my words, ma'am. Just place a sign on that bed
of yours, offering it free to whoever wants it, and
'twill be gone in the morning.'

So I did make a sign, nothing fancy, just cereal-box
cardboard and a loop of the white string I use for
tying up roses. I hung it from the headboard.

NO LONGER WANTED
PLEASE TAKE AWAY

It was not gone in the morning. Nor on the morning
after that. I wasn't really bothered, though. First,
because I was just relieved to have it out of my living
space (the new bed was fine, incidentally, with a
comfortably firm mattress). Second, because I had
turned my full attention once again to my garden and
in particular the herbaceous border. September is my
month for cutting away faded and dying stems from
border perennials, tidying up the plants but leaving
as much foliage as possible. Also, the summer bedding
plants have to be dug up for composting. On a
brighter note, I lay foundations for next year's display.
Most of the spring-flowering bulbs need to be planted

so they'll have established roots before the onset of winter.

I was doing just that, sowing a batch of crocus and hyacinth, when I heard a voice over my shoulder.

'God bless the work.'

I turned around. It was my neighbour Tess, her face visible from the nose up, speaking from behind the high garden wall. She is a short woman; I guessed she was standing on a box or something.

'Hello, Tess, how are you?' I said, but returned to my planting, not overly interested in her reply.

'Oh, I'm fine,' said Tess. 'The big question, though, is how are you?'

'Fine, also,' I said.

'Fine?' she said.

'Yes,' I said, and with great reluctance I got up from my task and turned to face her with a glare. 'I. Am. Fine.'

'Yes . . .' said Tess, backing away slightly and nearly losing her footing. When she was stable again, she continued. 'Anyway, it's marvellous to see how well you're taking the whole thing, but –'

'But what?'

'But I thought you should know . . . he's moved into one of the B 'n' Bs below facing the beach.'

My husband, obviously.

'With that young girl in tow.'

Of course. The one from McCarthy's Insurance Brokers.

'Yes. Thank you, Tess,' I said, and made to turn away.

'I also thought you should know,' Tess added, 'that she's only twenty-six.'

Oh.

'That's about your son Tony's age, isn't it?' she said.

I glared at her again. For a moment I contemplated asking if her vast knowledge extended as far as knowing the girl's bra size. Surely, in this matter at least, I was not the last to know.

I said nothing. I turned my back on her and knelt back down to the task in hand.

'One more thing, as well,' she chirped. 'I think you should know that there's been a few people complaining about that bed blocking the footpath.'

Later that afternoon, I was back on the sofa having a little rest when the doorbell rang. 'Tony!' I thought and nearly tripped over the coffee table on my way to open the door.

It was not Tony. It was the man from No. 2, president of the Residents' Association.

'It's about the bed, I'm afraid,' he said. 'You just can't leave it there; it's blocking the right of way for pedestrians.'

'Can't they just go around it, temporarily? My hope is that it won't be there very much longer.'

'No,' said the man from No. 2. 'The able-bodied person might manage it. But what about the people in wheelchairs? And the blind folk?'

Yes, admittedly I had forgotten them.

'And another thing,' he continued, his face turning a little redder, 'it's attracting an antisocial element.'

'Oh?'

'Yes. I saw some with my own eyes last night around midnight.'

His own eyes and a pair of night-vision binoculars, more likely.

'A boy and a girl, on their way home from the pub, didn't they spot it? And the pair of them jumped in. For a kip. Or whatever!'

Or whatever. Nothing new there.

'And bad as it is, in this lovely weather, what about when it rains? Then it'll turn into an awful mess. It might become a bolt-hole for vermin.'

For vermin. That too, I now knew, would be nothing original.

'Think of the impact on tourism in the area.'

I thought.

'So, then?' he said with an air of finality, his face very red now from the effort of getting out his piece. 'You'll move it, will you?'

'What, me personally? No, indeed! I won't touch it.'

'No, not you personally,' he said, taking a big breath and handing me a business card. It had the phone number of Kilrane Waste Disposal Ltd. 'I recommend this crowd.'

He bid me good day.

Rather than jump straight to his lordship's command, I went back out to prune the drooping clematis and honeysuckle from my archway. After teatime, though, I wanted to get the matter dealt with, once and for all. I dialled the number.

'All right,' said the girl. 'That'll be eighty-five euro plus VAT.'

Robbery! But I wasn't in the mood to ring around comparing prices.

'And how will you be paying today?' she asked.

I called out the credit card number.

'I'm sorry,' she purred, 'but that number appears to

85

be invalid. Do you have another card with which to pay?'

I tried the debit card. Again it came up invalid. I said I'd ring her back.

So my cards had been invalidated. My immediate thought was to ring my husband on his mobile and demand their revalidation. And tell him of my outrage. And my disgust. And my . . .

But no. Really, I did not want to speak to the man at all. He was probably lying in bed reading a post-coital tabloid beside his 26-year-old 38D from McCarthy's Insurance Brokers. In a greasy B 'n' B.

I checked my purse and found forty euro. Used purely for essential groceries, it would last me several days. Disposal of the blasted bed could wait.

'I think you should know,' said Tess the next morning, 'that we're all very much on your side in this. Everyone agrees that he's acted abominably.'

I was busy planting cuttings of berberis and griselinia in the winter cold frame.

'I mean, really, I'm shocked when I hear reports that the pair of them can be seen quite openly down at the chipper around seven every night. And she flaunting a ring that he bought her. Not an engagement ring, obviously. But, still, a ring!'

The berberis I was holding was extremely prickly. I wondered what it would feel like if it were thrown in someone's face.

From inside my house came the faint sound of the phone ringing. I dropped what I was doing and ran in without any goodbye to Tess. I was thinking the likeliest caller would be Tony. It wasn't. It was a telesales man promoting water filters.

'I thought we had an agreement,' said the man from No. 2 when I answered the doorbell again late that evening. Beside him on my doorstep stood a young garda. The timing, post-showering, was not ideal; I was dripping and in my dressing-gown.

'You've given me no option but to call in a member of the force.'

'But –' I began.

'But nothing,' shouted No. 2, his face getting even redder, even faster than before (my dressing-gown was of the sensible sort, but perhaps there was a glimpse of my calves showing). 'Twenty-four hours later the bed is still here. Furthermore, I rang up Kilrane's myself and you're not on their list of jobs for tomorrow. Plainly you have no intention of dealing with this matter.'

'It's not that simple,' I said, but was shouted down again.

'It is. That simple,' he bellowed, looking away from me and addressing the young garda. 'I even gave her the phone number and everything. All she had to do was pick up the phone and order collection. Pay by cash or credit card. That's all.'

Yes, that's all.

'It really is a disgrace,' said No. 2 in conclusion, 'an absolutely uncivic, unneighbourly disgrace.'

The young garda was leafing through the pages of a small handbook. He came to the right page and looked up to address me. Mournfully.

'Missus, this gentleman here has asked me to read

87

to you the relevant by-law pertaining to the abandon-
ment of any kind of article or articles that are
manifestly in themselves, or may be construed as such
to be, litter, rubbish, debris and/or any other kind of
waste (as previously defined in the preamble to the
Environmental Protection Act (1985)).'

'All right, garda, read on,' I said, and pulled the lapels
of my gown together against the chill. I was more
amused than annoyed, now that I knew I was not the
only person being bullied by the man from No. 2.

'Ah hahum!' coughed the garda, and he took a deep
breath but never got to begin. Instead both he and
the man from No. 2 were suddenly and simultaneously clasped around the shoulders by someone who
had tiptoed up the front path. My husband.

'Ah, Jaysus, lads, how's it hanging anyways? Am I
in trouble again? Are ye here to dish out the red
card?' he said, laughing. At nothing, obviously. But
it worked. The man from No. 2 looked a little less
heated, and the young garda breathed out in relief.
Everything was going to be okay after all – now that
they were dealing with a man, instead of a woman
in a dressing-gown.

Within thirty seconds the pair were happily on their
way out the gate with my husband's smiling assur-
ance that he'd get the bed removed on the morrow.
He shouted after them about Liverpool's chances of
winning a match. Then he turned to me once more,
his smile slipping sideways.

'Fucksake! You're making a holy fucking show of
yourself!' he said. 'Leaving our bed on the main
street! With that stupid sign hanging on it! And look
at you, out and about in your bloody dressing-gown
like some kind of washerwoman!'

He had never used such bad language, such aggressive language, with me. Of course, he was free of all restraints now.

'I am not the one making a show of myself,' I said, 'with a girl less than half my age.'

'Yes!' he said, 'half your age and double your libido. In fact, probably a hundred times your libido.'

That hurt. I felt like crying but I did not.

'Anyway,' he continued in a more conciliatory tone, 'that isn't the reason I came up here. I wanted to see how you're getting on. If you needed anything.'

I was still digesting the last comment. I stared at him and took in a few details. He was emitting a powerful blast of aftershave, no doubt something to match his new woman's perfume. Also his clothes were new, a bit more stylish, a bit younger. So much was visible, but there was, I reckoned, a fairly good chance that he might also have transformed underneath. Maybe finally clipped his toenails, begun to change his underpants daily instead of randomly when the notion occurred.

'Money,' I said. 'You cut off my cards.'

'Oh, yes,' he said, 'mine were cut too, though. I'm afraid the solicitor insisted on freezing the accounts. It's just for an initial period until the separation and redistribution of our estate is figured out.'

Solicitor?

Separation?

Redistribution of our estate?

My husband had many things already figured out.

'In the meantime I can give you some cash from the arcade. I'll go and get it in the car.'

Off he trotted. He (it used to be we) owned an amusement arcade down near the beach.

'Sorry about the change,' he said, handing me a small but heavy pink sack. 'There's a hundred euro in fivers and four hundred in two-euro coins.'

My money – no, my allowance – weighed about four pounds.

'So,' he said, 'the other thing is the bed. Seeing as you obviously don't want it, I'll come around in the morning with PJ's truck. We'll pick it up around 10 a.m. I mean structurally that bed is perfectly fine. I'll definitely be able to find a place for it, whenever I get out of the B 'n' B and have fixed up in a new gaff. In the meantime I'll store it in PJ's garage.'

So that was that, sorted.

That night I got very little sleep. I did, however, have a dream.

It began in the back porch with me putting on my brown leather gloves. I went out to the garden to transplant a cyanotis that was not thriving in the corner. The soil was frozen, so I stabbed at it with a spade but made little headway. A tiny little porcelain doll leaned its head over the fence, and, though it did not look like her, I realized at some level that it was Tess. She addressed me in her usual way.

'I just thought you should know that your husband and his other woman are around the front in that bed.'

I brought the spade with me and walked quickly through the house to the front. The two were in the bed all right, but it was no longer just a bed, it was a vehicle. It rolled on its castors away down the street and I rushed to follow. By the time I caught up, it was parked outside the chipper. I peeked through the window and saw my husband and the young woman from McCarthy's Insurance Brokers up at the counter ordering smoky bacon burgers.

I sat up on the bed and it floated gracefully onto the beach. The tide was coming in, but it was now like a raft and I used my spade as an oar until we were out past the waves. I was exhilarated, I was free.

'Where will we go?' I asked the bed.

'To a distant land,' said the bed.

I woke up and for a few sleepy seconds felt absolutely wonderful.

At 7 a.m. next morning, I put on my gloves. I did not, however, go gardening; rather, I went out to the street. For the first time in ten days, I was going to touch the old bed. Inspired by my dream, I had it in mind to move it myself, rather than let my husband simply redeploy it in a spare room somewhere as if it were just another object. It was definitely not just another object. I had three hours before his truck came in which to push it down the sloping paths of Tramore to the beach, about five hundred yards away. Once there, I would shove it into the sea.

That was the theory anyway, and it had seemed quite plausible when I was cuddled up in my quilt. In practice, however, the bed was way too heavy. I pushed hard against the headboard and moved it about two inches. Damn. It was on castors! Why couldn't it just roll smoothly, like in my dream? Perhaps because, as I found when I inspected them, the castors were no longer circular. They resembled nothing so much as tiny little flat tyres. Feck it! I stomped back in home for a cup of tea. There was still some time until my husband arrived, though, and I duly came up with another plan. After a bit of rummaging around on the back porch shelf, I found a saw.

It was a quarter past ten when I heard the revs of PJ's truck backing up outside. I didn't get up off the sofa; I tried to keep my attention on the television. Eventually, as I knew it would, the doorbell rang. Not once, not twice, but continuously, as a fat stubby finger pressed it down hard.

'Hello,' I said, opening up to find my husband. 'Did you want something?'

'Very funny,' said my husband; 'you know bloody well what I want. Where is it?'

'Where's what?' I said in my best innocent tone. 'You really will have to explain yourself.'

'No sign of it,' said PJ, coming around the corner from the back of the house. 'I checked the bins, the hedges, all around the garden.'

'For what?' I said, and by now I was enjoying the scene too much to suppress a smile.

'We only noticed it after we'd hoisted the bed onto the truck, ma'am,' PJ said. 'One of the legs of the bed has been cut off and is gone missing.'

'That's terrible,' I said, managing not to laugh.

'The bed's kind of useless without it,' he said. 'If we found it, though, maybe we could stick it back on with dowels.'

'Best of luck with your search, then, lads,' I said, and went to close the door. My husband stuck his foot in the way.

'No, you spiteful bitch,' he shouted and elbowed in past me, 'I know well it was you, so I'm searching the house.'

Shrugging my shoulders, I wandered out with PJ and had a look at the three-legged bed sitting forlornly on the truck. My husband meanwhile searched the house and, of course, failed to find the wooden leg. Not because I wasn't the culprit, but because I had buried it in the garden deep under a bed of cyanotis. By the time he had given up looking he was in an even wilder state of frustration. Not a hundred per cent sure whose fault it was, he began to spout abuse under his breath at everything and nothing in particular. F**king, sh*tting, b****xing, w*nking, etcetera, as his tantrum gathered momentum.

Just then the man from No. 2 walked past. Or rather did not walk past. He was after all a person who did not fear to get involved.

'Excuse me,' he said, tapping my husband on the shoulder, 'could you please stop that bad language? Think of the impact on tourism in the area.'

My husband turned and for a moment looked as if he might dish out a very different kind of impact.

'C'mon, 'tis time we got going,' said PJ.

So PJ jumped up into the cab. My husband was about to follow when something caught my eye and I had a moment of inspiration, the kind I usually get hours after I've had an argument – when I think, way too late, of what would've been the perfect word or gesture. This time I knew exactly what to do.

'Just one more thing,' I said to my husband, as I picked up the card that I'd noticed on the ground. It was the sign saying:

NO LONGER WANTED
PLEASE TAKE AWAY

93

Before he quite knew what I was doing, I'd put it over his head and around his neck. I started to laugh.

'Cop yourself on!' he said, and swiped it off quickly but it was already too late. I'd framed the image in my mind and I laughed quietly all the way into the house.

And as I put on the kettle.

And as I sent off a text message to Tony.

And as I phoned and made an appointment to see a solicitor.

And even after I finally began to cry, because in the end it was okay. I did no longer want him and he had been taken away.

10

King versus queen

This is the story of a quarrel that occurred long ago. The deserts of Iraq were then the green meadows of Mesopotamia. Two neighbouring kingdoms, Akkad and Elam, had capital cities separated by barely a furlong. It was a wet furlong, though, namely the River Euphrates. Through forgotten ages, the two kingdoms had always been at war. But, being equally potent, neither could ever conquer the other. In the time of which I write, it came to pass that two fine diplomats did arise, Sargon and Murabi, one in each camp. Each won the role of royal adviser and persuaded his respective monarch of the merits of peace. Hostilities ceased and there were three tranquil decades of prosperity. Citizens from the two kingdoms, however, were still utterly forbidden to cross the river. The two diplomats were an exception. Through to their old age they continued to negotiate with a view to promoting further harmony. Eventually they managed to engineer a marriage of the newly crowned young

97

successors, the King of Akkad and the Queen of Elam.

The morning after the royal wedding started early for Sargon. Barely past midnight, he was awoken and summoned to the king's bedchamber. Briskly he mounted six flights of stairs to find the king in his bed, head propped up on three pillows, shouting angrily. The queen was conspicuously absent.

'Yes, you cringing idiot!' said the king. 'You may stop squinting under the bed. She is gone. The Queen of Elam has left me. Is that a smirk I see forming on your ugly chin? Is it?'

It certainly was not. Sargon was at least as distraught as the king, possibly more so.

'This matter is to be kept hushed up,' said the king. 'I shall not have the rabble laughing and speculating about goings-on in the royal bedchamber. Say that she has returned to collect her belongings. Also, I want you to carry out a second mission.'

Sargon was only half listening; he was scanning the large bedchamber for some sign of what had caused the row. What had the king done to her? What had she done to him? What had brought about such a violent rupture just a day after they'd first met? By his pile of clothes on the chair, it could be assumed the king was fully undressed. That the queen had undressed also, at least partially, was evidenced by a sandal she'd left behind in her haste. What had happened next . . .

Sargon's reverie was interrupted by a shout from his master: 'Now repeat! What did I just ask of you?'

'You wish, sire, to exact a small revenge upon the queen for her downright unreasonableness,' said

Sargon, who could listen and think at the same time. 'You wish me to conjure up a plan by which this might be accomplished. Preferably by dawn.'

'Okay, so you were listening, Sargon. I should never doubt you,' said the king, less harshly than before. 'You may go and attend to it at once. On your way please summon me a concubine. No, make that two concubines . . .'

'He is a pig, pure and simple,' said the queen, when she and her pet (an orphaned kid goat) were finally alone with Murabi.

'What did he do, ma'am?' inquired Murabi, just as peeved as Sargon had been by the falling-out.

'He –'

But the queen was interrupted by a crashing sound on the lawn outside her window. They ran downstairs to investigate. On the grass were scattered clumps of straw, and in their midst the broken remains of a missile – what had been a hollow wooden ball.

'What does this mean, Murabi?' asked the queen, putting her precious little goat down for a moment. 'Is it a message from the gods?'

'No, ma'am,' said Murabi, who was scanning the perimeter of the crash site looking for something. 'I think its provenance is rather closer to home.'

'You mean Akkad?' said the queen, as a faint but high-pitched tone rang out in the distance. 'But how, why?'

'How? By means of a giant catapult,' said Murabi, and as he spoke he plucked from the grass an insect of some kind. 'As to why? I can only presume that it relates in some way to last night's difficulty with the king.'

'Oh, he is such a swine!' said the queen, 'and a stupid one if he thinks I'll be intimidated by a missile of straw and wood.'

'Aye, ma'am, the straw and wood are harmless, but they formed a ball and what of the contents thereof? That is the question.'

Gesturing that he had something in his fist, Murabi opened it a fraction to let the queen see what was trapped inside. It was a cricket. Even as Murabi crushed it tightly, the background din began to get much louder.

The wooden ball had contained five thousand crickets. On impact they had hopped free and fanned out across the lawns and gardens. Once established in a plot, each male dug itself a little burrow. Then they stood outside and began rubbing their wings together. The high-pitched vibrations of even one cricket are perfectly audible to human ears over twenty yards. Verily, the chorus of five thousand sent the queen and Murabi indoors clutching their ears. The piercing sound continued unabated all day, until Murabi finally deduced the most diabolical aspect of the prank: the hum is a mating song to summon female crickets and continues until one happens by. Each of the hand-picked crickets was male.

That night it was Murabi's turn to be roused early from bed. He entered the queen's bedchamber. Her little brown goat was asleep in its cot at the foot of her bed, but the queen was very much awake. She had to shout to be heard above the insect chorus.

'Murabi,' she yelled as she put on her sandals, 'it's an absolute outrage. I order you to prepare our soldiery. The truce between Elam and Akkad is officially over. We shall invade before dawn.'

'Ma'am,' said Murabi soothingly, 'an invasion sounds like an excellent and indeed totally justifiable idea. Perhaps before I sound the alarm, however, you'd let me share a possible alternative with you.'

'All right, you have one minute,' said the queen, staring intensely at her brown sandals.

'Well, ma'am,' said Murabi, 'it's been thirty-four years since we were last at war with Akkad, but at no stage during that time has our army been disbanded. Rather, starved of direct conflict, military minds have turned their attention to developing new methods of attack.'

'Go on,' said the queen, who had decided the brown sandals were not quite right for a battle. She ripped them off.

'Well, this was all done in secrecy, far from the capital and the prying eyes of Akkad. Testing generally took place in Jeddah. Numerous modes of remote attack were –'

'Get to the point, Murabi; your time is up.'

'Suffice to say, ma'am, that we too have developed a catapult like the one that was used against us this morning. Plainly Akkad has the ability to fire a missile into a specific garden over four hundred yards. We too have that capability.'

'But how's that better than just invading?'

'Ma'am, it has the advantage that such an attack is outside the terms of the peace accord. If none of our soldiers crosses the water, then no rule is broken and the problem doesn't escalate. Second, it has the merit of allowing you to target your attack on the king himself. Surely there's no need for an invasion when you bear his innocent people no ill will.'

'So you're saying,' said the queen as she took the

opportunity to inspect her toenails, 'I can send him back a swarm of crickets?'

'Yes.'

'Blah!'

'Well –'

'How about some other insect? How about' – and the queen's eyes gleamed for the first time all day – 'locusts!'

'Locusts? It's short notice. But we do have a few thousand on standby. As for sending them, yes. Once bound thickly in straw they generally survive transit.'

'Then make it happen, Murabi, and make sure they're hungry ones,' said the queen, and jumped back into her bed. She placed two thick plugs in her ears and shouted, 'On your way down you can also call off that invasion I ordered.'

At daybreak the crickets finally gave up calling and began to disperse. The news was not so good for the King of Akkad, though. He was awoken by something crashing through the branches of his apple tree. By the time he was on the scene, eight thousand locusts were already nibbling at everything green. In an hour things were brown. Although a dozen servants set about beating them away, the locusts scattered only when the food supply dwindled. It gave the king such a blinding headache that he had to retire to bed.

From a position of repose he shouted at his adviser: 'Dammit, Sargon. Surely you could have seen this coming. A reprisal should have been prepared for. If we'd got them at impact, those locusts could have been drowned.'

'Forgive me, sire, but we had no idea that Elam

had developed the same long-range capabilities as ourselves.'

'Well, you know now!' said the king, who was in bed, his head, as usual, propped up on three pillows. 'And as for that little ninny! Tell me, if you will, how perverse is the mind of a wife? I send my estranged spouse a few harmless crickets and am repaid with a ravenous horde of locusts – totally disproportionate! Just for that I'll have to send her something by return. And not crickets this time, or locusts either. I'll show her!'

The king beckoned Sargon closer and whispered what foul cargo he wanted the next missile to carry.

'Oh, please, sire,' said Sargon, 'not poisonous ones, I beg of you.'

It was lunchtime in the queen's castle when the next missile arrived. It hurtled through the ground-floor front window into the kitchen just as food was being prepared. Amid the hustle and bustle of cooks and servers, a hundred snakes were suddenly unleashed. Non-poisonous, thanks to Sargon's intervention, they nevertheless created a riot of confusion as the staff yelped and shrieked. Some climbed counters, while many escaped out through the in-door. The snakes poured into the dining room, scattering the throng, and made their way to every corner of the castle. When one slithered into the queen's chamber, she beheaded it with her sword. Then she turned to Murabi.

'The swine! Now let me tell you what I would like you to send back to my porcine husband.'

She whispered in his ear.

'Ma'am,' said Murabi, 'I beg of you, not diseased!'

*

103

At dusk, Elam showed it too could launch a ball with amazing exactitude. The fourth-floor side window of Akkad's castle was walloped open by a projectile filled with sixty rats. At Murabi's insistence they'd been washed and were not especially diseased. Nevertheless they provoked chaotic scenes throughout the household, as the intrepid little explorers worked their way down each level, rummaging in dimly lit rooms, gnawing at fabrics and turning up in the king's sugar bowl.

The third day of the quarrel saw further attempts at aggression by both sides, but these ended in failure. The scorpions fired by Akkad were shattered by the impact of landing; the wasps of Elam exited at the nearest window and flew straight back to their nest. Maggots, frogs and fleas were all launched without causing much disruption. As frustration built, each monarch tried to find the insult that would trump all others.

'Sargon,' said the king from his pillows, 'why don't we forget about the catapult and use birds? It should be possible to train them to fly over Elam and do something.'

'Train them to do what, sire?' asked a weary Sargon.

'Oh, I don't know,' said the king. 'Something! And whatever it is we could also train some bats and get them to do it at night!'

The queen's ideas were more fully formed.

'Out in his garden, what's left of it,' she said with a wicked smile while stroking her goat, 'my husband has a pond in which he has three purple fish. They're his pride and joy. What I want you to do, Murabi, is to train some bigger fishes to swim over there, go into the pond and eat his fish. All right?'

Perhaps Murabi did not look enthusiastic.

'No?' said the queen playfully. 'Then just send over another ball of rats.'

Murabi still did not look enthusiastic.

'Oh, right, then, spoilsport. What?' asked the queen.

'I think,' said Murabi, 'it's time that you and I took the boat.'

Murabi and the queen (and her goat) crossed the River Euphrates and were met by Sargon and the king. The goat was left to run around in the courtyard as the quartet supped wine politely in the castle. There was an awkward silence, eventually broken by the king. He said he wished to withdraw to his chamber for a quiet word with his wife.

Sargon and Murabi agreed but followed the royal couple at a discreet distance up the six flights of stairs. When the door to the bedchamber was closed, the two old diplomats pressed their ears to the timber. 'Hopefully,' Sargon murmured, 'we will now find out what it was that caused this stupid quarrel in the first place.'

The King of Akkad vaulted onto his bed and sat with his head propped up on three pillows, as was his wont. The Queen of Elam remained standing, her speech quick and to the point.

'I'm not going to complain of the crickets and the snakes. Let you mention not the locusts and rats. All I want is an apology for your behaviour on our wedding night.'

'Certainly not.'

'Then I suppose this visit has been a waste – good day!' said the queen, turning to go.

'Hold it there,' said the king sharply, but then tried a more conciliatory tone. 'Ahhm . . . my dear lovely wife. I don't have an apology, but I do have a solution.'

'Go on.'

'Well, the thing is, I've never shared this bed before.'

Outside the door, Murabi raised an eyebrow at Sargon. Sargon whispered, 'Concubines don't count.'

'The issue that arose on that first night was unprecedented. This is the bed I've slept in since the day I left my mother's breast. This,' the king said, pointing, 'is the bedspread I've always slept under. And these' – he gestured with his thumb – 'I've always had just these three pillows. The reason there're three of them is lost in time, I don't know why. Anyway, on our wedding night, everything was going great until you suggested that I give you two pillows and settle for one myself. Don't you see – that somehow put me on a lower level than you? In my own bed! And me a king!

'But I now realize that it was just the same for you when I insisted on taking two pillows and leaving you with just the one. Why would you, a queen, tolerate someone looking down on you? No wonder you flounced out in such a temper.'

'Right so far,' said the queen. 'So?'

'So,' he said, jumping up from the bed in a single bound, 'I'm now going to do what I should have done on our wedding night.'

The King of Akkad picked up one of his enormous goose-down pillows and flung it out through the window.

'So now it's just one pillow each!' gushed the Queen of Elam.

The two old diplomats, Sargon and Murabi, crept away from the door. They were afraid to look at each other and kept their hands to their mouths until they were halfway down the stairs. Finally, on the third landing, the laughter they'd been stifling erupted. They bent double. They cackled until they howled. They held each other, and tears ran down their faces. They trotted down the remaining flights, still laughing, but the merriment came to an abrupt end when they emerged into the courtyard. They were confronted with a grisly sight: there lay a fat goose-down pillow, and poking out from underneath was a pair of furry shins. The shins of the queen's little goat. He was perfectly still. And perfectly dead.

For a moment neither Sargon nor Murabi said anything. They stood in silent contemplation.

'Well, the timing could be worse,' said Sargon with a wry smile. 'If my king is any use at all, she'll give no thought to that unfortunate goat until daybreak . . .'

'Yes. I believe we can fix this,' said Murabi, picking up the small carcass. 'Let's call up our soldiers and get to work. We have seven hours to search the two kingdoms for an identical kid goat.'

11

Ladies! Does your husband spend every evening stuck in a newspaper?

LADIES!

DOES YOUR HUSBAND SPEND EVERY EVENING STUCK IN A NEWSPAPER?

Is he never helpful around the house?
His chores left forever undone?

DESPAIR NO LONGER!

Help is at hand in the form of Dr Iphigenia Whitlock's Reanimating Solar Tincture. Just one spoonful daily will transform your malingering man into a hardworking hero!

DR WHITLOCK'S AMAZING DISCOVERY!

A pioneer in the study of male malingering, Dr Whitlock has discovered the root cause of men's reluctance to do their chores around the house. The tiredness they complain of is actually due to an impure, impoverished and scrofulous condition of the blood. Dr Whitlock's patent tincture is specially formulated to infuse the bloodstream with elements of purification and reanimating force derived directly from the Sun. Within minutes of taking a single spoonful the subject is guaranteed to lay down his newspaper and gather his tools to carry out some much needed task.

✳ *Amazing Cure!* ✳ *Works Quickly!* ✳
✳ *Easy to Administer!* ✳ *Free Gift!* ✳

THINK OF ALL THAT NEEDS DOING!

Nearly every home has a backlog of tasks left undone by the man of the house. Whether it's fixing a leak under the sink, replacing loose slates on the roof or simply mowing the lawn – all these jobs will cost a tidy sum if you have to hire a plumber, carpenter or gardener. If you use Dr Whitlock's tincture, that won't be necessary, however – your own private handyman will take care of everything!

Despair no longer!
**Fill in the mail order form
and receive your first bottle within days.**
In addition, receive a Special Surprise Free Gift!

Act today!
Now!

12

The flatmate who knew too much

'Is that – oh my God, it is! That's Carol.'
I almost dropped my glass of wine in disbelief but there could be no doubt. It was definitely her, Carol Storan, whom I hadn't laid eyes on for eight years. I handed my drink to my husband and made a beeline over to where Ronan, our host, was pouring her a vodka.

'Hey there. Remember me?' I said, tapping her on the shoulder.

She turned around and for a moment she wore just a polite smile, plainly not placing me at all. Then the penny dropped.

'Fruitcake!' she said, throwing her arms around me. I hugged her back and found myself starting to cry. As did she.

'Do you want a shot of lime with that?' asked Ronan.

She ignored him and we stood for a full minute in a tearful embrace.

*

Carol Storan was a woman I shared a flat with back in the day. It was for just one year, but that year – 1999 – was the worst in my life. When I met Carol I was in an awful state, having just broken up with my boyfriend of six years, Mark. Looking back, with the benefit of now having some self-esteem, I could see that it was an abusive relationship. He bullied me relentlessly. He was probably unfaithful too. At the time, though, I was distraught at being dumped and felt life had passed me by. My friends were all getting engaged, planning weddings, buying houses and one or two had had their first babies. I, in contrast, was back on the scrap heap. I had clung on to Mark years after it became apparent that he was a jerk. I thought the alternative was to wind up alone. I was twenty-nine.

After moving out of Mark's place I needed somewhere to live and answered an ad in the paper. That's how I met Carol. She gave me the box room but I didn't really mind. I planned to make my stay a short one.

'I've done something stupid,' I said to her the next evening when she found me lying on the bath mat. I had indeed done something very stupid. I had swallowed sixty iron tablets. At my side were two notes I'd written, one to Mark, the other to my mother. Each had taken several drafts.

'Right, Little Miss Fruitcake,' she said matter-of-factly. 'Let's see if we can't sort this.'

She forced me to kneel up to the toilet. She made me get sick. Repeatedly. She counted the half-digested tablets as they landed into the bowl and when I got to forty she let me stop.

I fell asleep quickly. When I awoke I had a wee and found my urine had turned black. (It stayed that way for a week.) Otherwise I was fine physically. The whole

Mark thing had not gone away, however. I rang in sick next day and stayed in bed crying. I no longer wanted to die but I wasn't too enthusiastic about living either.

'C'mon, we're going for a walk,' said Carol, and, despite my objections, that afternoon I found myself strolling in St Anne's Park. We sat on a bench and I poured out my heart.

When I eventually looked up, Carol was crying. And it wasn't because Mark was such a control freak.

'Yes, Little Miss Fruitcake,' she said, smiling through her tears. 'I have troubles too.'

So she told me about her recent trip to England. And all about having had an abortion.

'So this is the famous Carol,' said my husband, Warren, when he came over to hand me my drink.

Carol and I were sitting on a bench in the short corridor to the back door.

'Carol,' he said as he shook her hand, 'this wife of mine used to mention your name in every second sentence when I first met her.'

'Is that right?' said Carol. 'But then she forgot me, eh?'

'God, no,' I said, 'I never forgot you. It was just you went to Australia and I know I should have written more often. Then you changed address and I kind of lost track.'

'I'm only teasing, Fruitcake,' Carol said, smiling and putting her hand on my knee. 'It was my fault totally. I got so into the Australian lifestyle that I forgot all about my former life back in the rainy country. I met a man and got married, y'know, had a house and everything for a few years . . .'

'But not now?'

'No,' she said. 'We divorced a few months ago, which is what has me here tonight. I only flew in a few days ago. I've had enough of Oz. I'm coming back to Dublin.'

'Oh, Carol, that's wonderful news,' I said.

'Yeah, it's working out really well so far. Ronan's an old friend of my brother, and thanks to him I've lined up a job in Loreto doing maternity cover. Now all I have to do is find a flat. I'm sleeping on my sister's sofa and her kids' new game is jumping on their Auntie Carol at six in the morning.'

I looked at Warren. Warren looked at me. He didn't hesitate. 'You must come and stay with us. We have a spare room. We'd love to have you over.'

'No, I couldn't impose,' she said, but we cajoled her.

'Okay,' she agreed finally. 'But only until I get my own place.'

Just then we were called in to dinner. There was a seating plan: Warren had been put beside Carol; I was down at the far end of the table. I was disappointed that we couldn't continue the reunion, but since Ronan was Warren's boss, I wasn't going to make a fuss.

'Go on,' said Carol, laughing, 'it'll give me a perfect opportunity to get to know this husband of yours and after dessert I'll give him marks out of ten.'

I took my designated seat but I wasn't much company for those around me. I spent far too much time trying to see how Carol and Warren were getting on. And when I wasn't stealing glances up the table, I was lost in the past.

*

The abortion filled Carol with guilt and regret, and throughout the first half of 1999 we were about equally miserable. The only consolation was that we were miserable together. Our mutual sadness helped forge a deep friendship. Outside of work, we spent most of our time together, having long chats, having long silences. There were many more tearful walks around St Anne's Park and then, for a change of scene, along Dollymount Strand. We stayed in every night, eating chocolate HobNobs and watching *Ally McBeal* or *Sex in the City*.

Carol saved my life when I took the iron tablets. But she saved it for a second time during that wilderness period. None of my coupled-off friends were interested in hearing about Mark. He was a slimeball, they all said, end of story, now move on. But sometimes you can't just move on. You have to talk it out of your system.

By summer, we both felt a little better. We were ready to take tentative steps back towards a social life and started going to the nightclubs of Harcourt Street a few times a week. In September, Carol decided to go to Australia for a year. She wanted me to go with her, but I was just too much of a home-bird. On the tenth of December I met Warren at a Christmas party. Carol departed for Perth on the second of January.

After dinner, Carol and I got together again and reclaimed the bench in the back corridor. We had so much to catch up on.

'Your life hasn't stood still, Fruitcake,' she said. 'Marriage, mortgage and motherhood, eh?'

I told her all about Jack (three) and Ciara (one) and asked if she'd had any herself.

'God, no,' she said, 'no children, no husband, no house, hardly even a country – I'm as free as free can be.'

'Yes,' I said. I thought, but did not say aloud, 'Which is wonderful when you're twenty or thirty. Less so at thirty-eight.'

'But you! My God,' continued Carol, 'you've come a long way from the girl on the bath mat, waiting to die.'

Yes.

I switched topics.

'So what did you make of Warren?' I said.

'He's nice.'

Oh dear.

'Yes,' she said. 'He's very, very . . . nice.'

I knew just what 'nice' meant to Carol. Nice was boring and bland. Nice was a damning indictment of my having taken the safe option with a harmless man, an uninteresting man.

'I gather,' she said, 'that Warren doesn't know how we first became friends?'

'No.'

'I see.'

But I knew that she did not see.

She began to tell me about the benefits of having moved country in the middle of a tax year. She'd be able to claim tax back in both jurisdictions. Or something like that. I don't know exactly because I was not really listening. I was explaining to myself – once more – why I had never told Warren about my suicide attempt.

At the start of our relationship, certainly, it would have been a stupid thing to reveal. From the moment

I met him it was clear that Warren was a completely different kettle of fish from all my previous boyfriends, Mark especially. He was honest, kind and considerate, and that was just for starters. I would sum up by saying that he was a gentleman. I saw two things clearly: first, he might well be a keeper and second, he mustn't know that I was actually a fruitcake.

I gradually told Warren the story of my life, Mark included, but not that one thing, the suicide attempt. He did not need to know absolutely every last thing about me. Because, really, it had been the action of a different Me. Our relationship blossomed and my self-confidence soared. I became so different from the old Me that that awful event became as removed from my real life as something I had watched on a soap.

'Now, then, ladies,' said Warren, 'may I get ye a top-up?'

We handed him our glasses and he disappeared.

'I love his accent,' Carol said. 'Where did you meet him?'

'He's from Belfast but we met at a work party in the Hairy Lemon, the Christmas before you left. I never got to introduce ye.'

'Jeeees!' said Carol. 'The Hairy Lemon. I had forgotten that place existed until you mentioned it. Is it still there?'

'The last time I looked.'

'And Break for the Border?'

'Ditto.'

'And Jute?'

'Gone, I'm afraid, replaced by an internet café.'

That set Carol off reminiscing about our 'wild' days before she left for Australia: getting chatted up by middle-aged farmers with white bands on their ring fingers, being asked to buy a line by a hoodie in Abrakebabra and me – too drunk, too innocent to understand – asking, 'A line? For what charity?'

'God, yes, we had some good times,' she said. 'Especially you, you mad thing!'

She was grinning at me as if we were sharing a joke, but I didn't know what she was getting at. And I wasn't sure I wanted to.

'Remember the New Year's Eve party when you –'

She was cut off by Warren's return. She gave me a conspiratorial wink to suggest that we both knew exactly what she'd been about to say.

The two of them began to talk about property prices.

New Year's Eve 1999 wasn't just any old New Year's Eve. But, even though it was the end of the millennium and the dawn of the 2000s, somehow I wound up at a crappy party on Dorset Street with a bunch of people I didn't particularly like. Though I'd met Warren three weeks earlier, our relationship was too new for him to cancel his plans to see out the millennium with his family in Belfast. He kissed me goodbye at the Airport Express bus stop on Eden Quay on the morning of the thirty-first.

Carol and I went out early that night and followed our usual pattern of going to the pubs of King Street, and then Harcourt Street, but by 11 p.m. we were in a taxi back to the Northside. Through an alcoholic haze, it seemed like a good idea because there was going to be the mother of all parties. Some guy said. Some guy was wrong.

I knew hardly anyone except Carol. And the guys

were all big sweaty oafs constantly asking my opinion about the Y2K bug. And the music was nothing but Pulp and Prince. And there was no wine so I had to drink punch. And it was already 11.45, too late to go somewhere better. We'd never be let in at that stage. And then the clock said 11.55. It was five minutes until the ending of an old thousand years and the beginning of a new. The doorbell rang and, since no one else was going to do it, I opened the door.

'Hello, gorgeous,' said the man standing there.

It was Mark.

He took one step closer and I leaned forward to kiss him.

I don't like to think of what happened next. I am filled with shame when I contemplate how all reason abandoned me. The bottom line is this: when Carol came looking for me ten minutes later, she found me upstairs in one of the bedrooms and I was with Mark. The same Mark whom she'd heard me moan about endlessly. Mark whom she'd never met, but could doubtless recognize from all the times I'd shown her my old photos. And the night I'd taken a scissors to many of them. He was sitting on the bed and I was on my knees. My hair was tied back. I was giving him a blow job.

Carol didn't have to say anything. Her yelp of surprise brought me to my senses. She closed the door and I stood back up, drunk and unsteady.

'Finish what you've started!' Mark moaned but I ignored him and stumbled for the door. By the time I'd made it downstairs, Carol had disappeared.

'Come back, you bitch!' shouted Mark from the landing, but I had to find my friend. I went out of the front door but it was no use, there was no sign of her. Just then my mobile phone beeped to signal a message received. It was a lengthy one, from Warren, saying what a great girl I was and how he couldn't wait to see me again.

I sat down on the step and burst out crying. I felt terrible about what I'd done. But I was weeping for how I'd let down Carol. More so than Warren.

'Earth to darling!' said Warren, waving his hand in front of my face.

I had been staring into space while he and Carol discussed the merits of buying a doer-upper around Synge Street.

'I think it would be better to rent for a while,' I said. 'The market still has some way to fall. Maybe as much as fifteen per cent.'

'Jeeeees, will you listen to her,' said Carol, sounding decidedly tipsy. 'So sensible. God, Warren, the things I could tell you – from before you tamed her . . .'

Right! I had heard more than enough. I excused myself and made my way to the bathroom. I locked myself in, sat on the toilet seat and tried to figure out what to do next.

I never told Warren about giving Mark a blow job. Or half a blow job. Or whatever. It was a terrible mistake that I put behind me, and in the eight years since I've never even dreamed of being unfaithful. Looking back on that awful night, I tell myself that we'd only been going out for three weeks at the time. Our relationship wasn't a definite thing. Neither of us had yet uttered the words 'I love you'.

However. Warren has made a habit of buying me flowers every year on the tenth of December. He is a hopeless romantic, celebrating the anniversaries not only of our wedding and engagement but also of the night we first got together.

'It started in the Hairy Lemon,' he tells people; 'it was love at first sight. Since then we've had eyes only for each other.'

So it would be most unwelcome news if Warren found out that three weeks after our 'love at first sight' I'd put a piece of my old boyfriend in my mouth. Most unwelcome news. And the longer he talked to Carol the likelier it was that something would just slip out. Warren would be very hurt. If I had lied about this, then what else?

Our marriage did not need this. Our marriage did not need Carol.

'Warren,' I said when I returned from the toilet, 'I just got a text from the babysitter. Ciara has woken up and she's screaming her head off. We have to go home.'

'Oh, darling, that babysitter loves to exaggerate,' he said. 'Ciara's probably just whingeing. Give it five minutes and ring back to see how she is then?'

'No, Warren,' I said. 'We have to go now. Could you get our coats from the bedroom?'

He headed off with a peeved look on his face.

'My, Fruitcake,' said Carol, who was drunk and happy and utterly unaware of any tension, 'you sure have that man well trained.'

'Thanks, Carol,' I said, and then I took a breath. 'Em, Carol, the thing is, about our offer of accommodation earlier, I'm afraid it really wouldn't be all that suitable.'

'What?'

'No,' I said. 'It's just that Ciara is due to go into her own room. That's the room Warren offered you. I'm afraid she still wakes a lot during the night. So you'd get very broken sleep with a bawling baby.'

'Oh.'

By now Warren had arrived back and was hovering at my elbow. I could tell by his posture that he was angry but I continued on regardless.

'Apart from that,' I said, 'we live out in the sticks, so getting into Loreto every day would be a nightmare.'

'Oh,' she said again. The significance of what I was saying was slowly percolating through the vodka haze.

'Oh.'

'Here,' I said. 'I'll give you my number.'

I took my handbag off Warren, pulled out a scrap of paper and scribbled on it.

'Don't worry: if you ring me tomorrow,' I said, 'I'll have figured out the best agencies to go with. I can drive you around to look at places.'

Carol looked stunned. I leaned forward to give her a hug goodbye but she did not squeeze me back. Then I handed her the slip of paper and she brightened slightly.

'So you'll drive me around as I look for a place?' she said.

'Absolutely,' I said with a smile.

'Call Fruitcake,' she read off the slip of paper. 'o86 9215690.'

'Yes,' I said, nodding. Beside me, Warren was about to speak but I shot him my most furious glance, a look that meant 'We'll discuss this later; shut up if you ever want to have sex again.'

Presumably, my gentlemanly husband was going to point out that I'd written down the number wrong. It was, in fact, 086 9216509.

'I don't think you've ever treated me so rudely,' Warren said when we were safely out in the taxi. 'And that lovely lady Carol, what possessed you to turn on her as you did?'

All the way home he ranted. And in bed afterwards, until he fell asleep. The next morning too, he stood outside the shower and complained at me while I shampooed my hair. I made no attempt to contradict him since he was, for once, one hundred per cent in the right. Nor did I ever answer his repeated question: 'And why did Carol keep calling you "Fruitcake"?'

13

When you're in love with a
pregnant woman, it's hard

Dublin, Ireland, February 2008

'I hope,' said Steph, 'the doctor will be able to see if it's handicapped.'

It was a Friday afternoon and we were sitting in a waiting room for the first ultrasound scan of our unborn baby.

'Jesus, Steph!' I said. 'How could you even think such a thing, let alone say it?'

'Well,' she said, 'it's just I'd like to know either way.'

'Jesus!' I said. 'Jesus, Jesus, Jesus!'

That thought had never crossed my mind. Of course not. It's a dreadful admission, but up until that point in the pregnancy, sixteen weeks on, I hadn't really fully engaged with the reality that a baby was coming. A baby that might be perfectly healthy or might not. After the initial shock, when Steph made the big announcement, I had kept my focus on projects at work and blocked out the impending upheaval. I confessed as much to Steph.

'Well,' she said, 'it's a little harder to ignore when

you're the one actually carrying the can. Indeed the one who, until it stopped last week, was feeling nausea, morning, noon and night. Now that I've a fragile little person inside of me, I've read all the pregnancy books. Some twice. I now know the hundred things that could go wrong. This baby could already be blind or deaf or suffer from dozens of congenital defects. The statistics are in the books. The reality could be inside my belly. And yes, if there is some problem, then we'll probably manage somehow. But obviously I do not relish a future life of managing somehow. I have the deepest admiration for parents who raise handicapped children. They are heroic. I, however, do not want to have to be heroic. I'd need some warning at least.'

Jesus! Jesus!

'Look, Steph,' I said, taking her by the hand and taking a deep breath before ploughing ahead in my most explicitly 'supportive' tone, 'you really mustn't worry yourself about terrible things that will probably never happen.'

'You feckin' fool!' she said but with a smile. 'I am soon going to be a mother of a precious fragile little person. My fate from now is to be ALWAYS worrying about terrible things that will probably never happen. Whether it's spina bifida or autism or meningitis or abduction or it stepping out in front of an articulated lorry!'

Jesus . . .

I picked up a magazine and started to flick through it for distraction. As Steph laughed at my discomfort, a nurse emerged from the scanning room and called out her name.

*

According to the consultant, there was nothing to worry about. A skeletal image of our baby glowed green on the screen and seemed to possess the requisite number of arms and legs. Its heart was properly formed and pumping away gamely. The width of its neck fold (often, said the consultant, an early indicator of congenital defects) was also within range.

When we walked out of the door of the clinic, Steph looked elated. We got to the car and she came round to my side for a hug. A long, long hug. 'Right, then, lover-boy,' she said, catching her breath with a laugh, 'take me wherever it is you're taking me.'

Because for the last few months I'd been so busy at work, because we'd hardly had any real quality time together, I had booked us a night at the Radisson Hotel and Leisure Centre outside Cavan town. Friday-evening traffic was brutal along the M50 and all the way to Dunshaughlin. After that we made good progress and checked into our room a little after six. I switched off my mobile phone and buried it at the bottom of the suitcase.

'So,' I said, 'do you want to try the spa or go down to their restaurant?'

'Neither,' said Steph. She walked over and closed the curtains. Then she opened her blouse. God, she was beautiful. The bump was hardly noticeable but I'd swear her breasts had already gone up a cup size or two.

'Feck the health and beauty spa,' she said, pulling at my belt while I unclasped her bra, 'and we'll order food from room service later.'

'Yes,' I laughed. 'Much, much later.'

*

'So, lover-boy,' Steph said, as we lay tangled together in the warm afterglow of a bout of brilliant sex, 'that ultrasound scan? Seeing the little critter on a screen? Did it make it seem real to you?'

'It did,' I said. 'It finally did. I realize now that I'm going to have to cop on and get more involved.'

'Good,' she said, and snuggled in closer on my chest.

Yes, it was good. Thinking about the scan, though, reminded me of an incident four weeks previously when I'd felt differently. Steph had rung to say she'd discovered blood-spotting in her panties – possibly the first signs of an impending miscarriage. She was crying and hysterical. I dropped everything and ran out to the car. I remember being frantic with concern, but it was entirely for Steph, not even remotely for the baby.

Now Steph's face was hidden beneath her mop of black hair. I parted the fringe with my finger and then slowly traced a line along her skin with it. In behind her ear, along her neck and down to circle a nipple. Then on again down an elegant curve to her perfect apple-shaped bum. Jesus, she was all this and funny and clever too! A goddess and no mistake.

'Hmmmmmmmmm,' she said, purring happily.

'I love you,' I said.

'Hmmmmmmmmm,' she said.

Yes. I did love her, so I was really going to have to cop myself on.

We sat up to a small table in the room and ate the food that we'd ordered from room service.

'Listen, Steph, I meant what I said earlier about

getting a lot more involved in this pregnancy. Tell me what sort of things I can do.'

Steph smiled and shook her head. 'You've got your earnest look on,' she said. 'Anyone would think you actually meant it. The reality is that once this weekend is over, you'll be back in business mode. Working until all hours, with little or no time for me.'

'I'm sorry that's how it's been,' I said, 'but all that's going to change. I swear. Absolutely.'

'Okay,' she said. 'I'll test you. Just take this coming Wednesday. I'm taking a half-day from work to go into town shopping for baby. Just a preliminary trip. It's still too early, too tempting fate, to actually buy stuff. Nevertheless, I'll be figuring out which baby buggy I want, which cot, which bouncy chair, etcetera.'

'Fine,' I said. 'No problem. I'll take a half-day too and meet you in Henry Street.'

'I'll believe it when I see it,' she said, trying to sound cynical but looking pleased none the less. Then she ate the last bite of her sandwich, gave me a peck on the cheek and jumped back into bed.

'Hang on,' I said, 'I'll be finished with this carbonara in a minute.'

'No need to hurry, lover-boy,' she said. 'I'm exhausted. I have to sleep immediately.'

'Really? But it's barely after 9 p.m.'

'Yeah,' she said. 'It's the stowaway in my belly that does it. And anyway you've already had your ration of passion for tonight.'

'Totally, yes. But no,' I said, 'I was hoping that you'd tell me more about this pregnancy that I've been paying very little heed to.'

Steph reached over, opened the drawer of her locker

135

and retrieved a book, *Advice for Mothers-To-Be*. It had the lived-in look of a well-read book.

'This one is the best. I carry it with me at all times,' she said. 'Why don't you have a flick through it?'

As Steph fell asleep, I switched on the bedside lamp and began to read.

Did you know that a pregnant woman should avoid going anywhere near cats? I certainly didn't. Apparently there's a very high risk of toxoplasmosis, which has dire consequences for the baby. Similarly gardening: handling soil is a complete no-no. As is standing in front of a microwave when it's in operation. As is taking a very hot bath or going into a sauna. Or eating certain types of cheese. Jesus! I put away the pregnancy manual and switched off the light. I stayed awake, though, and contemplated the situation.

Obviously, Steph's pregnancy had been unplanned. My initial reaction when she told me was not just shock. I felt panic and outright dismay. Having a kid was something I'd envisaged in the faraway future. The timing was not right. Now was not convenient. Not when there were so many things that needed to be sorted out first. Again my mind drifted back to the day when Steph thought she was having a miscarriage. The fact is that as I drove to her, a shameful thought did cross my mind: that a miscarriage would not be such a bad thing – a problem flushed away down the toilet.

But after seeing the ultrasound, after having spent a heavenly evening with Steph, it was obvious that I needed to rethink my priorities. With or without my input, this pregnancy was happening anyway. Over the previous weeks, whenever we spoke, Steph would mention her constant nausea. I'd largely chosen to ignore it, barely mumbling a condolence. I'd have to be far more attentive over the remaining five months as she began to encounter all the sufferings I'd read about – chronic constipation, blinding headaches, back pains, insomnia, difficulty breathing, darkened amniotic fluid . . .

And the baby . . . I thought back to its little green skeleton on the monitor. I thought about the fact that it was fifty per cent made of me. I realized that whatever about bad timing, it would be a wonderful thing.

But had Steph, I wondered, taken the correct folic vitamin supplements that would increase our baby's chances of good health by twenty-two per cent? I restrained myself from waking her to ask.

'But is it not obvious to anyone,' I said next morning as we chomped through breakfast in bed, 'that there is a fundamental design flaw at the heart of the whole process?'

'Huh?' said Steph, biting toast.

'The baby's head, Steph! I just woke up to the fact last night. The head will be about the size of a melon and has to squeeze out an opening that is a great deal smaller.'

'Oh, you just realized that, did you?' she said, starting to laugh, thinking this was funny when it was definitely not funny. 'I went through the phase of stressing about that weeks ago. And now you go and remind me. Tell me again, though: will it be like a cantaloupe melon or a gaia?'

'Oh, feck you,' I said, but she only laughed harder and I couldn't help myself joining in. It was nearly a minute before I could speak again.

'Anyway, love,' I said, 'I suppose you're right. It's probably a worry every woman who ever lived has had. And it always works out okay?'

'Yes, darling,' she said. 'Always . . . except for those cases where the baby gets stuck halfway, where they have to catch the baby's head with forceps and pull . . .

'Or suction it out . . .

'Or cut into you to make the opening larger . . .

'Or break one of your bones to ease the pressure . . .

'Or push the baby back in and cut open your belly to drag it out.'

Jesus! I hadn't read the book as far as the section on labour itself. There was a moment of silence while I composed my reply.

I said, 'Oh.'

Then Steph put down her toast and started to cry.

For two moments I didn't know how to react, but then my reading of *Advice for Mothers-To-Be* came to the rescue. Her tears were probably a manifestation of the mood swings described in Section 3. They weren't really her fault, but were caused by hormones, no doubt. The book had advocated they be met with patience and understanding. I put away our breakfast trays and held her in my arms while the sobs intensified into fully fledged wailing.

'It was just,' Steph said, 'talking about labour made me realize that I'll probably have to face it on my own.'

'No,' I said.

'Yes,' she said.

'No,' I said, 'I will be there. No matter what.'

'Even if the contractions start when there's an important meeting at work? What if you happen to be with –'

'Stop, Steph. I've told you definitively. I'm sorry for the way I've buried my head in the sand up to this point. But no longer. Now I am accepting and even looking forward to this baby's arrival. I will be there to see it happen.'

By and by, her sobs subsided entirely. We lay perfectly still in the warmth of one another's arms for ages. Then, half an hour before we had to check out, she picked up my hand and placed it where she desired.

'If it's a boy, then Macdara or Oscar, or, if I'm feeling particularly brave, Montwell,' said Steph, as we wound our way back through Kells.

'Montwell?' I said. 'Jesus, Steph! Are you sure that's even a real name? What about something simple like John or Gerard or Thomas?'

'God, no,' said Steph, laughing with mock contempt, 'those are all old hat. My little boy, if it is a boy, that is, has to have a cool name.'

'What about calling him after your father?' I said, determined that my poor little boy (if he is a boy) shouldn't be bullied relentlessly over his odd name in the playgrounds of the future. 'Michael is a fine name.'

'My father?' she said. 'This is the same father who as yet doesn't even know that I'm pregnant?'

'Oh,' I said. What a fool I was. I had taken a wrong turn and now our conversation must move towards more serious matters entirely.

'Of course I haven't told my parents yet,' she said. 'The convention is that you tell no one until twelve weeks for fear of a miscarriage. Then, once I'd waited that long, I decided to wait until the ultrasound scan.'

'Because . . .'

'I think you can guess why.'

I could.

She was waiting for me to arrive at the correct frame of mind. She was waiting until conditions were such that we could drive down to her home place in Mullingar and tell her folks the joyous news in person. Together.

We drove on in silence, as she looked out of the window and I turned it all over in my mind.

It didn't take too long for me to formulate a plan of action. Because I loved Steph and was falling in love with the idea of this baby, the time had come to get my life and new priorities in order. When we hit the city, I would drop Steph at her apartment in Kilmainham. Then I would go home and tell my wife all about Steph and the pregnancy. It was time, before she made any big plans for our tenth wedding anniversary, to tell my wife I was leaving her.

14

Love in the time of washing clothes by hand

Celine is the landlord's daughter and the dark-eyed fiery belle of a village in Gascony. Just eighteen years old, with her life before her, she is wild, adventurous and carefree. Then Peregrin Giffard, a handsome, daredevil student barrister, bursts into her life one hop-picking season. With his dancing eyes and charming wit, Peregrin seduces the naive young motherless girl, unlacing her bodice in the hop field under a million stars. In the blissful afterglow, he proposes marriage. The ceremony takes place one hour later, by candlelight, in the pastor's haybarn. On the morrow Celine awakens to bad tidings. The pastor has died in his sleep before registering the marriage. And of Peregrin, there is no trace. He has absconded to Paris.

She writes him fifty letters but receives not one reply. Nine months to the day, her baby arrives. Celine is driven from her childhood home by the scandal-mongering of her pious neighbour, Madame Elmere, and by the disapproval of her dear papa. On the morning Celine's coach is leaving, Papa goes for a very long walk, without telling anyone how long he'll be. He doesn't even say goodbye . . .

Life in Paris is worse than expected. Celine's lodgings are a hovel, and when she calls around to Peregrin's law firm they say that he has flown to Italy in a hot-air balloon. She returns to the hovel, seeking nothing more than a good cry. Even that is denied her: the baby's nappy needs changing . . .

Down to her last *sou*, Celine must decide between buying a pretty new clasp for her hair or milk for the baby. Luckily she runs into Bibby McKenzie, a Scottish laundrywoman who lends her enough to buy the milk as well. Bibby is strong-limbed, with a moustache that is noticeable only in daylight; her eyes glint with good humour, and she sees the funny side of every situation. They become fast friends and with Bibby's help Celine enters the laundry business. One day, while Celine is washing a gentleman's coat, an old newspaper falls to the floor and opens on the announcement of the marriage of Peregrin Giffard to his new bride, a rich heiress. Her hands grow itchy from all the soaking in detergent.

Celine's meticulous washing techniques build her a spotless reputation. Many more clients seek her out and soon every noble family in the 7th arrondissement is employing her services. She has to take on staff to cope, then more and more, until finally she is able to stop working and concentrate on management. She pays Bibby to change the baby's nappy. Her hands are no longer itchy.

Love enters Celine's life for a second time in the shape of Jacques Danton, managing director at the detergent firm. Jacques is older, more mature; he carries a reassuring air of solidity and steadiness. At first their late-night dinner is strictly business, but then he sends away the servants and brings her out onto the roof. There are stars in the sky. For a moment this makes her think of the hop field and Peregrin: feckless-betrayer-Peregrin, married-to-another-woman-Peregrin. Angry with herself, Celine allows Jacques a kiss. Soon he is caressing her bodice. It feels reasonably pleasant . . .

Her happiness is short-lived, however, smashed by the heavy hand of history. The peasants are starving and the middle classes have been reading dangerous philosophical books; big changes are in the air. An angry mob storms the Bastille and the French Revolution gets under way. Months of riots and street-fighting force all the nobility to stay indoors. They don't need their laundry done as often as before. Celine's business collapses. The baby, now able to crawl, slips and falls down the stairs . . .

There is a sound of sawing and hammering on the Place de la Concorde. The revolutionaries are building the first guillotine. Jacques persuades Celine that they should leave all this crazy madness; why not emigrate to Switzerland? She agrees: all that snow and chocolate sounds wonderful. Tearfully Celine kisses Bibby McKenzie goodbye and they set off on a coach stacked with cases. A while later they come back briefly, having forgotten to pack the baby.

Ten miles from the border, at a tavern in Montbéliard, there are only two other guests. They seem shy but after a few drinks open up sufficiently to introduce themselves. Louis and Marie. A very sociable game of four-handed whist follows, until they hear a racket outside the door. The revolutionaries burst in and arrest all four. Bound and gagged, thrown roughly on the floor of a wagon, Celine realizes exactly who her fellow-card players were . . .

How desperately unfair to stand on the steps of a guillotine when you've done absolutely nothing offensive! Celine and Jacques are about to be executed purely for playing cards with the wrong people. First they chop off King Louis's head and then Marie's. Rather gamely Jacques offers to go next, which is just as well. As his head is being taken away in a basket, the crowd gasps at a strange spectacle in the sky. It's Peregrin! In a hot-air balloon! He lands close by and runs over to Celine to explain everything . . .

The reason he left so suddenly after their wedding night was because of an urgent secret diplomatic mission from the Ministry of Defence. But he did ask the pastor to explain. If the old fool subsequently died, then that's unfortunate. The letters Celine sent were never forwarded to him, since not even his ambassadorial superiors knew exactly where he was. The society wedding she read about in the newspaper referred to an entirely different Peregrin Giffard, a distant relation.

'And,' says Peregrin, 'I gather you've had my baby!'

'Oh, no,' says Celine, 'in all the commotion I left it in Montbéliard!'

There's a parting within the spectators and out steps Bibby McKenzie, holding hands with the baby, who is now able to walk. Celine and Peregrin hug the old woman and the doughty young toddler. The revolutionaries, though, are growing restless, anxious to get on with Celine's execution. Cleverly, Peregrin throws a hundred *sou* in the air and in the mêlée they make their escape to the balloon.

Alone again at last, Celine and Peregrin float high in the sky, heading south. They seem to have forgotten the baby, but resolve to collect it from Bibby very soon. First, they must return to the village and get married again, properly this time, begging Papa for his blessing. Also wicked scandal-mongering Madame Elmere must get her comeuppance. After that, Spain beckons for a perfect honeymoon. In the meantime, Peregrin pulls Celine close and, with infinitely slow sensuality, begins to undo the laces of her bodice . . .

15

Right on the tip of my
wang dang doodle

Kerala, India, AD 960

Chola was the perfect woman with whom to have an affair. First, there was the fact she lived far away in Tanjore: never could it happen that she would have dealings with my wife. Second, there were her voluptuous good looks: lips, breasts and thighs, all were most pleasing. Finally, there was her enthusiasm in the bedchamber. Over the course of three nights, we tried every position. Most especially she gave me oral pleasure – and, unlike my wife, without ever making a face as if she felt sick. Yes, they were a wonderful few days, and, though the ride home took a week, I still glowed with the memory thereof.

Arriving late in the evening, I found my wife already in bed. I disrobed and began my ablutions. That was when I looked down and noticed something for the first time. Right on the tip of my wang dang doodle was a large pimple.

I'd never had such a spot before so there could be no coincidence. On top of providing me with ten delightful emissions, fair Chola, it seemed, had given me something else to remember her by.

151

'Are you not finished yet?' called my wife from the bed. A bead of sweat formed on my brow as I considered how to proceed. If my wife saw the pimple, she would surely guess its origin. I pulled my undergarment back on and went in to her. She was sitting up darning a sock and continued to do so after I nestled alongside her. After a while she said, 'Well?'

'Well, what?' I replied.

'Well, aren't you going to demand your conjugal rights, as usual?'

Normally I would. Superior though Chola was, that was a week previously and I was ravenous once more. But what if I passed on my pimple? Then surely my faithful wife would deduce the truth.

'No,' I said with an exaggerated yawn, 'I'm rather weary after the long journey. Goodnight.'

So that was that.

On the morrow, the pimple had got bigger and, in its lurid purpleness, considerably more hideous. Also, it was itchy. Determined not to panic, I told my wife I must go on business to the nearby town of Hebli. As a hard-working merchant, I go there often, so she passed no remarks. Once there I attended a physician of considerable repute; but one who knew nothing of me. I claimed a false address in Tanjore and told him of my complaint. Great was my relief when he pronounced the matter a trifle and avowed he knew just the right ointment. I left with a small brown jar tucked inside my jellaba. A discreet distance out along the road home, I paused and applied some to my wang dang doodle. It was soothed immediately.

*

That night, my ablutions again brought me up short. Though I'd applied the ointment hourly as instructed, the pimple was worse rather than better. In frustration, I placed a thumbnail at each side and began to squeeze at it. Perhaps I could pop open the blemish and excise the poison within. No. I found its contents more lumpy than liquid and the membrane too strong to burst. I pulled my undergarment back on and repaired to bed with my wife. She had brought us each a glass of tea. We sipped them quietly until she asked, 'Well?'

'Well, what?' I replied.

'Well, aren't you going to demand your conjugal rights?'

I could hardly use the same excuse twice and anyway a trip to Hebli never exhausted anyone. I decided to take a gamble.

'I was thinking of asking you to give me oral pleasure,' I said, and let the sentence hang for a minute. Her facial expression, as I knew it would, turned to one of grim apprehension. Then I continued, 'But, since you've made me this lovely glass of tea, I much prefer us to have a cuddle and then sleep.'

She smiled uncertainly, slow to trust in her reprieve. I put my arms around her waist and drifted into slumber.

Sunrise found me already on the road again, this time to Panjim. A thriving seaport, I surmised its doctors might well have more experience with ailments afflicting the sexual organ. By now the pimple was not only a gruesome eyesore and a wellspring of itchy irritation but it emitted a dull throbbing pain as well. I hurled the useless jar of ointment into a cornfield.

The waiting room at Dr Isfahan's establishment was crowded, and I came up with the ridiculous notion that people were looking at me peculiarly. Everyone else was either coughing or bleeding or supporting a broken limb. 'Perhaps,' I thought, 'they are all trying to guess the stranger's hidden malady.' I stared at the floor, perspiring mightily, until he called.

Isfahan was thorough; I'd certainly give him that. After ordering me to strip naked and lie on a table, he looked over my every body part before settling on the offending appendage. Abruptly he caught hold of it and flipped it back and forth a few times. Then he leaned in for such a close inspection I fancied I could feel him breathe on it.

'Yes, yes,' he clucked, directing his words, it seemed, to my wang dang doodle. 'You're a rare example. You're a most uncommon case. But don't you worry, little man, I have likely the lotion and precisely the potion. You'll soon be rid of this woeful disfigurement.'

Then he patted my appendage one more time and sidestepped up to my face with his demand for payment.

Disrobing that night, I was filled with anxiety. Though I had applied the lotion and drunk some of Dr Isfahan's potion, the pimple was as lurid and tender as ever. He had warned me not to expect an instant cure. The full course, a week's duration, must be completed, he'd said. In the meantime, I still had to face my wife. Again I squeezed at the pimple, pinching till tears ran from my eye. It achieved nothing. I entered the chamber to find her in bed with neither beverage nor embroidery. She looked expectant.

'Well?' I said.

'Well, what?' she replied.

'Aren't you going to tell me about your day?' I asked.

'Oh,' she said, plainly disarmed by this clever stratagem of mine. As anticipated she had much to say on the topic of what she'd done that day. So much, in fact, that the story was still not over when our candle burned out. She continued speaking in the darkness until her tongue slowed to sluggish and I floated away to unconsciousness.

I dreamed of Chola, fair Chola, caressing me, audaciously stripping me bare. I awoke to find that my undergarment had indeed been removed and my wife was straddling my legs. She had lit another candle and was inspecting my erect wang dang doodle even more closely than had Dr Isfahan. Not an inch from her eyeball was the hideous purple pimple. Hearing me gasp, she looked up and her countenance wore a strange smile. For a sleepy moment I thought everything was going to be all right.

The tip of my wang dang doodle is fine now. Isfahan's lotion and potion cleared up the pimple, just as he promised. What pains me still are extensive injuries to the stem of my appendage. They comprise a ring of deep gashes halfway down, where my wife bit me and clamped her teeth. Above these are the jagged scrapings she inflicted as I slowly drew her head up, pulling by the hair.

16

On inspecting a selection of toilet-roll holders

Leitrim, Ireland, July 2005

We were standing side by side in Home Hardware Superstore when I realized that, for the first time in my life, I was jealous of my younger sister, Ashling. It was not because she was eight months pregnant. Hell, no. I had plenty of time before my biological clock went off. She wasn't even a sexy mother-to-be like some first-timers. To be polite, I'd agreed that her bump was very neat but in fact she was blocking the aisle. Nor was I remotely envious of her job (the same old dull receptionist post she'd had since leaving school) or of her husband (the same old dull Michael she'd been with for just as long).

No, it was a stacked shelf of bathroom fittings that set me off. There were towel rails, towel rings, toothbrush holders complete with tumbler, soap dishes and toilet-roll holders; truly, the selection was vast. Sold singly or in sets, there were versions made from shiny chrome, clear plastic or Colorado oak. They came in all shapes and sizes: circles, squares, waves, fish and

Homer Simpson. And somehow, from this array, Ashling had to choose. Indeed, she had to choose three sets, because her newly built house had three bathrooms. (It was 2,500 bloody square feet! And that's excluding the conservatory.) I, meanwhile, would not be choosing even one set of toilet fittings, not even the classy-looking Polished Chrome Splash. Because I lived in a rented one-bed apartment in Dublin.

So what, you might say. So what, I too would have said, until the day before. That was when I got a tour of Ashling's new house, which was almost ready for moving into. It was stunning, in more ways than I could count. There was stone-facing on the outer walls and inside all around the fireplace. Her kitchen, of fitted pine and all integrated with a granite worktop, was nearly as big as my whole apartment. Most of the floors were polished wood and the remainder were tiled. All the lights had black wrought-iron lamp shades. And the paintwork was brilliant, and the carpets. And outside there was a cobble-lock patio. And in the master bedroom, a balcony. And from her kitchen window the view was downhill to the woods and a stream.

Having seen all this, I realized that I wanted what I thought I would never want. Having believed that buying 'stuff' was just many people's pathetic surrogate for living a properly meaningful and fulfilling existence, having preferred to spend my money on films, books, music and travel, on nights out with witty company, on adventurous things like mountain-climbing and sky-diving, having always been scornful of material things, now I was gripped by a shocking new realization: I still wanted all that but I wanted stuff too. And I wanted stuff now.

I supposed I'd better tell my husband.

'Let's just see if I have this straight, darling,' said Doug, outside in the car park where he had gone off for a quick cigarette. 'Previously you told me, many times, how Leitrim was such a boghole and how you spent your teenage years pining for the day you could get away from it.'

'I know. But –'

'And you kept me up nights raving about Dublin. About the fun we were going to have, drinking in Temple Bar and having Sunday-morning brunch in Ranelagh and taking evening walks along the Grand Canal.'

'I know. But –'

'So I finally agreed to leave Australia and move ten thousand miles to be where my lovely wife wants to be. And now you are saying you want me to move a hundred miles more. To the boondocks, the outback, the officially designated central point of nowhere. Is that correct?'

'. . . Yes.'

'Then my answer is equally clear,' he said, before taking an emphatic drag of his smoke. 'No. Bloody. Way . . . Darling.'

I had met Doug eighteen months before at a back-packer hostel in Cairns while learning to scuba-dive. He was athletic, good-humoured and had more zest in him than ten Irish guys rolled together. We hooked up out on the water, then later under the sheets. I'd kissed enough frogs to know a prince, and within a week I knew this was it. I extended my work visa and we married in the cathedral in Sydney. My parents came out for the ceremony, as did Ashling and Michael and a few of my friends from college. So they all met Doug for a few days and got to know him a little. And vice versa. But not exactly under typical conditions. Hence on this, our first trip home since we relocated to Dublin, he was still slightly 'on trial'.

Ever since we'd arrived at Mam and Dad's, Doug had played a blinder. I'd been on top form too, until the visit to the hardware shop. But over lunch that Saturday, I was too browned off to play the happy couple.

'This gravy is delicious, Mrs McManus,' Doug said, while I sat silent and sulking.

'That's a fine bookcase, Mr McManus, I can't believe you made it yourself,' he said, while I brooded over his rejection of my perfectly reasonable request that we review our plans.

'Michael, did I hear you're thinking of going out on your own with the oil-burner repairs?' he said, and I spotted the perfect opening.

'Yes. You did. He is. Well done, Michael,' I said quickly, 'but why not tell him, Doug, just what you think of that fine new house he's built?'

'Well, yes,' said Doug, turning to eye me suspiciously, 'it is very fine.'

'Oh, a bit more than that,' I added; 'it really is fabulous. So big. So many cool features.'

'It sounds like you're impressed,' said Ashling. 'With something of mine! Let me mark this date in the calendar.'

'Now, now,' said Mam, 'mocking is catching. What she really means, love, is she's surprised you're so enthusiastic, seeing as you never showed much inclination to move back here. Even when you so easily could have, after you'd finished college, like.'

'That, Mam,' cut in Ashling, 'is because she considers Leitrim to be Ireland's biggest boghole.'

'I do not,' I said, irritated that Ashling couldn't just concentrate on forking food into her voluminous stomach. 'I think Leitrim has improved enormously in the last few years. When we were growing up, there was feck all here, except a record number of potholes. But not since they did the roads and built a shopping centre in Ballinamore and there's that massive cinema in Carrick. In fact, I think Leitrim has become a fabulous place to live.'

'Better than wonderful Dublin, even?' asked Ashling, still unable to keep her gob shut.

'Yes, well,' I said, 'the traffic has got much worse. And property prices are so bad that Doug and I couldn't even contemplate buying and had to rent instead.'

'Do you know,' said my mother, smiling beatifically, as she tends to do, 'from the drift of what you're saying, it strikes me that maybe Dad might be able to make ye an offer.'

This was exactly where I'd hoped the conversation might go. All heads turned towards my father as he cleared his throat.

'Now, Doug, as you may or may not know, I was a schoolteacher before I retired last year. Vice-principal, actually. Anyway my father was a farmer and whereas he gave most of the farm to my brother Martin, I myself inherited the tail-end of the dog so to speak. I have four little fields up behind this house, not fit for much, really. By times, I rent the grazing out to a neighbour; now and then I save a sop of hay to sell the winter after.'

'Get to the point, Sean,' said Mam.

'So anyway, Doug,' he continued and addressed his serious face not to me, his elder daughter, but to The Man, 'the fact is that we do have one other site at the far end of the "estate". It has a bit of frontage out onto the road and the sightlines are adequate. Planning permission might take a while, but since your wife is a local you'd definitely get it by and by. Anyway, the truth is we were thinking of selling it soon and cashing in on this Celtic Tiger madness before the whole market goes belly up. But, on the other hand, if yourself and herself were contemplating leaving Dublin and coming down this neck of the woods, then ye can have it. The same as we gave a site to Ashling and Michael. Yes, indeed, and welcome.'

Excellent!

'That's too generous, sir,' said Doug, 'but thank you.'

'Thank you, indeed, Dad,' I said. 'C'mon, Doug, let's take a walk and I'll show you exactly where.'

'But –' said Doug.

'Ye'll need your wellies,' said Mam. 'The middle field is stopped for hay and there was a heavy shower this morning.'

The fourth of my father's little fields was an awkward triangular shape. It was wide at the top of the hill and tapered down along a steep slope to just the width of a rusty gateway onto the road. For most kinds of agriculture it was useless, but as a building site it would be perfect. Put our house right at the top and we'd have a view of three townlands.

'And,' I said, 'do you realize that it's worth the best part of 80K?'

'Flamin' hell,' said Doug, 'that is insane.'

'Insane but good for us that can have it free, isn't it?'

'No, darling,' he said, and produced a cigarette, his last, from the packet. 'It's just insane.'

He remained to be convinced.

'I suppose you won't understand, Doug, because I used to give out about home. But really things have improved enormously.'

'No,' he agreed, 'I don't understand.'

'And another thing I've become conscious of is how useful it would be to live near family when we decide to have kids. My mother and Ashling would both be available to babysit. And our children would have big lawns to play on, and a lovely small school to go to and –'

'And perhaps a pony while you're at it,' he cut in.

'Actually, yes, a pony would be nice for them. I don't understand why you find this funny.'

Doug sucked in a mouthful of smoke, then blew out a gale of laughter.

'Okay, wise guy,' I persisted, 'but what about the size of house we could build down here with 300K? We couldn't buy a kennel in Clontarf for that. And when you build yourself, it can be all personalized. It was only when I saw Ashling's house that I realized something about most other houses. Everything in them is just generic, just whatever was to hand at the moment it was needed, so it's all a bit bland. Whereas when you start with a totally blank canvas, the consciousness of the person who did the choosing is very evident. Don't you see?'

'No, darling, I do not see and I do not understand,'

he said. 'I came halfway round the world to live in Dublin, as we agreed. Now, barely three weeks on, you want to change everything. But I have already done more than half the compromising. I left my friends. I left my family. And, as you are well aware, even the winter weather in Cairns is better than what passes for a summer here. Flamin' hell, we're wearing wellies in July!'

'Okay,' I said. What he said was true and reasonable.

'And I'm just starting to enjoy Dublin. Plus I have the interview tomorrow and the prospect of an excellent job.'

'Okay,' I said, and a pair of tears leaked from my eyes.

Doug shook his head. 'C'mon,' he said, and held out his hand to me. 'It's time we were getting back.'

As we traipsed through tall rye grass, I couldn't help sobbing quietly. It was highly unlikely now that I would ever have a home of 2,500 square feet. Excluding conservatory. The most I would ever have was two bathrooms, maximum.

Back at Mam and Dad's, Doug moved straight over to our hire car.

'I'm just taking a quick trip into Ballinamore,' he said, 'to get a packet of cigarettes.'

I was left to go in alone and tell them the verdict.

Ashling and Michael were still there with my parents. They all looked up in anticipation.

'Well?' said Ashling, before I'd even removed my wellies.

I shook my head.

'Huh! I knew it wouldn't be good enough for Miss Cosmopolitan,' said Ashling. 'I just knew!'

My father was quieter but no less scathing in his way. 'Typical bloody you,' he murmured. Michael said nothing, only put his head back into a newspaper.

'Just what about the site didn't meet your high standards anyway?' asked Ashling. Why could my bitch of a sister not just go away and practise her bloody contractions?

'No, Ashling, stop a minute,' said my mother, 'give her a chance, it could be Doug that put a clamp on the idea. We don't know. Give her a chance to explain.'

And I almost said, 'Yes, that's right. It's all Doug's fault.'

The words had been composed and got as far as my tongue when I thought better and paused to reconsider my response. Truly I had dug a hole for myself. If I admitted that Doug was the problem, then, yes, I'd be off the hook in the short term. My loving family would be only too happy to offer me their condolences and consolations. It's quite understandable, they would say, for a foreign lad, perfectly reasonable and fair. But afterwards – this evening, when we'd driven out the avenue to head for Dublin – that would be the signal for the four of them to sit around the dinner table and pour out one more pot of tea. The postmortem would begin. On the weekend's proceedings, on Doug, on me, on our marriage.

'He seems a very nice lad, most polite,' my mother might begin, 'but it is a pity about the other thing . . .'

Gently at first, then with more bravery, more cruelty (his accent perhaps?), Doug would be slowly painted over in criticism. And no disapproval of him could possibly stop there. It would inevitably lead back to me. After all, I was the one who had married him in a whirlwind. An Australian, who we didn't know from Adam. Doug was and always would be my 'choice'. Thus he would always be my 'fault'.

So that was my dilemma. Look like a bitch for changing my mind about the site; look like a pathetic eejit if Doug changed it for me.

'Hell, no, it's me,' I said. 'I'd forgotten what a boghole . . .'

17

Thwack!

Confessions of a man standing on the first tee
at 10 a.m. on a Saturday, three-iron in
mid-swing, about to smack the living daylights
out of a golf ball

Wicklow, Ireland, November 2008

'Please don't,' my wife said, for approximately the 1,000th time.

'Don't what?' I replied, for the 1,000th time also.

'Don't try to wangle me into having sex.'

'Why not?' I asked, nudging into her half of the bed, sliding my hand inside her knickers.

'Because . . .' she began. There were various ways she might continue. She might say 'It's my period' or 'I'm exhausted' (both of these very popular). Other reasons she commonly gave were 'My neck is stiff', 'It's dangerous at this stage of the pregnancy' and 'I've only ten more pages in this book'.

Whatever the excuse, I never complied immediately. And I didn't this time. I stroked her gently, hoping to push the button, to arouse an animal fervour that would override her objections. It didn't work.

'Ouch!' she said. 'I asked you please. Don't!'

So I took my hand out of her knickers. I put my underpants back on, placing my erection into harness.

I picked up the newspaper and turned to the Sudoku. I couldn't focus. I pondered my wife.

One of her many fine qualities was that she was very good at sending out thank-you cards. Every gift we received, no matter how small, every gathering we attended, no matter how tedious, she would instantly acclaim with a carefully inscribed paragraph. In fact, such was her observance of courtesy that if I didn't restrain her, she'd insist on sending out thank-you cards for other people's thank-you cards.

As a result, everyone I knew complimented me. They said what a considerate person I was married to and how lucky I was. People also said how honest she was and how sincere, how intelligent and knowledgeable. She had a carefully worded opinion on every subject but never tried to ram it down anyone's throat. She listened to people and nodded at appropriate intervals saying very seriously, 'Hmmm. That IS interesting . . .'

She was, moreover, an excellent cook and showed considerable flair in her choice of carpet and wall colours for our home. She was a caring, capable mother of our two young children while still holding down a part-time position at Ernst & Young. Her work clothes were chic; her figure still trim. In summary, what the outside world saw was worthy only of praise.

But was I impressed by any of it? Was I lucky to have her? Was I satisfied?

Was I f—

I got out of bed and pulled on jeans and a T-shirt. I tiptoed quietly down the corridor past the kids' bedrooms and vaulted over the stairgate without opening it. Downstairs in the utility room, I picked up a three-iron and a few golf balls. I headed out into the night, onto the back lawn, still barefoot. I threw the balls down onto the grass and took a few practice swings. When I felt ready I stepped up to the first ball, luminous in the gloom, and let fly. Thwack!

At contact the club-head was travelling at 90 mph. If I made a proper connection, that acceleration was imparted to the ball. Due to its smaller mass, said ball then scorched away into the darkness at an angle of roughly 35 degrees and at speeds of up to 140 mph. Seven seconds later and two hundred yards away, I heard a faint thud as it hit the ground. Or a bush or a stone. Possibly a cow. But not a window or a person. We lived at the very edge of the village, and there was nothing at risk out in that direction but a boggy marsh overgrown with rushes and rhododendrons all the way down to the lake.

Thwack! I walloped another one and sliced it badly. Maybe I moved my head; maybe my stance was not properly parallel. Whichever, I really needed to get some proper practice on a golf course or driving range. That, however, was just another thing in my life that my wife would not facilitate.

I met her at a house-party fourteen years ago. We slow danced to fast music and waltzed drunkenly all the way home to her flat. The flatmate was already asleep in their twin bedroom so we lay on the sofa. After an hour of groping each other through our clothes, we finally undid both zips. Without taking off either knickers or underpants, we managed to have simultaneous orgasms. So began what were officially the happiest days of my life.

There's no cliché about the greatness and perfection

of love that I wouldn't use to describe those early times. We were students with only eight lectures a week. We spent our time wandering round parks and piers. If the opportunity arose we'd have sex: outside, in the woods, between the dunes, even in the toilet on the train. At night we renounced comfortable slumber for the romance of sleeping spoon-like in a single bed.

I left it too long to propose. Six years later that early momentum was long gone. I had been waiting for that day (promised in pop songs) when I would know, for sure, that this was *it*. It didn't happen. Instead the hope and conviction we'd started with was chipped away by arguments.

One of the arguments was about sex. It had declined in quality and quantity. But that was because of the business degree she was doing by night. Between that and work, no wonder she was exhausted. It would all sort itself out after the final exams.

Everyone we knew was getting married. It was the thing. It was the time. I proposed.

I panicked on the day of the wedding. The ceremony wasn't until 3 p.m. so I had time to think. I felt that something was wrong. My best man and the groomsman persuaded me to get out and get some air instead of moping around the hotel. They brought me to the neighbouring golf course. It was my first round ever and my focus was not great. After hooking a dozen balls into the rough, I stormed off the sixth tee, saying the wedding was off.

'But she's such a nice girl!' the best man shouted after me.

'Everyone agrees,' said the groomsman.

*

I went through with it but could feel a weight on my chest. The first time my wife and I were alone together was back at the hotel just before the meal. We had to go to the bridal suite to collect a camera left in her sister's coat. It was our first chance to get away from the crowd. As we opened the door, she was fretting about whether her fake tan was too much and complaining about her unreliable sibling who, on today of all days, couldn't remember 'the one small thing she was asked to do'. I said that I hadn't even noticed she was wearing fake tan and asked her to point out the sister's coat. When I turned around, my wife had slipped the top of her dress down around her waist and her breasts were swinging free.

'Now,' she said, 'do you see the difference between my ordinary skin and the bits with fake tan? I told that woman in the salon I wanted something really light, just enough to take away the pasty look. But she was in such a snot because I wouldn't take off my strapless bra, and I think she made it darker out of spite.'

Yes. There was indeed a layer of orangey-brown colour on her arms, face and neck, but not on her breasts. God, did they look white! God, did she look sexy! I gasped and felt the weight leaving my chest. I dropped the camera and strode towards her. Manfully.

The honeymoon in Naples was fabulous, both of us agreed, but perhaps for different reasons. My wife loved the cuisine, the architecture and the fact that she managed to send off her first twenty thank-you cards for wedding presents. My big thrill was having sex daily for the first time in ages.

The day we flew back my wife felt nauseous. We picked up a pregnancy test on the way home from the airport. Back at our house, I hadn't even finished unloading the suitcases when the toilet flushed and she ran out to me, whooping. In her hand was a thin blue line. We hugged and kissed and spun around in a waltz.

Later that night she said, 'Please don't.'

'Why not?' I asked.

'Because of morning sickness, silly!' she said, smiling.

The radio alarm glowed 22.45.

Morning sickness lasted for fifteen weeks and was certainly not confined to the morning, rarely easing off until a few seconds before sleep. It ended just at the time we moved a few miles out of Dublin to the house we live in now. Thus my wife went from being too sick for sex to being too stressed. By the time the move was complete, the bump was getting bigger and she developed backache. When the physio brought some relief there were only six weeks to D-day. Sex at that stage can do awful things to the foetus. And anyway it's a bit perverse, I was told.

So there were many reasons to not have sex and they were all perfectly valid. I didn't mind, really. It's not as if we never had sex throughout the nine months. There were a couple of times. But most of the sex in our bedroom was what we watched on Channel 4.

Her mother and father came to visit us for a weekend. Supposedly this was in order to see our new home. Really it was an excuse for mother and daughter to go into Dublin shopping. The snag was my father-in-law, who hated big crowds.

'Darling, will you please entertain him?' my wife asked, standing so close that I could feel the bump.

'Okay . . .' I said reluctantly. It had been established at various family gatherings that my father-in-law and I had absolutely no rapport.

'He likes golf. Why not take him to a golf course?'

'But I don't play golf. I've only ever played about five holes in my life.'

'Darling? Please . . .' she said softly. I glanced down. Her blouse was open at the neck. For hormonal reasons, her breasts had got a lot bigger.

I chauffeured him to the golf course in silence. We played the first hole in silence, interrupted only by the clunk of my drive smacking into a tree trunk. Luckily, the ball bounced out onto the fairway, but my second shot sliced it firmly back into the woods. From behind me I heard a heavy sigh.

After three holes I was playing so badly that I decided to give up. Perhaps I could just carry my father-in-law's bag?

Tut-tut, he wouldn't hear of it. He would, however, beg leave to give me a few words of instruction.

'Stand in a bit closer to the ball,' he said, 'and straighten your back. You've been stooping down too much.'

With nothing to lose, I did as he said and lined up to the ball.

'And don't lift your head!' he said.

I took a shot.

Thwack! The ball flew long and straight, bounced once and rolled up onto the fourth green, stopping just a yard from the flag. I ran down the fairway after it, delighted with myself, hungry for more glory. I couldn't wait to hit it again.

Along came Katie, our darling daughter. She was, and is, wonderful, beautiful and intelligent. This, though, is not a story about Katie's wonderfulness. This is a story about not having sex.

Katie cried non-stop for the first five months. There was no pattern to her feeding; her sleeps were predictable only to the extent that they were always too short. She had colic from day one and when that eased the teething took over. Night was no different to day: she howled until someone attended her, seven times between midnight and 8 a.m. We took it in turns but were both constantly exhausted. So we did not have sex. For a perfectly valid reason.

That same reason also militated against my being able to visit a golf course. After work I had to go straight home to relieve a woman driven demented by minding a difficult baby all day. At weekends it was a similar story: to go golfing would have been an act of unspeakable selfishness. I was not a Neanderthal. I had been raised by my mother to be sensitive. I knew the importance of putting down the toilet seat. I was unafraid to try my hand at changing nappies and burping.

Still, these were the nights when the frustration really started to build. The nights when I began to take furtive trips out to the back lawn with my three-iron.

You can imagine my surprise when Katie's six-month check-up coincided with my wife having a bout of unquenchable lust. Night after night, we found time when previously there had been none. I was so glad that I did not stop to ask myself why. I did not always use condoms, though my wife was not back on the pill. After two weeks the nausea returned. So did the little blue line. That very night my wife turned to me, smiled in a most apologetic way, and said, 'I'm afraid I'm going to have to ask you to take your hand out of my knickers.'

The tape was rewound to the beginning. We played it again note for note.

Along came Mae, our second darling daughter. She was, and is, wonderful, beautiful and intelligent. This, though, is not a story about Mae's wonderfulness. This is a story in which golf plays an important part.

Mae was another impossible baby and fell into a liveable pattern only when she was six months old. To celebrate I went down to the local golf club and signed up for membership. It was something that had been on my mind to do ever since that brilliant round of golf with my father-in-law. Though I'd bought a set of clubs, in the intervening two years I'd only managed to play on my back lawn. That was all about to change. My wife agreed that I could have every Saturday morning off from helping with the babies. In return she would go to the gym on Sundays.

I arrived at the course at 7 a.m. that Saturday and a 'Thwack!' on the first tee confirmed that I could still hit it. But the Saturday deal didn't last long. Two weeks later we had to go to a christening. My wife's nephew. Then her niece's first birthday, followed by her sister Colette's fortieth. Shortly after that came a barbecue invitation (in April) that my wife was too courteous to refuse. We drove seventy miles to be washed out by rain. It seemed that Saturday was not ideal for golf. My wife still went to the gym on Sundays, though.

A ray of sunshine appeared to break through when my wife came out of the shower one night and dropped her towel most pleasingly.

'No, it's okay, darling,' she said, as I ripped a condom from its wrapper.

'How is it okay?'

She wanted a third baby, preferably a boy this time, if at all possible. I rolled on that condom with particular care.

'So are you clearly stating,' said my wife when discussing the matter calmly over breakfast, 'that you definitely don't want another baby and will not be changing your mind?'

'Yes,' I said, while spooning yoghurt into Katie. 'Categorically! Two is enough.'

'And you won't change your mind later and start pining for a son?'

'Yes,' I said firmly, as yoghurt dribbled down a frilly dress, 'the price we're paying is just too high.'

'Hmm,' said my wife, 'if that's the way you want it, I'm not going to force you to do something you don't want to do.'

That very morning she made the necessary phone calls and a fortnight later she was hospitalized for a 'procedure'. Without further discussion, her tubes were tied up and our family was now officially complete.

There were also exciting developments on the golfing front. Despite getting to practise only on a haphazard basis, my standard of play had improved dramatically. Over the winter I scored well in competition and brought my handicap down from 28 to 16. I set my sights on the prestige event in March, the Captain's Prize.

If I couldn't get to the course on a Saturday, I redoubled my practice sessions on the back lawn. Hitting each ball only once was becoming an expensive habit. One day I went down to the lake, hoping to retrieve a few dozen. The ground was softer than I'd anticipated, coming up around my ankles, making a mess of my runners. I plunged onward until I had sunk knee deep and had to admit defeat. Retreating to the pier, I found an excellent vantage point. The balls were still out there, all right. Light enough not to sink, they pockmarked the muddy flats with a hundred dots of white. I just needed to come back with a bucket and a pair of tall wellies.

The night after she got her tubal ligation stitches out, we had sex, and for the first time in ages my wife had an orgasm.

'Don't bother,' she had said, as I moved my tongue in small circles, 'it probably won't work.'

But I insisted and for a change I was right. She had one and then several more in quick succession. She could hardly breathe for five minutes after. It was longer still before she could speak.

'Thank you so much,' she said.

Annoyingly, though, this was yet another false dawn and did not lead to any upsurge in sexual activity. Quite the reverse, in fact, as my wife began a none too subtle campaign of avoiding me. She started going to bed absurdly early, like 9 o'clock, just when I was watching something decent on TV. Even if I hurried upstairs as the credits rolled, the lights would be off and she would be snoring.

I learned my lesson but she changed her tactics.

I'd go to bed early, only to find she had some crime drama she desperately needed to stay up to see. I'd wait up in bed until midnight, grimly fighting off sleep. Sometimes I conked out. Sometimes I held on and she would eventually arrive yawning and saying, 'Darling, I'm afraid I have to say no. It's much too late for any of that.'

The day before the Captain's Prize, my wife 'reminded' me that we were booked to go on the morrow to another christening lunch of another sister's baby. It was entered on the wall-planner, apparently. The wall-planner my wife had put up recently to help make our lives run even more smoothly. Had I not checked it? No, I had not. I fumed. I fulminated. I accepted my fate.

That night we were both awake and in the same bed.

'Please don't,' my wife said for the 1,001st time.

'Don't what?' I replied, for the 1,001st time.

'Don't try to wangle me into having sex.'

'Why not?'

'Because –' she began, as usual, and then stopped. 'Because the truth is there is no "why not".'

'Huh?' I said, unsettled by this new tack.

'There is no "why not". There is no reason. Why should there have to be? Why must it be up to *me* to explain? Why must it be always my *fault*? Why must I be *always* the one under pressure? The fact

is that I simply don't want to. And I haven't wanted
to for ages. And I don't think I'm likely to want to
any time soon. Can't you imagine what it's like
having to do . . . that . . . thing . . . when you've no
desire? It's not very pleasant, let me tell you.
Anyway, you orgasm so easily that I think you'd be
as happy with a blow-up doll! I've discussed your
demands for daily frequency with Colette, and she
thinks you're being totally unreasonable. Frank only
wants to have sex once a fortnight and that suits
them both nicely. Though, God knows, I can
honestly say that if I never have sex again, I really
could not give a hoot!'

Blow-up doll!

Discussed me with Colette!

Never have sex again!

I suppose I must have looked stunned. She switched
to a conciliatory tone. 'On the other hand, I accept
what's obvious. That you still do want to. Have it.
For recreational purposes. Or whatever. I do respect
that. And to that end I have been thinking about a
possible compromise.'

I was still too shocked to interrupt.

'Even though I don't really want it, I'm prepared
to have sex once a fortnight on the following conditions.'

Always brilliant at brokering a deal, my little peace-
maker set out the terms.

'One. There's to be no pressure on me for sex on
any other night.

'And two, you're not to be wheedling me into any
of those funny positions you sometimes try.'

Truly, I did not know what to say. I nodded
weakly.

'That's brilliant, darling,' she said with a huge smile, 'such a weight off my mind!'

After giving me a quick hug, she lifted up the quilt and exposed my naked penis.

'As for tonight,' she added, 'I think it's gone a bit limp.'

Indeed it had.

The next day I got up early and gathered my golf gear. My wife apprehended me in the hall, swinging the belt of her dressing-gown playfully.

'I'm afraid to have to tell you, but I think you must be forgetting something, darling!' she said, laughing, cheerful as could be, making humorous quotation marks in the air. 'Re-Mem-Ber! My sister? Her baby? The christening?'

My reply was almost as witty.

'Fuck you and fuck your fucking christening.'

That was eight months ago.

We have no plans to separate. It seems odd but there is still something between us that resembles love. Maybe it's just habit and history. She's still, after all, the lovely girl the whole world praises. Still pretty when she goes out of doors, she is good-natured, ladylike, reliable, intelligent and hard-working, still a good person to live with. Also we have two lovely girls. And I do not want to miss out on their lives. Some might say the kids would be better off if we did separate, rather than being trapped in a hostile environment. But I don't think it is hostile. It's just not a situation in which they see their parents hug or kiss that often.

Tonight, though, I will slide my hand under my

184

wife's knickers and she will not say, 'Please don't.' She will let it happen because it is exactly fourteen nights since our last time.

We will have intercourse in the 'spoons' position. Always that position. Obviously I would prefer some variety but this way is best for two reasons. (a) Positions that involve us facing one another are no longer appropriate. At the best of times, sex is slightly ridiculous – panting, rocking, perhaps groaning – so you feel absurd if you look into blue eyes that are looking back with total detachment. (b) 'Spoons' has the added advantage of allowing her to continue to read her book.

When I am finished, my wife will mark her page, put down the book and turn to me with a wonderful smile on her face. She will mop the fringe from my sweaty brow as she would a little boy's. She will kiss my cheek and whisper the words: 'Thanks. That was very nice.'

It's not ideal.

Perhaps you might say that it's equally bad for both parties; a tragic misalignment of libidos. But no. I want sex daily. She doesn't want it ever. At the rate of once a fortnight, that means she's the one getting her way ninety-three per cent of the time.

Also, she has started to wear leggings around the house. She knows I detest leggings. Making any effort to look attractive while at home has dropped off her to-do list. I fear it's only a matter of time before she chops off her beautiful shoulder-length hair.

So, yes, I am now on the lookout for an affair or indeed a fling. Ideally, I'd like to find a blonde who is pretty, curvaceous and hungry for energetic but meaningless sex. Easy to say, not so easy to do. Unfortunately there is no queue of shaggable women forming outside my office door. Furthermore I'm nervous of various possible consequences – being caught, disease, pregnancy, attachment. Maybe one of the new temps might seduce me at our next Christmas party (I'll have to remember to take off my wedding ring).

As to that Captain's Prize contest? I came in third and won a nice little crystal bowl. My wife ignored its existence for a long while. Then she used it when pouring off the grease from the grill. Then she redeployed it for feeding the cat. Then she drove over it.

Nowadays, I play golf whenever I bloody well please. During the week, I work long and late for Sheehan & Kiely, often coming home only after the kids are in bed. My weekends, then, should perhaps be reserved for spending quality time with my family. But no. Each Saturday I spend both morning and afternoon out on the golf course. Later I might go home and spend time in the kids' playroom. On the other hand, if there's a rugby match showing on the clubhouse TV, I may be further delayed.

One last thing.

I went back down to the lake only last week to get those golf balls. This time I had a bucket and tall wellies. Strangely I found not even one, though I clumped over and back across the oozy marshland. Perhaps there were some in the tufts of vegetation? A haggard old cow meandered by on the headland and eyed me suspiciously as I used the three-iron to poke and bash at rhododendrons. No. It was to no avail. The balls had all been sucked up, dissolved and digested by the sludge.

18

Piddle faster!

'**P**iddle faster, Vera,' shouted my husband through the keyhole. 'We're going to be late.'

Imagine? Piddle faster? How exactly can you piddle faster? But, then, that's my husband through and through. Nothing I do is quick enough for him, least of all getting ready to go out. Still, I hoped things would be more relaxed on our honeymoon.

I came out here a virgin. I didn't have an older sister or girlfriend to tell me what to expect. I had no idea, but I certainly imagined that a good deal of the holiday might be spent in bed. I even thought an occasional breakfast might be missed. How wrong I was.

'Rome, Vera,' he tells me repeatedly, 'is a once-in-a-lifetime opportunity. We must be thorough. Make sure to see everything that's recommended in the book. And we must take photographs to show everybody afterwards.'

Since he sounded in such a strop, I did actually try

to piddle faster. I scrunched my stomach and forced the muscles to push. I probably shaved off a second or two. That wasn't enough. When I emerged from the lav he was gone. On the bed lay a note. Squiggles of rushed writing.

'Hurry! Use map and catch up! Gone ahead to see the Spanish Steps, then Trevi Fountain, then Pantheon, then Coliseum. Then Lunch.'

19

The mother-in-law who made very few demands

*T*he last Ice Age saw huge glaciers covering much of northern Europe, Asia and America. In 13,000 BC, however, these began to retreat, revealing a thin bridge of land connecting Russia and Alaska. Hunter-gatherers in Siberia were quick to seize the opportunity and walked towards green pastures dimly visible on the other side . . .

'Come on,' said Jarum, 'or we'll never get across!'

In his fist the young man carried a spear; across his shoulders was a leather bag. It contained a few stone tools, a fire-making flint and a dozen hazelnuts for snacks. Walking beside him was an older woman he called 'Mammy'. He carried her luggage also, in a big reed basket. Inside were three changes of clothes, a hair-comb and a pouch of pigments she used to colour her lips.

Behind them was Jarum's wife, Clov, who was weighed down with more practical effects: tent poles, skins and rolls of furry mammoth hide.

'Is she always this slow?' said Mammy. 'I suppose it's too late now to say I told you so.'

'I am coming, you pig! And you pig's mother!' said Clov under her breath. Just to annoy them she dropped her load and halted completely for a moment to adjust her hair.

'I did tell you so, son, didn't I?' said Mammy.

When Jarum started gesticulating, Clov turned her back on him entirely. While rubbing her abdomen she looked out into the northern sea. This close to the glacier, the tide was slow and sinister, pushing its way through the slush. When she was good and ready, Clov picked up her basket and followed.

The 25-mile Bering land bridge existed for only about a year. As the ice receded, a knock-on effect was the pouring of billions of gallons of water back into the planet's oceans. Those who crossed the bridge towards the latter end of that time would have noticed the surrounding sea levels rising and the water lapping on either side. Such formidable walkers as the Siberian hunter-gatherers could have crossed it in a single day . . .

Except when they were bringing a slow-moving mother-in-law. Except when her daughter-in-law was in the middle stages of pregnancy and sulking about her mother-in-law having been brought in the first place. Except when both women dawdled so much that they were forced to make camp for the night halfway over.

There was little shelter to be found on the tundra but Jarum cobbled together two tents from the contents of Clov's basket. His mammy, meanwhile, took out the pouch of pigment and dabbed an even coating on her wide lips. Clov lit a fire and rustled some sort of supper out of their meagre rations. Mammy winced when she tasted hers, put it back in the bowl and declared that she'd prepare breakfast herself. Then she retired to her tent and the young couple to theirs.

Ten minutes later, Jarum was stroking his wife's abdomen, murmuring 'baby'. Then he heard his mother calling: 'Jarum, oh, come quickly, Jarum.'

He shot up and nearly knocked down the tent in his hurry to see whether a polar bear had attacked her. He returned to Clov in a little while after fixing down the corner of his mother's tent. A draught had been getting in at her.

Just five minutes later, the young couple had advanced to passionate cuddling when the calling began again: 'Jar-um. Oh, Jar-um.'

Jarum said to Clov in alarm, 'Maybe it's snow-wolves.' Luckily he was wrong again. There were just some adjustments required to her pillow.

On the last occasion that Mammy called, Clov and Jarum were not stroking or cuddling; they were having a row in which Jarum tried to explain for the umpteenth time why it had been necessary to bring his mother with them.

(Jarum's father was long since dead, having been killed in a mammoth hunt. Being something of a beauty, Mammy had had no trouble attracting other men but three subsequent husbands had also met with untimely deaths. Now, considered bad luck, no man would touch her, even as a concubine. Thus it behoved her only son to see to her needs. Which weren't so very many. All told, she made very few demands. And anyway she probably wouldn't live much longer. Couldn't Clov be patient?)

More slowly than before, yet dutiful all the same, Jarum went out to Mammy's tent to find her complaining of hunger. She was now ready, she groaned, to perhaps have that food, which she'd not been able for earlier.

Next morning, they gathered their things and made rapid progress now an end was in sight. After two hours of walking, Mammy discovered something terrible.

'Oh, no, Jarum. No, no, no,' she shrieked. The poor woman could hardly get the words out in her grief, but her son eventually established that she'd left something vital behind at the last camp – the pouch of lip pigments.

'We have to go back,' she moaned.

'Don't be ridiculous,' said Clov. 'That's two hours each way, four hours, just to be back where we started. We'll just get you new ones on the other side.'

'Now, Jarum, I make very few demands,' shrieked Mammy. 'But they wouldn't be the same shade. I need that shade.'

Her son did not like to disappoint.

'I know,' said Jarum. 'I'll go back on my own. Running there and back, I can easily do it in half the time. Meanwhile the two of you just sit right here and take a nice little rest.'

Clov shouted loudly, 'No, Jarum. I'm sick of this old woman's silliness. I specifically ask that you do not go off on this stupid errand.' But her husband had already turned tail. Incensed, she looked back to see her mother-in-law's dry lips barely concealing a smirk.

*

Around the world, melted ice lifted the sea levels by up to ninety feet and brought cataclysmic flooding to many places. Not least of these was at the Bering land bridge, which was abruptly drowned, becoming the Bering Strait. The period when it was possible to walk from Russia to America came to an end . . .

Two women saw Jarum returning in the distance. As he came closer, his hand was aloft in triumph; it held the precious pouch. Mammy hurrayed in delight and ran out to meet him. Clov stayed put. She watched as mother embraced son, but then her eye was caught by a huge wave coming out of the north. She stood up but was walloped back down. The wave of freezing water passed over on its way to the southern sea, tearing over the land bridge as if it weren't there. Clov tried to get up but there was another wave on its heels and she was flattened again. Slowly she crawled towards higher ground and after five minutes the waves quietened somewhat. She stood up to see if the others had survived. They had. Both Jarum and his mother were standing only a hundred yards away. But those hundred yards were now filled with sea.

'Don't worry, I'll come and get you,' shouted Jarum, and began to paddle across through the treacherous currents. Soon he had to resort to swimming. Unfortunately the Siberians were not a maritime people, and, athletic though he was, Jarum wasn't up to swimming through a whirlpool where the freezing waters of two oceans were colliding. He tried several times but nearly drowned and was swept back to the Siberian shore.

Clov began to cry while Mammy remained unusually

silent. She was trying to comb her hair back into some sort of proper order.

'I'm just going to take a minute, catch my breath and think,' shouted Jarum to his stranded wife before the heavy waves started again.

By mid-afternoon, further encroachments by the waves forced them to stand two hundred yards apart. Jarum had tried swimming again but it was hopeless. With only a few hours of daylight left, they had to make a hard decision. To stay in the vicinity overnight would be fatal; further waves would surely attack in the dark. Furthermore, they'd lost all their food and camping gear. Without these things, death from exposure was inevitable. The only solution, said Jarum, sobbing even as he shouted across, was for Clov to go on towards the new land, and for him and his mother to go back to Siberia. Thus both parties would find food and shelter by nightfall. Once home, he would collect the materials for a raft and return to make the crossing. All Clov had to do was wait.

Clov was a practical girl. Though her face streamed with tears, she blew a kiss and then did as bid, setting off east.

Mammy was not so practical. Only ten minutes into her journey, she retrieved the pigment from her pouch and paused to apply some more to her lips. Jarum growled, tore it from her, and threw pigment and pouch far into the sea.

When Jarum returned in three days, loaded with wood and string, the channel had already widened to a mile. Again, his lack of maritime experience told against him. He was unable to make headway against the ripping cross-currents. His raft smashed, and, his heart broken, he decided to camp at the edge and see if perchance the waters might recede again, go away as quickly as they appeared. That hope was forlorn. He stayed by the waters for three weeks and they simply pushed him back and back as the strait widened. Through days of hunger and thirst, he stared intently at the far shore, hoping for even a glimpse of his lovely wife. One night Jarum was attacked and hadn't the strength to resist. The snow-wolves ate him.

Clov waited for him a long time – but not for ever. She had a baby to consider; to the south lay food and a warmer sun.

Still very attractive for her age, Mammy found another husband. His first gift to her was some pigment of just the right shade.

20

If I'd thrown the baby
half a second earlier

Cork, Ireland, 2007

I nearly killed my daughter Amy when she was just eight months old. It was accidental. I'd been cuddling and tickling her while sitting in an armchair in the living room. I stood up and moved towards the kitchen, playfully tossing her into the air as I went, as I often did. She gurgled and screamed with excitement. As we came to the doorway, I didn't pause. I was oblivious to the doorframe of wood and solid concrete until the split second after I'd thrown her out of my arms. I was too late to snatch her back, and my eyes followed her helplessly. Her head disappeared from my view, on an arc just past the other side of the frame. She dropped back down into my hands. Nothing had happened.

My wife was upstairs getting dressed, but her sister Denise was sitting in the living room and saw everything. She was there to babysit while my wife and I went to the cinema. She gasped in fright. Rather than admit what had almost happened, I kept my composure and continued to play with Amy, albeit more carefully. I felt a surge of sweat in my armpits. Nonchalantly, I explained to Denise about mixing six scoops of powder for the baby's bottles. I talked extra loudly. *Nothing had happened*.

In the cinema afterwards, I replayed the scene in my head.

Definitely . . .

1. Amy missed a head-on collision with solid wood and concrete by a tiny margin.

2. I had thrown her with such force that she then flew upwards, way past the top of the doorway.

So, when I had stridden out through that doorway . . .

1. *If I had thrown her a quarter of a second earlier.*

Some part of her face would have clipped the doorframe. She'd have taken a knock on the nose and forehead or maybe the chin. She may well have bled and certainly would have screamed her head off. This would've been upsetting and hugely embarrassing because it was totally my fault. Amy would have got over it, though, in a matter of days.

2. *If I had thrown her half a second earlier.*

She would have got a violent wallop from the wood or the concrete on some part of her head. Maybe I'd have broken her nose. Or her jaw. Or smashed her few teeth that had cost us so many nights of wailing. Maybe I'd have smacked the top of her skull. Maybe she'd have lost her sight or hearing.

Or maybe the force would've broken her neck and left her whole body paralysed. Maybe all her future life of running and playing and jumping and hopping and skipping and sliding and falling and laughing would've been denied to her. Maybe her mental age would've been frozen right there at eight months. Maybe all the potential of her wonderful life, all the searching and the finding, would never have had a chance to happen.

Maybe my wife and I would have been condemned to making the best of it. Caring 24/7 for a poor misfortunate girl whose life remained long, but was one of slow suffering.

Or maybe she would have died instantly on impact.

And it would all have been my fault. Entirely. For a moment's stupidity.

My wife would have blamed me and could never have forgiven me. And she'd have been right. So our marriage would have been wrecked as well.

Half an hour into the film, I felt like getting up and leaving the cinema. I was plagued by a looped rerun of the moment of near disaster. I couldn't focus on the plot and lost the thread. My wife, however, sat oblivious, even laughing when appropriate. I reached across the darkness and clasped her hand. I leaned back, closed my eyes and tried to focus on the most important fact: I had been very lucky. The terrible thing had not actually happened. My baby was fine and my marriage still intact.

A wave of extreme exhaustion overcame me and I began to fall off to sleep. In the last few seconds of consciousness, though, I made two resolutions:

1. Effective immediately, I would stop throwing Amy into the air.

2. In a few months' time, I would definitely rent this film on DVD.

21

Twenty-three days
before the crunch

I t's noon on a Monday and I can hear my father, only three feet away, through a thin plasterboard wall. He is supposed to be at work but has come home early. It is plain from his grunting and the rhythmic knocking of the headboard that he is having sex. It is less apparent with whom.

My excuse for being at home in the afternoon is more respectable. I have just over three weeks until the Leaving Cert. It's pointless, at this stage, to go to school. Classes are just a distraction. It's all about study; it's about sitting alone with my notes and trying to transfer their contents into my skull. When the crunch comes it won't matter whether I understand this information, just that I be able to regurgitate it onto the page.

Anyway, today is Day 1 of my 23-day revision schedule and it has, admittedly, got off to a slow start. The plan was that I'd walk down to the library after breakfast and work there until three or so. Instead I had no breakfast and spent the morning attempting to study while lying in bed. Bad call. After only a few pages I found myself 'resting my eyes'. It's okay, I assured myself, I'm just letting the information sink in by pondering it more deeply. I fell asleep.

I was awoken by the sound of a car door slamming in the backyard. Very strange, I thought, since my parents were at work. And our postman cycles. I got up to investigate and peered out through the curtains. It was Dad, locking his car. He was the only one I could see. He called out in a loud whisper, 'Wait a minute, sexy,' to someone who was already at the back door, below my window and out of sight.

I closed my bedroom door and held my breath. Dad and the other person came inside and I heard them murmuring down in the hall. It was impossible to make out the words, but easy to make out the gender of Dad's companion. Then, without further niceties, they came up the stairs in what can only be described as a gallop. Clump, clump, clump went his loafers, click, click, click went her heels, as they rushed past my door giggling like fucking imbeciles. They burst into the master bedroom, nearly taking the door off its hinges.

I'm supposed to be at the library. Dad thinks the house is empty and hasn't bothered to check. That's why I now bear witness to this outbreak of adulterous behaviour. It's appalling but not surprising. In fact the rhythmic sounds from next door (getting a little faster now) confirm something I've suspected for quite some time: my parents' relationship is on a slippery slope to breakdown.

They are a typical pair of lower-middle-class (but snobby), Mass-going (but essentially godless),

FF-voting, *Winning Streak*-watching, *Sunday Independent*-reading, Eagles- and Bee Gees-listening idiots. They argue constantly. Mostly this is because Dad is (according to Mum) 'an insensitive clodhopper with no regard for my feelings or needs'. Examples of his thoughtless behaviour include:

1. a propensity to clip his toenails at the wrong time and in the wrong place (the correct time and place has never, to my knowledge, been established);
2. pacing around impatiently when she's taking the trouble to look especially nice before they go out;
3. inappropriate use of the designated guest towels;
4. placing of his mug on the coffee table without a coaster;
5. turning up the volume on the TV too loud on account of being half-deaf;
6. always putting his toast on for a second turn, always walking away and letting it burn, always stinking out the house for days after. Etcetera, etcetera.

The immediate result of these trespasses is a rebuke. Then a counter-opinion and a walk-out. Then a cold shoulder and a long evening of silence. The three of us sit side by side by side making no eye contact, each watching the TV with grim intensity. Even if it's awful crap.

On the other hand my mother is also somewhat at fault, being (according to Dad):

1. a ridiculously over-sensitive nincompoop;
2. a person who can't stop trying to control every detail of everyone around her;
3. a fusspot;

4. far too quick with the tears;

5. well able to dish it out yet not so ready to hear a few home truths herself.

But what is wrong with my father that, after twenty years of living with her, he can't anticipate what's going to drive her into one of those sulks and nip the problem in the bud? I've certainly had to do so myself.

The recent tensions aren't entirely a bad thing. When they're mad at each other they tend to be nicer to me. It's quite amusing, Dad bringing me cups of tea and chocolate biscuits. He starts asking me questions about Lykke Li. Pretending he likes her new song and wondering if I have it on my iPod. What does he know about any music recorded since 1985? Jackshit, that's what. And Mum then, just as bad, showing an elaborate interest in how was my day at school. Asking if I ever want to talk about my 'feelings'. Screw that!

On the other hand, less amusing is the evidence I came across when snooping around their bedroom looking for something interesting. In Mum's toiletry bag, there was a box of capsules called Fexepam XL 50mg. According to the information leaflet they're for depression, and/or severe and persistent anxiety. The dose was one daily and nineteen were missing.

Without warning the racket on the far side of the wall stops. Dad must be finished punishing the headboard. Finally! I breathe a sigh of relief. I could really do without distractions, particularly such revolting ones, while I'm trying to study. I open up *Chemistry for Today* and turn to the section on benzene. I've Questions 1, 3 and 5 totally covered but if any of this 'organic' stuff comes up, then I'm screwed. I wonder if this is my father's first little afternoon rendezvous? No, stop. All across my seven subjects, it's a similar story. There's stuff I can do and some I totally can't. In English, I'm relying on Yeats coming up this year, as he tends to every third year. If some smartarse in the Department of Education decides to fuck with the rota, I'm up shit creek. Particularly Kinsella: I haven't even read him, let alone learned off the notes. If that scenario plays out, I can kiss my 530 points and Architecture goodbye.

A new sound is emerging from the other side of the wall – moaning. What the fuck? Oh, I get it. Moaning from Dad's playmate. Jesus H. Christ! Presumably if he was a gentleman he'd have let her come first. Nevertheless he seems to be making an effort now. Trying to ensure that this isn't a one-off. That he'll have his wicked way again.

And then abruptly the woman shouts out, her words muffled through the wall but easily extrapolated in this context: 'Yes, Ronan! Yes, yes, yes. Oh, God, yes.'

I could do with going for a slash. There is silence now, though, so I'd surely be heard walking down the landing to the bathroom. Not that I have anything to be ashamed of. But I'd rather my presence in the house was not detected. I distract myself instead by pondering the identity of Dad's co-adulterer based on a shortlist of three.

It's a bit of a cliché, but suspect No. 1 is his secretary, Ms Wallace, whom I've met once or twice at the office and who certainly has some appealing qualities. In fact, I was reminded of her when Robbie told us this brilliant joke last week:

Man has three possible girls for the position of secretary.

The interviews consist of just one question, which he asks each of them.

'If you found a 100-euro note on the street, what would you do?'

Girl A says she'd stick it straight into her purse and keep it.

Girl B says she'd take it to the nearest church and put it in the poor box.

Girl C says she'd place it in custody at the garda station, and if it wasn't claimed within a year and a day, then legally it would be hers.

So which girl did the man pick for his secretary? The one with the biggest tits, obviously.

Suspect No. 2 is Mary O'Brien, a friend and neighbour whom Dad is always praising as a much more sensible woman than Mum. 'She doesn't be always fretting over matters of no consequence. Why can't you be more like Mary?'

On the other hand . . . no. Like so many women of her age (dunno exactly, ancient, maybe fifty-one) Mary has kind of given up being a woman. She's a person still – I'll give her that – but not a woman as such. Her hair is cut to boy length and her body is of a similar tubbiness all the way from her shoulder to her ankles. What curves there once were have been swamped by bulges.

Suspect No. 3 . . . actually, I can't think of any other candidates.

So it has to be Ms Wallace.

Someone gets up from next door and saunters past my door to the bathroom. By his heavy footsteps, I know it's Dad. Needless to say, there is no en suite in this stupid old-fashioned kennel of a house. He leaves the bathroom door open and I hear him slashing away merrily. He pads back to the bedroom and out comes the pitter-patter of some tinier feet. Ms Wallace – it probably is Ms Wallace. I scramble over to the keyhole to look but it's hard to determine. The woman who flicks past is not naked but is wearing my mother's dressing-gown. Jesus! Make yourself thoroughly at home, bitch, why don't you? She, at least, is polite enough to close the door. All this pissing means I can't ignore my bladder any longer: I am bursting for a slash. She vacates the bathroom and I am tempted to take my turn. But no. I'm not leaving my room.

I look around the room to see if there's anything I can go into. A jug, a glass, a mug, an empty Coke can, anything. But no. Mum tidied up in here last night, so there's nothing. Then I have a bright idea. What about doing it straight out the window? It overlooks the backyard so there's no risk of being seen. The piss will flow down along the slates, into the gutter and away. Perfect.

The window is quite high, though, so I pull my chair over alongside. I open the window outwards and stand up on the chair.

Problem.

I do not believe this. I am foiled by the fucking inside windowsill, which is ten inches wide. In order to do the deed, your schlong would have to be about twelve inches long. Though it pains me to admit, mine isn't. I push it out as far as I can but it's still too short. I suppose that once I got going the trajectory would carry it out over the frame. But not at the start or the dribbly finish. It's fucking typical! The stupid fucked-up way that everything in this house has been designed.

*

I simply have to go.

I slink out my door heading for the small toilet downstairs. I am padding ever so gently, in bare feet, when suddenly the master bedroom door opens behind me. Without thinking I turn and face it. There is a moment of horror and suspense. Will it be Dad or Ms Wallace?

It's Mum.

She looks shocked. As, I'm sure, do I. She recovers first.

'I thought,' she says, 'that I heard burglars in the hall. And I thought you were going to the library.'

'Aahm, no,' I say, swallowing hard. 'I fell asleep doing Geography.'

'So you were asleep, then?'

'Yes.'

'Good . . . that's good.' She looks mighty relieved. 'You need your rest in between study sessions.'

There is a moment of awkward silence as we both search for ways to continue or conclude the conversation. I can't think of anything so I turn and carry on down the stairs. In the small toilet I finally get to unleash my urine, which breaks all previous records and lasts over the two-minute mark.

'So it was Her with Him all along,' I mumble to myself, feeling drained both physically and mentally. Fucksake! The fucking fucked-up idiots. As if I don't have enough to contend with, only twenty-three days before the crunch.

22

Once upon a time

A forest in the middle of Europe, 1376

Once upon a time, there lived a poor wood-cutter who had nine children, all boys. One day the fifth lad, Tom, overheard his father arguing with his stepmother. Tom was astonished to hear that they intended to abandon the children in the forest.

'I will drop shiny little pebbles along the way,' thought Tom; 'then I'll know the way back.'

Next day the woodcutter brought his sons on a trek into the woods and promptly deserted them. Some wept and others trembled in fear, but Tom was calm and confident, for he had executed his plan.

As they followed the stones, the boys came to the house of the Three Bears. Famously hospitable, the Bears were not found wanting. Mr Bear brought them inside and cobbled together benches to seat all nine. Mrs Bear then lavished porridge upon the little urchins, and they scooped through second and third helpings. Baby Bear even let them play with his ball until they burst it. Two hours later, and not before time as far as the Bears were concerned, the boys finally departed.

It was nightfall when they reached home. Unsure of their welcome, the children crowded around the window and looked inside the humble one-room dwelling. On the dinner table were numerous serving plates and in the centre the carcass of a large turkey. Every speck had been licked clean. Their father and stepmother were still in their seats, bloated and asleep.

Two weeks later Tom was again in the right place to hear his parents hatch another diabolical plan to get rid of their children. This time he didn't get a chance to collect pebbles but instead filled up a bag with sawdust from beneath his father's workbench.

The sawdust worked just as well as the pebbles. Though this was a deeper, darker part of the forest, Tom quickly established their direction home. On the way, they noticed an enchanted palace that was surrounded by particularly dense vegetation. Being wiry little fellows, they penetrated the shrubbery easily and went inside. All the inhabitants were asleep. Some guards were slumbering standing up, which the lads found hilarious. They knocked them over, daubed jam on their faces and made some unlikely pairings hold hands. Tom found a pretty princess asleep in her bed. He gave her a slobbery kiss on the mouth but she grimaced and kept her eyes shut. In reprisal, he tied her shoelaces together.

Eventually the boys continued on home and again they made it by nightfall. Looking in the window, they saw that the table was covered in bottles of wine and beer. Every one of them was empty; two tall glasses held only dregs. Their father and stepmother were still in their seats, drunk and asleep.

Tom's final piece of espionage took place three weeks later, when whispered voices again let him know that his parents were hatching a plan. This time he was overly casual and made no preparations. He just assumed he'd have time to load up with pebbles or sawdust once more. His father, however, hurried him out of the door the next morning and he could only grab a loaf of bread.

The woodcutter brought his children into the remotest valley of the province. When Tom went to pick up his trail of breadcrumbs, it was gone. The birds and mice and insects had eaten it. Tom wept. He blamed himself.

Thankfully the other brothers picked up the baton of leadership and they boldly headed off in a random direction, arms round the shoulders of an inconsolable Tom.

Presently they came to a huge house, where a kindly Giant woman lived. She invited them in for tea and again it seemed as if they had landed on their feet. But this time they had pushed their luck. On an armchair by the fire, her husband, the Ogre, lay asleep. She told them not to wake him since he especially liked to eat children. The boys began a game of 'dare' to see who would touch him: one grazed his boot, another brushed his knee and then brave Tom flicked his ear. The Ogre awoke and, though the Giant woman hid the boys in the cellar, he could smell them and opened the trapdoor. They seemed to be cornered but a newly energized Tom somehow discovered a loose grating and they squeezed out in time. The

Ogre gave chase and the boys ran out along his avenue and then into the thickest of the trees, hoping he'd soon give up. But he didn't: the Ogre hadn't tasted child flesh for a very long time and craved it. Their slight bodies were able to get through the thick vegetation quickly. But every time the Ogre got to a clearing he almost caught up with them in a few long strides. For an hour this continued, before finally the monster fell heavily.

Ten minutes later the boys took a risk and stopped. There were no giant footsteps behind them. Over the next hill they cheered at the sight of their own home sweet home: from 360 possible directions they'd somehow chosen the correct route and, having run all the way, they were back in double-quick time. The nine brothers went over to the window and looked inside. The table was bare, the chairs vacant. They could see nothing, nobody.

Their parents were inside, but under the table, where they couldn't be seen. They were naked except for the woodcutter's socks. He was moaning and she panting when they were suddenly silenced by Tom's rapping on the window-pane.

'Daddy, Daddy,' called a few of the boys.

'Where's my step-mammy?' called out the youngest of the bunch.

The woodcutter rolled off his wife and they continued to lie side by side under the table.

'Do you see?' whispered the stepmother as she reached for her knickers. 'Do you finally accept that I am right? There really is no alternative.'

'Okay, okay,' said the woodcutter with a sigh. Outside he could hear the boys shouting and throwing pebbles: they were using the unfortunate goose for target practice again.

'No matter what it costs!' continued the stepmother. 'The next time we want an evening alone together, we'll just have to pay a babysitter.'

23

My daddy is a teller of
fantastic tales

Kirina, Mali, 1284

'I said no,' shouted Mammy as Daddy tried to kiss the side of her neck. 'I won't give you money.'

Daddy's face turned very mad. He picked up the chair and banged it off the floor. One of the legs broke. Mammy sighed and shook her head – just like she does at me when I spill corn. Then she went out of the door and down to the market, where she minds the fish stall.

'Darling daughter. Come here,' said Daddy, spotting me crouched behind the water urn. 'I have a question for my tall clever girl.'

'What, Daddy?' I said. I was still a bit worried about the chair. It was our very best chair!

'I need to know where Mammy hides her money,' he said, and took me by the hand.

'I don't know,' I said. But I did know.

'I need it badly,' he said, and pulled me closer, kneeling to look me straight in the eye, 'and I will now explain to you why.'

*

229

Daddy told me one of his best-ever tales. He needed the money to buy a new chair to replace the broken one. But there was more to it than that. Daddy's helper on this adventure was, as usual, going to be Diata, the good-hearted snake. In order to get the new chair they would have to go to Mali City, overcoming many obstacles along the way. There would be a rickety bridge hanging high above the river, horrible wild dogs that would attack without warning and then a swamp full of talking frogs. Yet somehow Daddy and Diata would make it through. And buy the new chair in Mali. And bring it right back here to our hut.

It was more than just words. Daddy acted out the actions and the voices of every man and animal they would meet along the way. When he was finally finished we were both breathless, but he did not need to ask me again. I went and got him the gourd where Mammy hides her money. Then he kissed me and ran outside.

When Mammy came home from work, she checked the gourd and saw that her money was gone. I thought she might smack me but instead she just sat at the table and cried.

'He will place bets,' she said, 'and lose it all.'

I did not know what the word 'bets' was. However, I was quite sure that it had never been mentioned by Daddy. I put my arms around her neck and hugged her tightly.

'No, my lovely mammy,' I whispered. 'He has gone to Mali City for a new chair. And helping him will be Diata, the good-hearted snake.'

24

After Baby No. 3

Tipperary, Ireland, August 2008

I n the delivery room, as the consultant was sewing her torn flesh back together, my wife, Rachel, grimaced and told me: 'We've definitely done our bit for the continuation of the human race; enough is enough.'

In my arms, still bloody, still strangely purple in colour, lay our third child. Tiny fingers, teeny toes, little-bitty ears, a big huge head.

'Yes,' I said, 'the time has come for us to retire from any further baby-making.'

So we were agreed.

The problem arose later as I was leaving the delivery suite to collect Babies No. 1 (aged 3) and No. 2 (aged 18 months) from their granny. Rachel pointed out sweetly that since we were of one mind about it, I should therefore get a vasectomy.

Mother and new infant came home. Sex simply wasn't an issue for a while. No sleep, stitches, sore nipples from breast-feeding and continuous post-partum bleeding were contraceptive enough. Five weeks later, though, hungry Baby No. 3 was switched to bottles of formula and began to howl slightly less often, and for slightly shorter periods of time. We flopped naked into bed one evening and lay in an exhausted embrace.

I made moves.

'Why can't a cuddle just be a cuddle?' Rachel said, more tired than angry.

'It can. But it's been a few weeks and you look so sexy and –'

'Oh, yes,' she said sleepily, 'and I feel so very sexy. Let me count the ways! My belly's still enormous, my breasts have gone lopsided and there are clumps of my hair falling out in the shower.'

'Hmm. Okay. So, would that be a "no" for today but a "maybe" for tomorrow?' I said, in what I thought was a conciliatory tone.

'It would be a "no" today and "no" tomorrow and "no" until we thrash out the serious issue of contraception once and for all.'

'But –' I began.

'No buts,' she said gently. 'Look, sweetheart, I'm sure that if you thought about contraception at all, you thought of it as something I would handle. But I can't.'

'You can't?'

'No, I can't.' She paused and yawned. 'The consultant said that because of my blood-pressure problems I can't go back on the pill. Not without the risk of deep-vein thrombosis or an embolism.'

'And those deep-vein throm things would be bad, I take it?'

'Yes!' she said through slightly gritted teeth. 'Very. Bad.'

Rachel works as an administrator in Limerick Hospice, hence her familiarity with all things medical.

'I've investigated the possibility of a tubal ligation and I'm just not happy with the risks. So that's why I suggested that you should think about getting a va—'

'Don't even say it,' I interrupted.

'All right, then,' she said. 'I've got a temporary solution.'

Rachel bounded from the bed and scrabbled through the mess at the bottom of her wardrobe, emerging with something in her hand.

'Here you go,' she said, laughing, 'big boy!'

She opened her fist to reveal an old foil-wrapped condom, from when we used them years ago. It was wrinkled but still intact.

'God, that was fantastic,' said Rachel. 'I'd almost forgotten how.'

The night that followed, though, was not so good. Baby No. 3 woke at 1 a.m. and I got him back to sleep with a bottle. He was just settled when Baby No. 2, who was having a bout of teething, woke shrieking at 2.15 a.m. needing a spoon of paracetamol and a cuddle. Not to be outdone, Baby No. 1 strolled into us around 3ish wanting to come into our bed. At 4 a.m. Baby No. 3 woke again, full of the joys of life and wanting to stay awake. He took two hours to settle.

I gobbled a hurried breakfast while trying to spoon yoghurt into a reluctant Baby No. 2. Mouth shut and arms open, she knocked a few messy spoonfuls out of my hand onto the table. Then she proceeded to play with them, drawing a picture of a neigh-neigh. Though she's a budding genius, it was not a particularly good likeness. I decided she wouldn't starve and gave up. I went over to Rachel and hugged her from behind as she washed Baby No. 2's bottles at the sink. There were already six of Baby No. 3's cooking in the sterilizer.

'If I'm out and about, I'll get a packet of new ones later,' she said.

'What, new bottles? New babies?' I said, puzzled and yawning.

'No. Condoms, silly.'

'Oh,' I said. 'Hmmmm.'

'Hmmmm, what?'

'Well, it's just –'

'Just what? Is it the sock thing?'

I nodded. Rachel was referring to a comment I'd once made about using condoms. They drown out the sensation, turning the whole experience into a frictionless one. The previous night, I had indeed felt like I was 'doing it' through a sock.

'I've already told you about a much better form of contraception,' Rachel said. 'In the meantime, unless we want another baby, it's condom sex or no sex.'

Later that evening, there was a chemist's bag on Rachel's dressing table. I looked inside to find she'd bought four packets of twelve.

A month later there was a quiet day at work. I took out the calculator and reckoned how many condoms we'd need to completely evade our fertility until Rachel's menopause. She was aged thirty-four so that gave approximately fifteen years, at perhaps a rate of two or three sessions per week. (I also allowed a dozen extra per annum for when we might get the odd weekend away.) The answer was 156 boxes of twelve amounting to approximately €3,808. It was good value, but my difficulty wasn't measured in euro. The frictionless phenomenon, bad enough on that first night, was really causing problems beneath the sheets. I was taking ages, still toiling away long after Rachel had come. One drawn-out session had made her miss the episode of *CSI* where Horatio gets shot. No climax for me either. I admitted to myself that it was time to look at all the options.

I told my assistant Orla I was going to be busy all morning checking her work on the weekly figures. I locked myself into my office, logged on to the internet and typed 'forms of contraception' into Google. I printed out a few pages and reviewed two possibilities at lunchtime over a brown baguette.

1. *Rhythm method: avoiding sex around mid-cycle when the woman will be ovulating. Failure rate thirty per cent.*

That sounded high . . .

2. *Intra-uterine device: a small object made from plastic and metal, which is placed into the uterus . . . provides a physical and hormonal barrier to implantation. Failure rate nine per cent. Risks . . . infections, infertility, painful periods . . .*

Yuch!

I pondered and stared into space until Orla's face bobbed up just a few inches from mine. She was looking expectant. I covered the notes with my elbow and tried to seem casual.

'So, Mr Collins,' she said, raising her eyebrows, 'what's the decision?'

'Huh?' I said, alarmed and outraged at her ability to read my mind.

'The figures. Will they do?'

*

'I've made a provisional appointment for you with a consultant at the Barrington Clinic,' said Rachel that evening over dinner. Baby No. 1 had been throwing a fearful tantrum, so we'd put him out into the utility room to cool off. His background sobbing made me think I'd misheard.

'Clinic. What? I'm not sick,' I said, and rubbed my right eye distractedly. True, I had caught another dose of conjunctivitis from Baby No. 2. 'Or at least no more than usual.'

'No, not sick,' she said, and lowered her voice as if either baby could understand. 'I mean with the vasectomy specialist. Mr Keogh is his name. I thought you could go to find out a bit more about the procedure. He's supposed to be the best in Munster; he was recommended in an article I read –'

'Best at what?' I growled. 'Sticking skewers through testicles! You must be joking. Anyway, I found out today that it's not the only option. Remind me again Rachel, why you don't just get an intra-uterine device?'

Two weeks later, I came home from work to find a letter had arrived for me. Before I'd even got the envelope open, Baby No. 2 grabbed it and scuttled away in her walker, chewing a corner wetly. Baby No. 1 decided that he had to have whatever she had. A bad-humoured tug of war ensued before I ripped it from them and left both crying. I discovered that I was invited to attend Mr Keogh's vasectomy clinic and they'd even assigned me a patient number, EH13420.

Thankfully, it was a letter that I could tear into pieces and put straight in the bin. Just that afternoon,

Rachel had been to her gynaecologist, who'd inserted an intra-uterine device.

It was a big mistake to read the explanatory leaflet that came with Rachel's contraceptive. It contained facts of which I'd otherwise have been blissfully ignorant. Imagine a tiny copper wire that has been wound round a plastic stem. It has a monofilament thread, whatever that is, trailing from the base. More pertinently, imagine this little article is inside your wife. I began to worry about putting a certain part of my anatomy in its vicinity. I might be banging off a sharp bit of metal. I might even get caught up in the thread.

Rachel, however, was enthusiastic about putting it to use as soon as possible. As soon as all three babies were asleep, she took me by the hand, led me up the stairs and stripped off.

A while later, when Rachel had had a screaming orgasm and I'd done my best to fake one, she said, 'You looked like you were wincing. Why were you wincing?'

I told her why.

'Damn it,' she snapped and switched off her bedside lamp. 'There's simply no pleasing you.'

Over the nights that followed, I tried to put the device out of my mind but I simply couldn't. I kept imagining I was brushing against it and shrivelled at the thought. Eventually I had to admit defeat. I apologized to Rachel for asking her to have it put in. I asked her to have it taken out. I suggested that instead we have a go at the Rhythm method.

'It says you can have unprotected sex outside of Days 10 through 20 of the woman's cycle,' I explained.

'That's seventeen days per month when no contraception is necessary!'

'To put it another way,' said Rachel, 'all we'll be left with is having sex before my period, when I'm cranky as hell, or during it. Lovely! And that's assuming the kids go to bed and we're not so tired as to be comatose. Pah!'

Despite her scepticism, I was determined to make it work. First, I needed to know where she was in her cycle.

'Day 13,' she spat out.

Damn. Not ideal. I noted the date on my mobile phone calendar.

'Just eight more days,' I whispered romantically.

So Rachel had the device taken out. When eight days rolled around, however, when it would've been perfectly safe to have sex, some circumstance intervened and it didn't happen.

We did have sex (fantastic condom-free, device-free sex) on Days 22 and 24, then again on Day 5 of the new cycle. After that, the next convenient time (as allowed by our wonderful children) was Day 12. Rachel was most definitely in the mood – judging by her choice of underwear.

'But, darling,' I said, 'we can't. It's Day 12. How about I give you a back massage instead?'

'I don't want a bloody back massage,' she said. 'I want sex! Now!'

And several more tempting moments slipped by before Days 21 and 28, when we had sex more because we could than because we wanted to.

During the following cycle we found ourselves in a passionate clinch on the night of Day 11. Not so very different from Day 9. We decided to chance it. And paid for the pleasure in an anxious countdown until Rachel's next period arrived on schedule. It was obvious, even to me, that the Rhythm was not the answer.

I resolved to get some more data on the unthinkable. Rachel, facing a similar dilemma, would have phoned some friends but I couldn't possibly tell any of the guys I was contemplating having bits snipped out of my privates. While at work, I went back to the vasectomy websites I'd so carefully ignored. I told Orla I'd be busy with accounts.

. . . Vasectomy is a minor surgical 'procedure' performed under local anaesthetic and completed within thirty minutes. The surgeon uses a scalpel to make two incisions in the skin of the scrotum, one each side. The tiny vas deferens tubes are lifted, cut, tied and cauterized. The cut tubes are returned to the scrotal sac and the incisions closed with stitches.

So far, so horrifying, but there was worse in the small print.

You get the anaesthetic by way of a huge needle into the phallus.

There's smoke and sparks during the cauterization.

You can smell the sweet scent of your own burning flesh.

I chanced across a site called myvasectomy.com, where some American guy had posted step-by-step photos of his operation (taken by his girlfriend). The pictures left me feeling dazed. I was breathing heavily when there was a knock at my office door and the handle began to turn. It wasn't locked.

'Are you all right, Mr Collins? You don't look well. Shall I call a doctor?'

I was indeed quite feverish. I just managed to close down the incriminating website window depicting a surgically gloved hand and a naked American penis.

A week later, at 11.20 a.m., Babies Nos. 1 and 2 were in the crèche, Granny was minding Baby No. 3 and I was off work. According to Rachel, we needed to go into Limerick together to buy a second cot. Granny believed it, I believed it. But Rachel had set me up. Instead patient EH13420 arrived in Mr Keogh's waiting room.

I kept my eyes down and fidgeted with my wedding ring, sliding it on and off. The nurse called my name.

'C'mon, darling, it'll be all right,' said Rachel gently. She led me through the door.

Inside, Mr Keogh reached across his desk to shake my hand but I couldn't look him in the eye. My attention strayed to a shiny metallic object lying at his elbow, just an ordinary scissors, but a snipping scissors in the wrong place at the wrong time for me. My vision blurred, my left knee crumpled, and I lurched sideways to the floor and into the bliss of unconsciousness.

I awoke laid out in the back seat of the car. Rachel turned around in the driver's seat to glare at me but I didn't mind. We were in motion, presumably going home. I closed my eyes again and tried to worm my way back into a dream that was receding faster than I could catch it.

The next few months saw little progress in sorting out our predicament. Somehow our sex life muddled along – a combination of watching for the right days and using condoms on the wrong ones. Every time we had sex, one of us was getting short-changed. After years of going to Rachel's parents for Christmas, we stayed in our own home for the first time and that was good. Santa brought a huge tractor, a doll's house and some teething toys. The New Year had barely begun when Babies Nos. 1 and 2 came out in chicken pox and were banned from the crèche until the itching stopped. When Valentine's Day rolled around we managed to beg an assortment of babysitters and Granny to set us free for a mid-week break. We stayed in a hotel in Dublin and hardly left the room, just sleeping and having sex. Mostly sleeping. The holiday happened to fall on Days 13, 14 and 15.

In March, Rachel had used up all her maternity leave, unpaid extra leave and holidays accrued. Baby No. 3 started at the crèche to get acclimatized. After dropping the three kids and driving on to work, I looked in the mirror to see tears in my eyes and a reddening face. I let out an involuntary sob and felt a weight on my chest. Jesus! I was crying.

'Hay fever!' I shouted at Orla and locked the door.

I decided to stay late and phoned Rachel, pleading a backlog of work to get through. The babies were already back from the crèche and I could hear Baby No. 2 singing a phonetic version of 'Jack and Jill' in the background. Rachel was trusting, understanding, and blew me a kiss down the line. Two more tears formed in my sissy eyes.

The office was dark and desolate. Surfing randomly I learned sperm are manufactured in the testicles at a rate of 1,000 per second. A twiddle on the calculator revealed that in thirty-four days I could theoretically produce enough sperm to impregnate four billion women. Every single female on the planet.

My thoughts drifted. Even if I had the operation, all those sperm would still be churned out relentlessly. Only they'd swim down the vas deferens to meet with the blank wall of a cauterized wound. There'd be a huge pile-up of squirming tails. After a while the immune system would lose patience and treat them like an infection, eating them up. Their remains would be digested and put to other uses.

More sissy crying. Tears and sobbing!

I went back to the main vasectomy site and read about getting a vasectomy reversed. The prognosis is not spectacular, reversal being a much more difficult operation than the mutilation itself. Still, with advances in microsurgery, it might just be possible.

Abruptly I shut off the computer. In the bathroom I washed my tear-stained face and looked in the mirror. I narrowed my eyes and gritted my teeth.

I had decided to have a vasectomy.

At home the kids were all asleep; no one was sick and no one teething. The end credits of a film were rolling and Rachel had a chocolate-bar wrapper in her hand. Looking very intent, she was folding it into halves, quarters, eighths. Standing up to greet me, she put her arms around me and her finger to my lips as I began to tell her of my big decision.

We went straight to the bedroom, stripped one another and fell onto the mattress. I calculated that it was Day 4, so okay.

The sex felt like a dam-burst, as if something had been released in us. Afterwards she fell asleep quickly. I rolled onto my back and lay there, totally satisfied for the first time in ages. My bladder was full but I couldn't be bothered to go empty it; I just lay staring at the ceiling, savouring the moment.

Later in the en suite I stood over the toilet bowl and saw something familiar in the rubbish bin. After finishing my piddle I picked out the little plastic stick. It was a home pregnancy test and upon it were two bright blue lines in the shape of a cross.

It was definite.

We were pregnant.

What? When? Some day too early or too late. My legs wobbled and I had to sit down on the toilet to catch my breath. From a faraway room came the familiar howls of Baby No. 3 looking for a feed. I walked back into the bedroom, where my wonderful wife was still out cold.

I kissed her on the forehead and went downstairs to warm up a bottle. My shoulders were hunched but I was smiling. Four children under five – Christ! – but a little voice in my head, or perhaps lower down, was looking at the upside. 'Now that she's pregnant she can't possibly get any *more* pregnant. So no need for condoms. Or to ask what day of the month. Absolutely no need for a scalpel to make incisions in my scrotum!'

25

There are things even worse than dandruff

Limerick, Ireland, March 2008

'IS IT DANDWUFF, MAMMY?' whined my three-year-old daughter, for the fourth time. I'd been too busy staring at a speck stuck on the comb to answer her.

'Yes, Lauren, that's what I found in your hair, just a tiny speck of dandruff.'

I didn't mention that it was 'dandruff' with six wriggling legs and a belly full of her blood.

Earlier that day I'd received a phone call in work from her crèche. They rang to say that her hair had just been searched and they'd found numerous live head lice and their eggs. The lady then quoted from the crèche's 'Child Sickness Policy', Section 16.

To control the spread of head lice, we expect the child to be treated on the day that parent/guardian has been informed. If, on the next day, you have failed to treat your child and head lice are still apparent, you will be asked to remove said child immediately from the crèche until they are cleared of the infestation.

Stupidly I had left it to my husband, Marcus, to buy

Lice Lotion on his way home from work, but he claimed the chemist was closed due to an industrial dispute.

I showed him my grisly find.

'My God, that's awful. My poor little princess!' said Marcus. 'I can't bear to think of them crawling all over her. What can we do?'

'Well, the first thing *you* can do is take tomorrow off work. The crèche will almost certainly kick her out when they discover she hasn't been fully treated. I, meanwhile, have a major meeting with Anderson's that can't be rescheduled.'

'Oh! Oh . . . eh . . . well,' he said, and paused before composing the perfect answer, 'I have *two* major meetings and they can't be rescheduled either.'

The call duly came at 11 a.m. the next morning when they found more lice in Lauren's hair and asked that I collect her immediately. I went to see my boss, Jacqui, who can be, quite frankly, a cranky bitch. Apprehensive at asking for impromptu leave, I began by complimenting her new lime-green top, even though it was quite hideous. Then I got to my point. Surprisingly she was fine about it.

'Don't worry, I'll handle Anderson's. Just you go and do what you gotta do.' Her lips even curled upwards in a smile. (Though it was that smile of hers where the eyes don't participate.)

As I left her office, she shuffled paperwork and unearthed a purple ring-binder. It caught my eye but I'm not too good at reading upside down. She noticed me looking and hid it under her papers again.

'IS IT DANDWUFF, MAMMY?' Lauren whined at me again that evening. I'd bought the lotion and put it on for the requisite six hours so the head lice were supposedly dead. I just had to make her stand still while I combed through her hair and picked them out.

'Yes, Lauren, that's what I found in your hair, a little bit of dandruff,' I said again.

The miniature beast didn't seem remotely tired, let alone dead. He was clawing at the open air, desperately trying to find his way back to the warm haven of my daughter's scalp. I harvested ten more but before I was finished Lauren broke free and went over to her daddy's lap for a cuddle. 'My poor little bittle princess,' Marcus murmured in her ear, and her small arms squeezed him tight around the neck. Meanwhile I sorted some laundry and then emptied the dishwasher.

Marcus deposited Lauren asleep into bed. When he came back down, I showed him a piece of tissue onto which I had wiped fourteen head lice. One or two were still writhing. He wouldn't look.

'God, no! I can't bear to think of those minimonsters on poor Lauren.'

Next day Lauren was accepted back into crèche.

Everything returned to normal for about a week, but then the epidemic recurred and she caught them again. I rang Marcus to say that it was his turn to collect her, but his direct line rang out. I knew he was ignoring me. His mobile was powered off. Seething, but with little choice, I went into Jacqui's office and praised her voluminous floral-print smock. She said yes to my request for the day off. Then she produced the purple ring-binder. I had to ask.

'Oh, nothing much,' she said with her fifty per cent

smile. 'Just a private little thing I've been compiling, sort of a league table among the staff. Measuring stuff like punctuality, flexibility, productivity, instances of unscheduled leave . . .'

'So,' I said, replying with an equally insincere smile, 'how am I doing?'

'Well, you're not the worst,' she said, managing a laugh, 'yet.'

The third time Lauren was quarantined I actually caught my husband by ringing him from a phone number he wouldn't recognize. His excuses were many.

'The big boss is down from Dublin to inspect, so today's not really the day . . .

'. . . half the staff are out sick and we're up the walls busy . . .

'. . . the deadline for the Cassidy thing is 5 p.m. today . . .

'. . . on top of that, I have *three* meetings I just have to be at . . .

'And after all, gorgeous,' he said, 'I am the higher earner in this family . . .'

I hung up while he was still yakking.

The lower earner in the family asked for her third sick day in as many weeks. Jacqui decided to level with me.

'I'm not supposed to say but head office has decided we need a deputy manager to handle the increased workload. There'll be extra remuneration commensurate with responsibility, etcetera, and we'll be looking to recruit internally. A month ago you were in pole position but now I'm not so sure. I'll be asked my opinion, and on the basis of what I've got in this purple binder I'd say, "She scores well in every area but the big one: on the day I need her she might not actually *be here*."'

We received a letter from the crèche calling an emergency meeting of parents on the Friday night. We managed to get a babysitter and both attended.

'We've established that every single child in the crèche is infested again,' said the crèche coordinator.

'Yes,' shouted an angry Mr Moustache man from the floor, 'but from whom exactly did my child first acquire head lice? Which toddler was the primary vector?'

'Mr Buckley, this is not about blaming any one child,' said the coordinator; 'it's something that we must all deal with together.'

'I have my theories, you know! It was that little boy with the black curls, wasn't it, wasn't it?' shouted Mr Moustache. 'There's no point protecting the parent whose negligence brought this plague on us all.'

'Mr Buckley, please sit down before you say something we may all regret. There'll be another chance to air your views after our head lice expert has spoken. Ladies and gentlemen, I give you Mrs Paula Byrne from the Health Promotion in the Community Initiative.'

After applause, the science began.

'Head lice (*Pediculus humanus capitis*) are small parasitic insects. Their six legs are elegantly evolved to grasp hair shafts and provide a striking example of biological specialization . . . *blah blah blah* . . . cannot survive for more than a day without access to a person's blood . . . *blah blah blah* . . . female deposits more than a hundred offspring at a rate of six eggs daily . . .' The expert moved to her specific analysis of the lice being found on our crèche children.

'. . . Evidence of extensive overuse of chemical treatments, mutations arising have led to a new multi-resistant strain . . . *blah blah blah* . . . pyrethroids, malathion and lindane all rendered useless . . . *blah blah blah* . . . painstaking physical removal by combing is time-consuming, but the only option . . .'

There was a murmur of disapproval, and the assembly was not pacified when she said we'd all be getting a complimentary nit-comb to take home with us.

She said another thing that I'd noticed myself: the head lice were getting bigger: '. . . Typically they're four to five millimetres, but the average in this sample was six.' The muttering grew louder.

She prescribed a major clean-up programme to rid the crèche of any malingering lice and eggs. All floors and walls were to be disinfected, while pillowcases, sheets, towels and stuffed animals would have to be washed and dried.

The crèche coordinator interrupted to say that this would mean closing the crèche for two days: Monday and Tuesday of the following week. Furthermore, she was introducing a Zero Tolerance policy. Each morning thereafter children would be assessed in the crèche lobby and refused admission should any evidence of infestation be found. Many parents stopped whispering and voices of dissent could be clearly heard decrying the 'disgraceful situation'.

The expert invited questions.

'I've noticed a mangy sheepdog who hangs around near the wheelchair ramp in the evenings,' said Ms

Lanky Frizzy Hair. 'Could the lice be coming from him?'

'I've a shotgun!' shouted an anonymous male from the back.

'No,' said the expert, 'dogs have their own separate species of lice. Dog and human lice do not mix.'

'Well, what about the so-called quote-unquote "social inclusion" children from the tinker campsite?' said Mrs Layered Blonde Bob.

'I've a shotgun!' hissed the anonymous male again, not quite so loudly or so bravely.

'Different species, are they, as well?' quipped another entertainer.

'Please,' said the expert, 'head lice are equal-opportunity parasites with no respect for age, gender, hygiene habits or socio-economic status. The chances are that there're head lice in this room right now nestled in the scalp of One. Of. You.'

An angry buzz through the gathering suggested that many found this comment outrageous but I thought it funny. I looked over at Marcus to share the laugh but he was staring straight ahead, teeth clenched and scratching nervously at his sideburn. The meeting ended. Sixty parents poured out into the night, disgruntled, despairing of a cure and brandishing their shiny new complimentary nit-combs.

On the way home Marcus got itchy.

'Stop the car! Stop the car! I need to know right now!'

I parked on the roadside and he put his head in my lap. The light was poor but I quickly found my first egg.

'Oh, God! No!' gasped Marcus.

There were a dozen of them stuck to hairs above his right ear. There were a few more on the crown, and there was a massive live adult down around the nape of his neck.

'Looks like a girl one,' I said, laughing. 'How could this happen to the higher earner in our family, huh? Maybe I should just leave her there and she'll breed you a whole colony.'

He didn't reply.

'Hold tight, darling husband, your low-earning wife will come to the rescue,' I said, chuckling as I struggled to land her. She got away. Only then did I notice darling husband was trembling.

I pulled him up and saw a face suddenly drained of colour.

'Oh, sweet Jesus! It's just the thought of those creatures crawling all over me. And Lauren! Drinking our blood, breeding faster than rabbits.'

'Don't worry, I'll comb you properly when we get home; you'll be fine.'

'For how long, though? They just keep coming back and back. And maybe they've already noticed them at work. I'm sure Maria's been giving me funny looks recently. Maybe she's told the staff and they all know. Oh, God! Oh, sweet Jesus!'

The armpits of Marcus's shirt darkened with sweat. After taking the precaution of putting my hair into a ponytail, I hugged him and offered him a deal.

'Listen, Marcus, I've got the gun to my head at work, because of all the days I've taken off over this thing. You can help by minding Lauren next Monday and Tuesday, then I promise to comb every inch of that scalp of yours till every last louse is eradicated.'

'Of course, no problem,' he said. 'I'll do a bit of

work from home on the laptop; they'll hardly know I'm gone.'

We hugged again until he got another itch at the back and asked me to investigate. Just as he nestled his face down into my lap, a garda appeared and tapped loudly on the window.

Marcus sprang up, banging his head on the steering wheel. The garda tapped again so I rolled down the window and explained.

'Good evening, garda. I was just checking through my husband's hair searching for head lice.'

As he got back on his motorbike, Marcus whispered at me, 'I can't believe you! How could you tell him about the head lice?'

'But I had to. Don't you see how it looked? He probably thought that you were, y'know, committing an obscene act in a public place. Would you prefer he think that?'

He remained silent.

'Well, would you?'

During the ten minutes' drive home he scratched silently while I hummed a song.

'Sssssssh,' he said, 'I'm still trying to decide.'

I began a campaign to rid the head lice from our lives for ever. Marcus and then Lauren sat on a high stool near the window, where the light for combing was best. On Saturday I gathered a total of twenty-three lice and eggs from Lauren and nine from her father. On Sunday the death toll fell to ten and five. On Monday night I found only eggs, six and six on each scalp. On Tuesday night it was the same. I knew what that meant. They each had just one elusive louse left, a fertile female laying six eggs each night.

Wednesday morning, Marcus brought Lauren to the crèche but they found two eggs I'd missed and she was turned away. For a change it was him ringing me and he sounded agitated.

'But you said yourself you can work from home on the laptop,' I said.

'No, gorgeous. Please, no!' he said, hyperventilating. 'That hasn't really worked out too well. I've got nothing done the last two days. I thought Lauren would be happy to watch DVDs but instead I have to do painting and reading with her and the new game, washing and drying potatoes. Over and over and over . . .'

'There, there, dear,' I said, stifling a laugh, 'don't worry. I think I know just the solution.'

'Excellent, so you'll come home and let me go to work!'

Jacqui wandered in from her office wearing a pinstripe blouse, pleated skirt with ivy print and court shoes. The ensemble was appalling, but all designer and obviously expensive. If I were deputy manager, I'd be able to afford something with a similar price tag but more tasteful.

'No, darling. But when I come home I promise to have the final solution. I guarantee that you and Lauren will be totally lice-free by bedtime tonight.'

He tried to argue further but I switched off my mobile.

I spent my lunch break down at the chemist again. This time I bought no lotions; rather, an electric hair-clipper with Interchangeable Blades 4, 3, 2 and 1, with the last used for the tightest-possible cut.

*

I was home at 6 p.m. and by 6.05 Marcus's lice problem was history. So was all his hair. He gathered his clippings enthusiastically and watched them crackle away to nothing on the fire. Then he turned to the mirror for reassurance that he didn't look like a thug. He did a bit, actually, but I reassured him. He started composing his excuses for the staff at work. Had he done it for charity or a lost bet? He couldn't decide.

Phase 2 of my final solution ran aground immediately. I grabbed the hair clipper again and suggested he hold Lauren still for me.

'But!' said he.

'But what?'

'But, no way! It was fine for you to shear me, but Lauren? Lauren? After all it took to grow it . . .'

When she was younger, Lauren's hair refused to grow. Even when she was two it was so short that people assumed she was a boy. Older girls in the crèche used to tease her. It took fully three years to get to bob length so we'd never even trimmed it.

'I know what you mean,' I said, 'but we've been left no choice.'

'Yes, we have!' he said. 'Turn off that razor and get me the nit-comb, please.'

I said nothing. I got the comb and threw it at him. He called his little bittle princess over and began his search. Fit to burst with irritation, I decided to retire to the bedroom. He was holding the comb all wrong.

I came down at midnight to find them both asleep: she on her bean bag, he slouched on a chair behind her, the nit-comb in his hand. I inferred the louse had not been found. I pulled the bean bag plus Lauren over beside me on the sofa. I switched on the electric hair-clipper and she didn't wake. I brought the humming blade to the nape of her neck and she did not flinch. She smiled in her sleep, the smile of an angel.

'Damn it!' I whispered and switched off the machine. I wrenched the nit-comb from Marcus's grip and ran it through Lauren's fringe. Immediately I found the louse.

The biggest ever, she was seven millimetres long, and her belly was red with Lauren's blood. For a second I had her in my grasp, half on the comb and half in Lauren's hair. But I was unprepared. She squirmed free and disappeared back into Lauren's tresses. Though I combed the area frantically she was gone.

After making a cup of tea I settled down to the task. If I could find the enemy once, I could find her again. Except for the two sleepers' breathing, the room was silent and my concentration total. Slowly and methodically I worked through every section of her scalp and found nothing. I made more tea and resolved to be even slower, more methodical.

Towards the end of my fifth sweep, I finally encountered the louse again, clinging onto a hair shaft north of the left ear. With ruthless efficiency I plucked her up and out, well clear of Lauren's scalp. She was writhing on the comb when Marcus awoke suddenly and shouted, 'What? I do not have a receding hair-line!'

I dropped the nit-comb. When I retrieved it the louse was gone.

To show his remorse my husband stamped his shoes all over the carpet where the louse might have landed.

Then he lifted Lauren up into her bed. Then he took me to our bed and, trying desperately to make amends, committed an obscene act. Which was nice. Then he conked out again.

I couldn't rest. I thought about not missing any more days off work. I thought about the deputy manager's job and being a 'higher earner'. I thought about a lovely baby-pink designer suit in BT's that was out of my league. But intruding on the dream was an absurd recurring image of the head louse. Crawling slowly up the stairs, it was using every last ounce of its energy to get back into our lives. I gave up on sleep and went downstairs to the scene. Everything looked the same.

I picked up the nit-comb from the carpet and turned it over. There was the louse, still alive and getting thirsty. Before I knew it, she had climbed off onto my thumb. I tried to shake her off but she sank her feeding mandibles into my skin and clung on. I punched down with my other fist but succeeded only in breaking a nail. It took five thumps before she was defeated. Four legs were bust but two still clawed at the air. I went to the sink and washed her away down the plughole with hot water.

Which I left running all night.

And most of the next day.

26

Though I spend my days
slaving for our children,
though I lie awake at night
worrying about them, my
lazy husband is their
favourite parent . . .

Ong Peng and Woochi had yet another dispute over their toys. This time it was about the wooden horse, of which we have only one.

Ong Peng came in to my husband crying that Woochi had pulled her hair. Between sobs she explained that she had been on the horse first, so Woochi had no right to it until she chose to get off. Her daddy gave her a big hug and said, 'Yes, dear daughter, you are quite right.' She ran along happily.

Woochi appeared presently to defend himself against Ong Peng's allegations. It emerged that she'd been on the horse for a long time and wasn't even playing with it properly. Rather, she'd been staying on purely to annoy Woochi, since it was his favourite toy. When he politely asked her to dismount, she had scraped him in the face. That was hardly fair, said Woochi.

My husband gave him a pat on the shoulder, winked and said, 'Yes, dear son, you are quite right.' Woochi went away, smiling cheerfully.

My husband is a messy eater. Throughout all this I'd been sweeping rice from the floor around his feet and listening to proceedings. 'Husband,' I said in exasperation, 'both children cannot be right.'

He looked up and smiled at me. 'Yes, dear wife, you are quite right.'

27

The third passenger

Minnesota, USA, 1847

Somewhere between Rochester and Winona, with an abrupt grinding of brakes, our train came to a dead halt. I poked my head out into the corridor, hoping to catch a conductor, hoping for some explanation. None appeared, but a voice piped up behind me. 'Don't fret, sir. Chances are it's probably just a few light branches on the line. It happens pretty often along here. They'll have it cleared in ten minutes.'

I turned and took my seat again in the compartment. The gentleman who had spoken was seated opposite. I thanked him for his comforting conjecture. Now that the ice was broken, we proceeded to introduce ourselves. He was impeccably dressed: his shirt had a butterfly collar of the old-fashioned sort and he wore a cravat. In every respect he was well groomed and pomaded; the sort of elderly gentleman who looks younger but is probably well over seventy. I noticed his leather suitcase on the rack over his head. Upon it were his initials: J. N. A. In Gothic lettering, they served notice to the world: here is a man of substance.

'Ames,' he said. 'Dr Jacob Ames of Cedar Rapids.'

'Oh,' I said, unable to disguise my disappointment: polite conversation between us would probably prove impossible.

'And you, sir, your name and profession?'

'John Veale,' I said with a sigh, before deciding it best to just get it out, get it over with. 'I too am a practitioner. I've just recently graduated from the Thomsonian Institute in Boston and am on my way to set up a practice in St Paul.'

'Oh, I see,' he said. 'Then, young man, you are no doctor. You're just one of the many "Irregular Practitioners" currently swarming across this great nation of ours. That Thomsonian is a madhouse of "homoe-opathy" where they will, no doubt, have taught you to treat tuberculosis with nought but dried flowers and steam baths.'

'I think, with respect,' I said quietly (but firmly), 'that you're being unfair. Fact is that much conventional medicine is useless if not actually murderous. The barbarous overuse of purgatives and blood-letting has killed far more patients than it's cured.'

The train was still not moving. I resigned myself to several more rounds of this, followed by a long journey of avoiding eye contact. There was an interruption from my right. The third passenger in our compartment spoke.

'Gentlemen, hush!' he said. His face was obscured behind a copy of the *St Paul Chronicle*, but his voice sounded nervous. 'Suppose you all return to your former sociable silence, since politeness seems impossible!'

He put down his newspaper and there was a morose look on his face as he stared out of the window over my right shoulder. He was in some ways the opposite of Dr Ames, probably not very old but already reduced to combing his fringe forward onto a high forehead. Where the good doctor exuded confidence, this third passenger seemed in a constant state of nervousness, always searching for a prop with which to fidget. I fancied that he gave a sudden small involuntary shiver before shaking his head sadly and picking up his paper again. As he tried to resume reading, Dr Ames addressed him.

'But come now, sir, you seem a solid citizen. I trust that *you* have no time for any of these new-fangled fads like hydropathy and naturopathy and whatever other "pathy" it is this young man is peddling?'

I thought to protest at this unfair portrayal of my qualifications and reached toward my case, intending to produce my diploma, but just then the third passenger threw down his paper violently. 'To be perfectly frank, sir, when it comes to conventional medicine versus the irregular sort, my attitude is "a plague on both your houses". I have no regard for either!'

The ferocity of his tone left me dumb, but not so Dr Ames.

'Oh, now, sir. Your position is surely an intemperate one. After all, what higher calling can there be than to strive with all a body's might to save the life of a fellow man?'

'A high calling? No,' said the third passenger, wagging his forefinger, becoming more animated yet. 'I tell you solemnly, sir, that much of this mighty striving is, in point of fact, a violation of the Human

Temple. Let the human body heal itself as it may, I say! If extreme interventions be required, then better to be allowed to die in peace.'

'Well!' said Dr Ames, his lips pursed. 'I do declare! I never heard such –'

'Tell me, sir,' I cut in, 'your opinions do seem a little forceful. Is it perhaps the case that you've had a bad experience with one rogue doctor, or been disappointed by the empty promises of a single fraudulent faith-healer?'

'As a matter of fact, my experience was of several dozen,' he said, and focused his grey eyes upon me. He paused for a moment before looking away, and he seemed to be choosing his next words carefully. 'Not direct experience, I suppose. The incident that most confirmed my dim view of you "healing folk" happened to my next-door neighbours. They were a family visited by a horrific tragedy, but it's fair to say that the interference of all manner of practitioners made matters worse by a hundredfold. What started as a natural calamity was distorted by men like you, in ways that are against Nature, and eventually against our Lord Creator himself.'

He paused again for a moment but then began to elaborate without further prompting.

'Look out of that window, gentlemen,' he said. Ames and I followed his gaze up the rolling hills to where the sun was a low orange disc, sinking from the sky. Nestled among the slopes was a mansion built in the Neo-Palladian style; the pillars plain save for a single diagonal, the cornice a model of harmonic restraint.

'I don't know how to explain this coincidence,' said the third passenger, 'but before I give further details

I should remark that the horrific incident occurred in a house very like the one on that hill.'

This was no big coincidence, I thought. Mansions of that type, though they strained for individuality, were to be found all across the country, from Ohio to Minnesota.

'At any rate,' continued the third passenger, 'the incident of which I speak . . . it happened about twenty years ago in the town I'm from, Elgin, Illinois . . .'

The train shuddered. The unexplained halt was over. We began to roll forward.

'The Carlyles of Elgin were a happy family, comprising husband, wife and their little boy. Carlyle was in the textile business, importing raw cotton from Virginia, dispatching a thousand rolls of the finished fabric each week to the drapery stores of Chicago and even New York City. Energetic and innovative, he built up a small factory, inherited from his father, into the biggest of the North Country. It was inevitable that the family would one day move to a mansion commensurate with their wealth. Inevitable but ill-fated.

'The mansion was of three storeys and set on a hundred acres. While Mrs Carlyle was delighted with the move, her son, aged five, was positively ecstatic. Two full rooms had been set aside for all his new toys, the lawn was ideal for playing soldiers, and he even got his very own pony. Unfortunately, though, children can never be long satisfied. They are always looking to turn the world itself into their next toy. Bored one day, unattended by his mother or any servant, he conceived a dangerous new game. On the third floor he climbed onto the banister along the landing. Holding onto the banister with his hands, he slid his body over to the other side and placed his feet between the balusters. Thus he contrived to hang precariously over a 25-foot drop. Strong, nimble and fearless, the little boy then proceeded to compound the hazard by moving his feet stepwise along the balusters, left to right, then down the stairs to the second landing, then right to left along the landing, and then down again. At the bottom he whooped with exhilaration, a daring devil was he!'

At this point the third passenger swallowed hard. As he proceeded again with the account, he bore the visage of a finicky eater trying to swallow a bowl of spinach.

'The horrific incident (which led to all else) occurred one day when the boy's parents arrived home unexpectedly to find him engaged in this foolish game. Outraged and frightened by what he saw above his head in the hall, Carlyle let out a roar of reprimand, "Get down this instant, you rascal!"

'Initially, the boy was frozen to the spot in shock, while Carlyle rushed up the staircase several steps at a time. Then, however, the boy tried to comply with his father's wishes and to get down. In his panic, he lost his footing and shrieked in terror. Holding on as best he could with his hands, the boy struggled to regain a toehold, but his wild swinging only made matters worse. Grimly he held on with just one hand, then only three fingers, then one and then . . .'

The third passenger paused again in a state of some agitation. Reaching inside the breast pocket of his jacket, he fumbled for a few moments and then produced a cigar. 'Do you gentlemen mind if I smoke?' he muttered. No! We did not mind. We only wished he would tell us if . . .

'So there came a moment when the boy's falling was inevitable. And yet, as in many a catastrophe, that is the very moment that seems to last an eternity. The tragedy had not yet happened but absolutely could not be stopped. While her small boy dangled, his mother stood twenty-five feet below, fixed to the spot. Her husband had reached the top stair and had the closest vantage point from which to witness this horrendously prolonged moment. He looked into the face of his boy, his precious, precious beloved son, and saw a little mouth open in horror but no longer shrieking, no longer emitting any sound whatever. The right arm was outstretched, trying so very hard to reach his father but clawing only air. Worst of all was the dangling boy's eyes, locked onto his father's, wild in terror. The moment ended and he finally fell.'

'Good Lord!' said Dr Ames. 'How very appalling. And when they went to his body, was the poor boy dead?'

'No,' said the third passenger, bringing a match to his cigar butt and taking his first proper drag, 'far worse than that. He was alive.

'The boy's eyes were open but he was paralysed and incapable of any kind of movement or communication. He was carried to his bed and a doctor called. That local doctor, Oleson, took just twenty minutes over his diagnosis, but it was to be confirmed many times thereafter: the boy had broken at least thirty bones in the fall, including certain parts of the spine and skull. In addition he had many internal injuries, though their number and location were harder to specify. Yet still he breathed and his eyes were open. His parents held onto hope.

'"No," said Dr Oleson, "I'm afraid there can be no expectation of a recovery."

'"What, none?" said the Carlyles.

'"I'm sorry. But no. None," said Dr Oleson.

'For his trouble, the plain-speaking doctor was escorted from the premises and never sought out again. His medical analysis was the last honest one to be uttered in that accursed Elgin mansion.'

The third passenger was interrupted by a passing conductor, who stuck his head into our compartment. 'Gentlemen,' he said, 'I'm afraid we have run low on oil supplies. Ordinarily about this time, I would be lighting your compartment lamps. That will not be possible this evening. The management of Northern Pacific would like to apologize for any inconvenience caused.' He was gone before we could complain. Outside the sun had set but there was enough light remaining for me to look again into the face of the third passenger. Once again his habitual gloom turned toward anger as he continued.

'And so began the period that most particularly begat my aversion to all factions of the medical field. Another doctor was called. He assured the Carlyles that the boy could be saved. He set about the task of putting splints on each and every breakage. By the time he was done the poor boy was encased in sticks of wood. You could barely make out his two vacant little eyes inside what amounted to a timber cage. It took two dozen visits, however, before the doctor finally admitted that the resurrection would not be effected by himself. At the close of his last well-paid call he gave the Carlyles the name of a specialist in Chicago.

'Only much later would the Carlyles discover that the specialist was a former classmate of his predecessor. In the meantime they had dragged that poor broken boy by carriage to a hospital in Chicago. The specialist smiled optimistically and prescribed an operation, in fact a series of operations. Within hours of their arrival, the boy was stripped of his splints, had his eyelids closed and was put under the knife for the first time.

'Two months later, the boy was released from the hospital and brought home. Many of his bones were still broken. Now his skin was covered in gashes, the long straight wounds having been inflicted with scissors and saw. His mother set about washing and dressing them daily. Only when the wounds were fully healed, you see, would the previous doctor be able to put him back in his cage of wooden splints –'

'Well, now,' I cut in, 'I can see that these doctors may have been a little over-zealous. But, even so, upsetting as this case is, it only relates to two practitioners of the old school. I'm sure that if that poor boy could have been attended by one from my institute –'

'Stop!' said the third passenger, quite rudely. 'The Carlyles did eventually lose patience and respect for the doctors. Soon enough they began to look elsewhere for answers, and in due course faith-healing, flower-squeezing practitioners of every hue descended on that benighted Elgin mansion. I couldn't supply you with a comprehensive list but off the top of my head I remember his being treated with racoon blood, magnets, electrical currents, the application of leeches, immersion in hot baths, immersion in cold baths, and it seemed every single one of you medical men felt the need to round off the session by purging the boy's bowels with a tablespoon of calomel.'

The third passenger paused for another drag of his

cigar before continuing in a more conciliatory tone. 'So, you see my point, gentlemen? What angers me is that thirty or forty medical men attended that boy and, except for Dr Oleson, not one was honest enough to say that he could do nothing. Instead each one subjected him to their little bag of tricks when surely it was to no end, but torture. And why? Purely because the mansion itself spelled money. Every last one of them doubled his fee and walked away with a considerable wedge of dollar bills.'

I nodded sadly and so did Dr Ames. Partly because we agreed, partly because it seemed imprudent to cross him further. The compartment was quite dark; the last vestiges of daylight had drained from the sky. I thought the matter was now closed and leaned my head back for a small nap. But Dr Ames had another question.

'What was the eventual fate of the boy? I trust he died a peaceful Christian death in the arms of his family.'

Though the inquiry might have seemed innocent, it must have struck the third passenger like a hammer blow. I could no longer see his expression but in the gloom I heard him gasp and then he made a low moaning noise, followed by a short stifled sob.

'Dear me,' said Dr Ames. 'Excuse my manners, sir. I have been far too inquisitive. Come, let us forget about this unfortunate incident and discourse on some other matter. Mr Veale, what do you make of the latest goings-on in Washington?'

'Oh . . . well, the president does seem to be itching for a fight,' I said vaguely, knowing very little of politics. But the third passenger spoke again, this time in a hoarse whisper.

278

'Gentlemen, please excuse my emotional outburst, Dr Ames's inquiry was a fair one, and I am now determined that, however painful the telling, I shall answer it, if you will bear with me.

'In short, he did not die a Christian death in the arms of his family; rather, his passing was a diabolical abomination . . .

'The Carlyles, as I mentioned before, were a family blessed with both happiness and prosperity. Neither of these survived long after the accident. The prosperity was of course eroded somewhat by the vast medical bills that were accrued. More damaging was the lengthy period during which Carlyle totally ignored his business, engrossed instead in the quest for a cure for his son. Without his hand on the tiller, key deliveries to Chicago were missed and factory workmanship slipped from excellent to so-so to slipshod. Within a single year, the empire he'd spent twenty years building began to unravel.

'As for their happiness? Well, initially it was all for one, one for all. The parents were equally fervent in their desire to cure the boy at any cost. That little red-haired boy had been the very light of their lives: precociously intelligent, strong, brave, funny, he was everything good that a boy can be. They spent hundreds of hours side by side ministering to him. He lay there insensible, communication still impossible, but his two open eyes glistened from inside the wooden cage. The parents' talk consisted mostly of swapping anecdotes about this witty thing the boy once said or that horseshoe he'd flung round the spike, aged only two.

'In time, though, the husband grew doubtful about the treatments. He started to come to terms with the impending death of his beloved son. Not so the wife. If anything, her devotion to the boy deepened to obsession and she dropped all social ties with the outside world. Except doctors. Inevitably, perhaps, tensions rose between the two parents, until finally there was the nastiest of blazing rows.

'It emerged that the wife blamed Carlyle for the accident. After all, it was his shouting that had frightened the poor boy into falling. Carlyle too revealed his long-standing grudge. In the period after the accident she once let slip a casual remark about how the boy had "often done that feat before without injury". In other words, she had known of the dangerous practice and hadn't stopped him. So it was her fault, really, the accident inevitable. That night, Carlyle stormed from the house and wasn't seen for two days.'

'For a drinking binge, was it?' asked Dr Ames.

The third passenger nodded solemnly. 'The first of many, sir.'

By now the only light in the compartment was from the tip of his cigar. It bobbed up and down while he continued in a strangulated tone.

'Over the next eight years, that Great Deceiver Alcohol would slowly drag Carlyle into the pits of shame and infamy. He was set on a spiral of total moral disintegration. Drunkenness and hangovers, each chased the other's tail. The domestic rows only increased in frequency and intensity. Unwelcome in his own bed, he eventually moved into Chicago to a life of extra-marital affairs and then whores. Down the line lay bankruptcy and even briefly, until he found God, destitution.

'His wife, it turned out, was made of much sterner

stuff. When Carlyle left, it was she who retained the mansion. Though the divorce courts awarded her only a quarter of Carlyle's wealth, that proved quite sufficient. While he squandered his three quarters, she released all but two of her servants, lived frugally and managed just fine.

'Shortly after Carlyle moved out, there was a brief scare when it seemed the injured boy was nearing death. Carlyle was summoned from town. By the time he arrived, however, his wife had changed her mind and would not allow him upstairs. She said that the patient was much recovered; the danger had passed. She had found a practitioner who'd saved him at the brink. Carlyle, shamefully, was too drunk to argue. He lay on the couch and passed out. Late in the night, he awoke briefly and could hear his wife up on the third floor. Even through the floorboards, it was plain she was talking very loudly. Carlyle could not make out the words but he knew that they were questions . . .'

From out on the corridor, we heard the approach of the conductor and his dark silhouette announced, 'Gentlemen, the next station is Winona. Passengers wishing to alight should collect their belongings. We will arrive in five minutes.'

'Winona is my stop,' said the third passenger, and I heard him rustling his newspaper. He began to stand up, but Dr Ames took hold of his sleeve and said, 'Come now, sir. You still haven't reached the point of the poor boy's expiration. We may have to hold the train if you don't.'

'Oh, all right,' said the third passenger, sitting back down with a sigh. 'But I must warn you, gentlemen, that this was no ordinary death. I'm afraid it took place in very grotesque circumstances.' He took a deep breath and made for the finish line.

'Let me skip through the next ten years and say that the boy did not die until he was sixteen. It happened one day when Carlyle paid a visit to the mansion. After hitting rock bottom, the derelict husband and father had been infinitely fortunate to rediscover the grace of our Great Redeemer. Freed from those twin tyrants Alcohol and Wantonness, he finally felt worthy to approach his son. His unannounced arrival was timely, as his ex-wife was gone into town on some errand. The protests of old servants were easily brushed aside and he strode to the boy's bedroom door. It was locked. Two minutes of fiddling with a sharp knife were enough, and the door swung open.

'Inside the darkened bedroom the boy lay alone. Much had changed from how Carlyle remembered it. First the carpet, curtains and bedspread – all had been replaced with new patterns. Second, the boy was no longer in a cage of wooden splints. Third, his eyes, for so long open, were now closed. There was one thing, however, that had not changed and was all the more sinister for that.'

The third passenger paused. In the silent dark I leaned toward him as his voice fell to a whisper.

'It was the boy himself. HE hadn't changed. He was now sixteen years old, yet he lay there with the same small body of a six-year-old.'

Dr Ames gasped.

'Carlyle was in a state of utter shock, confronting, as it were, an image from a decade past. "Son," he shrieked, "are you alive or dead? What has she done to you?" His initial shock was as nothing when after a minute he was addressed by a voice from within his son. Perhaps you will find that description strange, gentlemen, but it was indeed a voice from within his son. It did not come from the boy's mouth: the jaws were quite still, the tongue incapable of movement. It had a hollow ghostly quality but was recognizably that of a boy. It said, "Alive, but very near death. As I've been for a long time. They have held me here in a deep deep sleep."

'Carlyle damn near collapsed in anguish. He stood open-mouthed and staring at his son as tears ran hot down each cheek. By and by, he reached a terrible decision. He stood behind the door and waited for his ex-wife to return. When she entered the room he put a knife to her throat . . .'

The train began to slow down. Winona was only a minute away.

'There was shouting and tears on both sides as Carlyle's ex-wife explained about the night he was near death, breathing erratically, ten years before. She called for a hypnotist as a last throw of the dice, anything to ease his pain. She had read of how the hypnotic trance holds the human body in suspension. In the event, the sleep had been so deep as to suspend their son's penultimate moments indefinitely.

'She said, "The important thing is, he did not die!"

'"Nor is he really alive," shouted Carlyle.

'"But I can talk to him; ask questions and his spirit answers."

'"For whose benefit?" yelled Carlyle. "Not his. This has to stop."

'So he again brought the knife close to her neck. Initially his ex-wife denied she'd be able to break the hypnosis, but eventually she agreed to try. She opened the boy's eyelids and placed all her focus on his right eye. Her palms made lateral strokes across his forehead and she began to speak to him of waking up.'

Brakes were grinding; the front of the train was already alongside the long platform at Winona.

'When the hypnosis was broken, there was a moment when the boy's eyes opened and managed a sparkle. Then something truly grotesque began to happen. His boyish body, held in suspension for so long, was instantly impelled (by its inner atoms, I s'pose) to take on the proper form of a sixteen-year-old . . .'

'What?' gasped Dr Ames, struggling for breath.

'The boy's arms rose up under the pressure of . . . rapidly elongating bones. Under the blanket too, his legs began to stretch. Yet matter cannot be instantaneously created. The body was attempting to restructure along adolescent lines using the smaller amount of flesh and bone of a six-year-old. The result was that the skin across his chest began to split and leak blood. Muscles ruptured everywhere, even as their ligaments were pulled past breaking point. From the boy's cheeks poked through a fuzz of hairs, joining to form a beard, while the skin itself collapsed away beneath it.

'As the mother backed away, screaming, Carlyle stood firm by the bedside. Somehow the paralysed monstrosity found the strength for one final motion. He raised his head from the pillow and reached toward his father. Carlyle looked into the face and saw a mouth open in horror but not emitting any sound whatever. The spindly right arm was outstretched, trying so very hard to reach his father but clawing only air. Worst of all were the eyes, fixed on Carlyle's, wild with terror. The moment ended, and the boy finally fell back onto the pillow. He was dead.'

The train pulled away from Winona. The third passenger had alighted just before the doors closed. Thankfully no new passenger had joined us. Dr Ames and I had the compartment to ourselves.

'Care for a cigarette?' he offered, and I was glad to accept.

After we'd lit up, I finally made my first reference to the third passenger.

'That gentleman! He truly was remarkable.'

'Yes,' said Dr Ames. 'Truly remarkable. I suppose you knew who he really was?'

'Oh, yes,' I said, nodding calmly. 'His emotional state during the account made it clear that he was no neighbour. Plainly he was the boy's father, Carlyle himself.'

Dr Ames smiled. He allowed himself a chuckle at my expense.

'No?' I asked. 'You have a better theory?'

'That,' said Dr Ames, 'was a man by the name of Poe. Halfway into our conversation I realized why he looked vaguely familiar. I recognized him from a photograph printed in the *Chronicle* just last week. Full name, Edgar Allan Poe. He's an author. He writes mysteries and ghost stories and suchlike.' Dr Ames took another puff. 'I don't normally go in for such tomfoolery, but Lord! Can't he just spin a tall tale?'

28

Imagine you are my wife

L et me start by asking you to imagine that you have a cat. Yes, not only are you beautiful but you seem like a very intelligent woman. I would be interested to hear what you think. This cat is jet-black but you can make him any colour, indeed any gender, you like. The important thing is that you have a cat and you're very fond of it.

Oh, you like cats, do you? Splendid.

Now imagine, if you will, that this cat suddenly gets killed in an appalling accident. It involves a plugged-in hairdryer and a sink full of water. It's nobody's fault, just one of those freak things. Electrocution is instant, so at least you can be sure the cat didn't suffer.

If you wish to probe the matter further, though, the accident was technically your own fault. The sink was full of water because you had filled it. There was a burned-out saucepan in there steeping. You had burned it while trying out a new recipe you had cut out of a Sunday lifestyle magazine. It was also you who'd been using the hairdryer, beside the sink, of all places. You were drying your hair while waiting to take something out of the oven. Still switched on, the dryer was left on the draining board for just a moment while you checked the casserole. The cat leaped up. Somehow both he and the dryer fell into the basin.

No, please don't get defensive.

As I said earlier, it was a freak thing and this cat was your precious friend, so nobody, certainly not me, seeks to cast any blame. I take the cat's stiffened body out of the sink, towel him off and hand him to you. You cradle him and talk to him and I encourage you to grieve for as long as you need.

Anyway, now please imagine that time has marched on and it's been six days since the poor cat's untimely demise. It is, any reasonable person would agree – and I think you are a reasonable woman – high time to think about disposing of his remains. As it stands, he has been placed in his old basket. There is no nice way of saying this: your apartment is beginning to be filled with the distinct smell, nay, the distinct stench, of dead cat.

Imagine that the options for his disposal are limited. You live here in the city, so there is no nearby field in which he might be buried. In addition, it's the middle of a particularly cold winter, just like now. Were you to take him to the park, it would be impossible to dig a hole in the frozen ground. Certainly not without a proper shovel, certainly not quickly. You would be discovered by one of the park attendants and they would doubtless take a dim view of your activities.

Also the river is frozen over, so an honourable

send-off into the waters is equally impossible. Crema-
tion too is out. Where could you attempt such a thing?
Furthermore – and I'm sorry to be indelicate here
– inside the skin it has started to decompose, so it's
not very flammable. Dousing with petrol would probably be required.

Now, moving sideways for a moment, may I ask you
to imagine that I am your husband? You laugh, but
it is not, I assure you, a disagreeable thing. I am a
nice guy and a good husband. I am not at all the kind
of man who will treat you badly. I can be relied upon
to hold open doors for you. On Sundays I will invariably bring you breakfast in bed.

Anyway, now that we are married, imagine once
more the situation with regard to your dead cat. The
problem of his increasingly noticeable odour. And the
difficulties related to the disposal of his remains.

All of which brings me to my point, which is to
ask you a question. How would you react if you were
to come home on the seventh day after the cat's
unfortunate death to find that the apartment was now
mercifully free of the stench? Which had posed a
serious threat to minimum standards of sanitation
and health?

What if you were to discover that it was your good
and loyal husband (that's me!) who had finally taken
action and dealt with the situation? What if he (that's
still me) sat you down and calmly explained that he
had placed the dead cat most respectfully in a carrier
bag – not just any old flimsy plastic bag but a quality
bag from one of your favourite boutiques? That he
had laid the cat gently on the fine perfumed tissue
paper that was still in the bag, sealed it shut and

placed it inside a bigger black refuse sack? And then placed the whole kit and caboodle into the garbage-disposal unit? Which is to say, he sent the cat's remains down along the chute that leads directly to the basement of your apartment building, down to where bags of rubbish are constantly falling into a massive wheelie bin, placed there by the janitor employed by building management.

What if I, your husband, was quick to stress that you could buy a new cat at the earliest convenience? One of the very same jet-black colour as the deceased. Or, in the event that you wanted a change, then perhaps a grey cat or an orange one. After all, you still have an opened bag of cat meal left over from the last little fellow. And you still have the cat bowl and all his other accoutrements. So why not get a replacement? It's a sensible idea.

And so I ask *you* now, imagining all of the relevant details, how would you react?

Would you break down in a fit of sobbing? Would you get angry and throw various articles at your blameless husband, who was only doing what had to be done?

No?

No?

Definitely no?

Good. That's good.

I thought so.

It gives me some consolation to have it confirmed that it is my wife who is the dysfunctional one in our relationship.

So now then . . . I'm in no hurry. Let's just say that my wife is unlikely to be waiting up. How about you? Your friends have all moved on to the nightclub, have they not? So, it's just you and me. Which is nice. Would you perhaps do me the honour of allowing me to buy you another drink?

29

Because I. Am not. You.

Mayo, Ireland, 2006

My stomach is still sticking out. My thighs are horrendous. My bum is a width only my husband Jim could (claim to) love. I'm two weeks into my diet and five pounds down according to the scales, but the mirror doesn't show any difference. I stand naked, pinching and stretching pinky white cellulite, trying to squint out some shrinkage. The doorbell rings. As I pull on my track-suit it rings several times more. As I suspected, it's Jim's sister. Smiling radiantly. Here for a visit. Un-announced. As usual.

She barely bothers with niceties as she bustles past me into the sitting room. She sits down one end of the sofa, roots in her bag for a clipboard and pen, and then pats the cushion beside her. I know there's no escaping.

'Now, if I were you, Kathleen,' she says, pen poised, 'I'd have his birthday cake baked in the shape of a car tyre. Since he runs the tyre-repair firm, I mean! And I'd carry the theme through with cute little

297

favours for all the guests; maybe bedside clocks in the shape of a rubber tyre? I saw some on sale in the car accessories shop on Duke Street.

'If I were you,' she adds, ticking the second box on her list, 'I would invite a few more people. You seem to have forgotten some important names that I would put on the guest list. And why not get person-alized invites specially done up with that adorable photo of him when he was only three and dressed as a spaceman? He really loved that outfit, y'know? He wore it all day, and as pyjamas all night, for six days straight at one stage! Anyway, I could definitely design some cards like that for you on the laptop if you like.

'If I were you,' she continues, 'I'd have special T-shirts made up for all the party guests saying I WAS THERE on the front and on the back WHEN JIM HIT THE BIG 4-OH! in assorted sizes and various colours. They'd be a lovely thing to have afterwards. I've researched a place in Galway where they print up batches for a budget price.'

But I hadn't asked for her help in organizing Jim's birthday party.

And I don't want her help in choreographing some overblown fuss of a party.

And I. Am not. Her.

Her mobile phone rings. It's her husband, Terence, summoning her home to find a modem adaptor for his laptop. That useless American lump can't ever seem to do anything for himself. Still, she smiles brightly and packs up her clipboard. She gives me a quick hug and kisses the air just past my cheek. I walk her to the front door and wave goodbye. She strides six yards to my gate, opens and closes it. Then she steps two yards to the left and opens the next gate before walking up the path to where Terence is already at their door, waiting.

My sister-in-law does not live next door on a permanent basis. It is Jim's parents' home but empty since they went into the nursing home. My sister-in-law's actual residence is San Diego, California, with Terence and their ten-year-old son, Cole. The three of them are over on vacation and will be going back soon, on the day after Jim's fortieth party. In the meantime, that woman will be in my hair, morning, noon and night. And there will be lots of fierce smiling.

Her relentless cheerfulness is not the main reason I find her such hard going.

First, there're her constant attempts to advise me – no, control me – by text message. From eight thousand miles away she feels it's her duty to text both Jim and me, reminding us of his mother's birthday, his father's birthday, their wedding anniversary, Mother's Day and Father's Day. Subsequent beeps tell us which gift to get. Then which second-choice gift to get if the first is unavailable. When we don't comply quickly enough, she buys it on-line, ships it and tells us to stump up x euro. Indeed, thanks to the long bloody tentacles of the internet, there is very little she can't stick her nose into from afar. Only last year we had to decide between two secondary schools for our twelve-year-old son, Cian. My sister-in-law weighed in with several lengthy e-mails sharing her research on both establishments. DEFINITELY SEND HIM TO BALLA! she concluded (and yes, in block capitals in case we missed the point). We went with St Gerald's and he's doing fine.

Second, I'll admit another reason is 'jealousy', or, as I would prefer to phrase it, 'Uncomprehending Annoyance with the Puzzle of Why Some of the Most Undeserving Bloody People in This World Seem to Have It All'. The first mystery is how she and Terence are so wealthy without ever seeming to do much work. I suspect some kind of trust fund, some shrewd stock market investments by Terence's father back in the seventies. Perhaps in IBM or Apple or Bill Gates when he was still in first grade. Or, better still, in lingerie manufacture, or some pornography distribution company – which would explain why the whole matter of where they get their income is never mentioned.

Also, how has she somehow shed the pale freckled skin that was her Celtic birthright for a permanently golden shade of tan?

The most irritating question, though, is how she went from being a size 12 to a size 8. Maybe even a size 6, I don't know, it's not like I go around checking her labels. The fact is that on her wedding day she was definitely a 12. As was I. Now, fifteen years later, she's got slimmer while I've moved up two divisions to size 16. On a bad day, 18.

Third, there're the hugs and kissing of thin air beside my cheek.

Which leaves in fourth place the relentless bloody smiling.

'She doesn't do it to be controlling, Kate,' says Jim when he comes home that evening. 'She tells you what to buy and where, so as to be helpful. Saving you hassle.'

'That's your interpretation,' I say, 'but I do not want that woman and her clipboard dictating our lives. Please make it clear to her that I am perfectly capable of organizing your party without her input. Unless, of course, you'd actually prefer her to do it, instead of me?'

'No!' he says, putting down his sports section with a sigh. 'In fact, I'll drop in next door right away and tell her.'

So he did. But not quite. Good old diplomatic Jim just couldn't resist a compromise.

'All she wanted was to be of assistance in making things special. She was very upset.'

Poor thing.

'So?'

'So, in the end, Kate, as an olive branch, I agreed to her having a small little separate event, in the old house. Something that would fit in with the main party here. She's putting together some kind of PowerPoint presentation of photos from my life – "When Jim was a kid" and so on. She assures me that it'll take only ten minutes to view. Fifteen tops.'

He pauses. He does not look me in the eye.

'So I was thinking that maybe an ideal time for it would be after the splendid meal you're going to cook. When the table has to be cleared, the party could adjourn briefly next door. Then we'll all come back for dessert and coffee and maybe a game of cards?'

He still does not look me in the eye. He picks up the sports section and hides.

I decide to relax about it. Indeed, over the next few days, housework and the mechanics of my horrible diet intrude. I have to cook every meal twice: one nice one for Jim and Cian, another dreary one for me. I am also distracted by Cian's school report. It's good overall but maths is a problem and he's already past the point where I can be of much help with homework. Maybe we should be getting him grinds . . .

My sister-in-law and her family visit us every evening when Jim is home from the garage and Cian from his summer camp. Terence flops into Jim's fireside armchair and gives us daily updates on how Mr and Mrs Frawley – our mutual parents-in-law – are doing in the nursing home and on the latest turn in their Alzheimer's. Cole disappears upstairs with Cian to play on the Xbox. My sister-in-law won't sit but flits about, giving us cordial advice on what bedding plants she'd sow in the front this autumn ('if I were you') and what colour curtains would look great in the utility room. She does not mention the fortieth at all.

By the time I turn my attention to the party again, it's too late for written invitations. I spend an afternoon on the telephone and ring everyone on my list (the list my sister-in-law dismissed). They can't believe he's forty. They'd love to come. I begin to plan the party itself.

Allowing for the inevitable no-shows, I estimate a crowd of about thirty. Thus the meal will have to be a buffet. Perhaps a choice of chicken curry or pork casserole, quiche for the vegetarians, baked potatoes, rice and lots of different salads. And fresh bread rolls or brown soda bread. And before that loads of crisps and dips on the coffee table. Maybe crème brûlée for dessert. And the birthday cake, of course. Chocolate, maybe. Or a nice Gâteau Diane. And, needless to say, massive amounts of every type of alcohol.

I'm going to need more plates and cutlery. I'm

going to need more glasses. When Mrs Frawley was still in the whole of her health, I used to borrow them from next door. I ring without even thinking and of course it is my sister-in-law who answers, singing, 'Helloooo!' I put down the receiver.

The next day Jim is called away to Copenhagen for some crisis talks at head office with his company's directors.

'This may take a few days, but I'll definitely be back for the party,' he says.

When I return from the airport, there is something unusual going on next door: I can't see the front door, as it is now surrounded by large black polythene screens. I go into my own house and mind my own business. Looking out the back door, I see sheets of black plastic in the back garden as well. I feel a slight spasm in my abdomen.

It is Cian who gives me the first inkling when he returns from spending an afternoon next door playing with Cole.

'Jeepers, Mam, it's awesome!'

'What's awesome?'

'All the stuff they have in Granny and Grandad's.'

'What "stuff"?'

'I don't know. All the cool stuff 'n' stuff.'

'Cian! What?'

'All the stuff for Dad's party.'

It is the day before Jim's fortieth. As Cian speaks a van pulls up next door. A man hops out and begins to unload from the side into his trolley. His delivery is in unmarked boxes. Whatever it is, my sister-in-law has ordered lots of it. A blast of acid reflux shoots up along my throat. It seems my dreary calorie-counted dinner wants to come back up. It tastes no better the second time around.

The time to panic has officially arrived. I thought that my preparations for the party were under control. But no. It's now obvious that my sister-in-law is planning far more than a ten-minute slide show. I am in a hostessing contest and am going to be found wanting. I have been far too unambitious. I should have invested in a clipboard.

I spend what's left of the evening driving over to Market Street, parking on double yellow and trying to make some vital purchases twenty minutes before closing. It does no good. The shops don't have what I want and the shop assistants, coats on, just want to switch off the lights and bring down the shutters. At six o'clock I am standing in the drizzling rain with an empty shopping bag.

At 8 p.m. the next day things are looking rosier. Jim is home, and he and Cian were a big help in the final few hours of preparation. The house is thoroughly tidied and festooned with balloons. The tables are laid out nicely and the food is all in hand. The three of us are showered and dressed to the nines. The doorbell rings and our first guests arrive.

By 10 p.m. I finally relax and admit to myself that things are going well. Thirty-five guests have made it, and they've all been fed and watered. I'm getting compliments – and requests for the recipe – for my potato and onion salad. (My secret ingredient is just a hint of chopped sage.) Every room on the ground floor is abuzz with conversation and laughter. My sister-in-law is here somewhere but has stayed out of my way. Then Jim approaches me as I'm collecting empty cans off the mantelpiece.

'So what do you think, Kate?' he says. 'She's been harassing me about going next door for the photo thing. Maybe I should go now with a few of the lads and get it over with.'

I can't really say no.

I should have said no.

Initially, Jim goes next door with six friends for just ten minutes. Then several come back to drag along their wives. Then they come back quickly to say that we should not miss the spectacle. 'This, you just have to see,' they say. I do not ask what is so amazing.

By half past ten I am alone in our house. Everyone is next door. Initially this allows me to clear the table and set it up for playing cards later. Then I have time to fill the dishwasher and put it on for a quick cycle. That done and the house still empty, I take the opportunity to sit down for the first time in hours. I can even take off my shoes for a rest. I sit and listen to the increasing racket next door.

But eleven o'clock comes and still nobody has returned. I put my shoes back on and go next door.

The polythene screens have been removed and purple spotlights now light the front of the house. The door has become the centre of a big swirling spiral.

Jim's friend Joe Nally is standing outside smoking.

'It's just like that programme we all used to watch as children,' he says. '*The Time Tunnel*. This is exactly how the tunnel looked when the two men fell into it and re-emerged in the time of the dinosaurs or Abraham Lincoln or whatever. Brilliantly done, isn't it?'

Yes.

Joe throws away his fag and accompanies me inside, where the old house has become unrecognizable. *The Time Tunnel* has taken us back to 1966, the year of Jim's birth. There are psychedelic lights kaleido-scoping round every wall. On two huge TV screens there is documentary footage of Vietnam and Arkle and Jim Frawley aged one, two, three, four, five, six, seven, eight, nine . . .

'Listen,' shouts Joe above the racket, 'she even got a DJ and every song he's playing tonight was a chart hit in that year: "Monday, Monday", "Yellow Sub-marine", "Wild Thing", "Paint It Black", "Pretty Flamingo", "These Boots are Made for Walkin'" . . .'

A life-sized cardboard cut-out of Jim stands just inside the door. It is dressed as a spaceman. Joe Nally is one of several people wearing the specially made T-shirts saying I WAS THERE . . . WHEN JIM HIT THE BIG 4-OH! My sister-in-law has done everything that she wanted me to do and much more besides. Here's the wheel-shaped birthday cake; there's the big stack of little wheel-shaped favours.

From out of the crowd Cian emerges – red-faced, sweaty, hair askew, obviously having a ball.

'Mam! Can I stay here tonight in Cole's bedroom? His mam said it's all right if I get your permission.'

Granted.

Then I come across Jim. He is surrounded by a group of people whom I did not invite. Lads from his misspent youth, two ex-girlfriends, people I thought he'd probably outgrown. Wrong.

'Hey, love,' he roars in my ear while grabbing at my bum drunkenly, affectionately. 'I'm glad you came over. It's great, isn't it?'

'Yeah. But it seems to be taking longer than ten minutes,' I say. He is in a bubble of alcohol and adulation and doesn't pick up the bitter tone. There is nothing to be gained from bursting it.

I turn to go and hear my sister-in-law's voice crowing to some admirer above the din, 'I always say you can never be too organized.'

I study her from behind. I have to admit that her dress is stunning, plainly a designer label. It hangs upon her size 8 figure properly, the way a dress is supposed to hang. Nevertheless I fancy that beneath the make-up her face has that pinched look of a woman who is thinner than she really should be. She is, incidentally, holding her clipboard.

Abruptly she turns around and I can't escape.

'Oh my God, Kathleen!' she says. 'What a lovely outfit you're wearing. It makes you look as if you've lost weight.'

Thanks.

'Yours too,' I say. 'But I really must be getting back.'

'What?' she squeals, looking down at her clipboard and ticking one of the boxes, 'but there's going to be a magician in a few minutes. And fireworks at midnight!'

'Wonderful,' I say as another blast of acid reflux climbs my throat, 'but I have to see about serving the desserts.'

'Oh, why bother, Kathleen?' she says. 'If I were you,' she says, 'I'd just stay here for the rest of the night. Everyone else is going to.'

She pauses before adding: 'Jim is certainly going to.'

I go home.

Feck the fecking fecked-up diet. I help myself to a crème brûlée and sit down to my table. Then I fix myself another portion and pour myself a large glass of red wine. Through the walls I hear the party whooping ever louder.

Jim chose Her. Feck Him and fuck Her.

A tear slithers down my cheek. I sniffle. I put my head in my hands.

Half an hour passes and I am resting my face in my hands on the table. Sleep is only seconds away when I feel the strength and warmth of a man's hand on my shoulder.

I sit back up abruptly but it's only Terence.

'Hi,' he says. 'All on your own? That's too bad.'

He moves over to the kitchen worktop and pours us two more glasses of red. He sits in the chair opposite. He tells me we have something in common.

'. . . being married to a Frawley. You have to admit that, while there are differences between brother and sister, they're also quite alike. I reckon a lot of it stems from the fact that Jim was born only eleven months after my wife. Were you aware of that?'

Yes, obviously.

'So from the time they were in diapers, they played side by side for years, forging an incredible bond. They practically had their own exclusive language; even to this day when they're together you notice it, words and phrases, running jokes and references to some specific incident that happened in the sandpit when they were seven and eight.'

'Yes, Terence.'

I am staring drowsily at the top of his chest where a button has come undone. A single silvery chest hair pokes through.

'And then there're all the pop songs, the TV programmes that they watched together. That of course is how she knew he obsessed over *The Time Tunnel*. You couldn't have known that, nor could anyone else.'

I switch to gaping at Terence's moustache. How could anyone think it looked anything other than ridiculous?

'So what I'm driving at is that there's a bond between that brother and sister that no one can ever get inside of. And I mean no one, not even a spouse. Personally,' he says, chuckling ruefully, 'I gave up trying with my Frawley years ago.'

I chuckle also.

'By the way, Kathleen,' he says, changing tack, 'I really love your dress tonight. And your hair. It's awesome.'

Jesus! Even drowsy and drunk I can't miss the signal. Terence is trying to make a pass at me.

'Did I ever tell you what I'd really like to do as a career?' he asks, and I shake my head.

'Well, the truth is I'd throw it all away if only I could become a professional writer of fiction.'

'Really?' I say with the mildest possible tone of polite but unenthusiastic interest.

'Oh sure, I've been keeping it quiet but I've wanted to be a writer all my life. And I've been actively writing in my spare time for nearly twelve years now.

Mostly short stories. Also two novels of a trilogy. Right now I'm generating ideas for a projected TV script.'

'Really?'

'Yup! But, before you ask, the embarrassing part is that I've had damn all published. So far, all I've got to show is one short story printed in the *Idaho Quarterly Review*. It earned me the princely sum of fifty dollars.'

'Really?'

'Yeah.' He chuckles once more. 'In fact I'm starting to come around to the idea that my stories aren't going to find success until after I'm dead. The problem is the damned publishers. They never give the little guy starting out an even break. You have to have an agent, have to know people who know people.'

'Really?'

'Yup! And anyhow the kind of fiction I'm writing is just too far "out there". Y'know? It's edgy, dangerous, completely different to anything you ordinarily see on the shelves. Publishers are just not willing to take chances. All they do is churn out the same old formulaic garbage.'

'Really?'

'It is,' he says, 'the curse of being just a bit ahead . . .'

He drones on and I am considering whether I can answer 'Really?' again when Terence reaches across the table and takes hold of my hand. His eyes seek contact with mine and they are hungry.

Ugh!

I jump up to go to fix us two more drinks. For a moment there is an awkward silence, but from next door comes the sound of shouting and cheering. Someone is making a speech.

'That'll be the birthday cake,' says Terence in a cracked, disappointed tone of voice. He really thought he had a chance! Now he seizes his opportunity to retreat. 'I've been told to take lots of photos.'

So he leaves. Phew! He is such an idiot. I almost feel sorry for him. I pour two glasses of wine anyway. I plan to continue drinking in bed and it'll be handy not to have to get up for a refill. Too lazy to undress, I flop onto the bed fully clothed and flick on the TV.

When I awake, I am still lying on top of the quilt. The TV is still burbling away. And Terence is between my thighs.

Whaaaaaaaaaaaaaaaaaat?

Yes, it's a fact. Though my senses are still drunken, still sleepy, still unwilling-to-believe. '*Terence is between my thighs!*'

My panties have been removed and my skirt is hitched to my hips. Terence is lying between my open legs with his trousers and underpants about his ankles. He is moving in a rhythmic fashion. The top few buttons of my blouse are also undone. Terence is pawing at one breast while licking the other. His eyes are shut tight in concentration and he is grunting, 'Oh, Kathleen, you're so curvy. So soft . . .'

This is a nightmare. I cannot believe that this idiot is actually trying to have sex with me. I'm so muzzy from all the wine that I'm strangely calm about it. Terence is not yet inside me but I feel a semi-solid willy banging a little too high against my pubic bone. Plainly I need to do something. With one hand I reach down between our bodies and grab hold of him. My intention is to dig in my fingernails and put a halt to his gallop.

Just then the bedroom door opens quietly. My sister-in-law stands there, silent for once, taking everything in. She is still carrying the damn clipboard, though surely by now the last box has been ticked and party-boy Jim is conked out on her sofa.

Totally oblivious to his wife, Terence continues rocking. My fingernails are poised, but I hold off. As he groans like a bull, my sister-in-law's customary smile is absent. In its place is an unfamiliar expression of anguish.

'Yes, that's it!' Terence shouts into my ear. 'Good girl, Kathleen!'

And still my sister-in-law stands there, transfixed, I suppose, by the awfulness of it all. I break the spell by looking her in the eye and uttering five words, five words that make her run down the stairs shrieking. The moment she turns away, I stick my nails into Terence's willy and he too lets out an awful howl. He rolls off me squealing, 'Sorry, sorry, sorry . . .'

And the five words?
Because I. Am not. You.

30

'You promised me Rome'

'Fuuuuck!' said Mary when she got home from work.

'Tough going was it, beautiful?' asked Joe, who was either already in bed or hadn't left it all day.

'You've no idea,' she said. 'I'm going to strangle that woman if she doesn't stop bossing me around.'

From under her shawl she produced a small bottle of wine. 'Here, I called at Malachi's on the way home.'

Joe grabbed the bottle and immediately uncorked and drained it.

'God, I needed that. Thanks, beautiful, you're a great girl.'

'I know. There's few enough would put up with you. So did you do any writing while I was gone?'

'Yes.'

'Yes, what? How many pages exactly?'

'Aahmm . . . three, I think.'

'Three, my eyeball! Show me. That parchment is

as blank as it was when I left. Did you even get out of bed today?'

'Of course. I –' Joe began, but it was too late. Mary had opened the cupboard.

'And you didn't even stir yourself to get bread. You are unbelievable! You know, I think you'd actually starve if left to your own devices.'

'That's not true, beautiful,' said Joe, and he got out of the bed. In two strides he had crossed their tiny dwelling. He pushed past her outstretched hand and embraced her as her anger turned to tears.

They cut an unlikely pair. Mary was beautiful with long lustrous black hair and a full youthful figure. Joe, a dozen years her senior, was tall and skinny with sticky-out ears and a scraggy red beard. His eyes were different colours: one blue, one brown.

'Sssh, now, beautiful,' he whispered, 'I'll go out in a minute for the bread. And we'll have fish. It'll be lovely.'

'Oh, Joseph, you're such a fool,' hissed Mary, pushing him away from her. 'It's not my dinner I'm worried about. It's just another example of the hundred things that are wrong. The thousand things that are not like what you said.'

'Hundred or thousand? A concrete example, please?' Joe said.

'Everything, you idiot! You said we would have money and I'd never again have to slave in the laundry. Wrong. Instead I'm working harder than ever supporting us both while you spend the day in bed daydreaming. You said after we married, we'd live in a palace, not this hovel! You said you'd take me to see Rome, maybe we'd even live there. You said you'd show me the Forum and the Coliseum. You said we'd go to see the giraffe in the zoo and have a picnic in the shade of the Pantheon. We were going to get front-row tickets for the Circus Maximus and the chariot Grand Final. Wrong, wrong, wrong!

'Instead we're still stuck in this dusty corner of nowhere. Instead we can't even get to Jerusalem, let alone the Eternal City. Instead —'

'Please, beautiful,' Joe interrupted, 'none of this is fair. I meant it when I said all those things but circumstances went out of my control. You know perfectly well how those plans fell apart. You know too how close they were to fruition. How close we were to Rome, how very close, if only —'

If only 'Eliphaz the Eloquent' had listened to Joe . . .

Before Joe had met him in 5 BC, he was just plain old Eliphaz, a minor preacher peddling second-hand proverbs in Tiaska Square, Jerusalem. After he hooked up with Joe, though, Eliphaz suddenly began captivating casual passers-by, where once they'd hurried past. True to his new nickname, he was articulate in expounding a fresh brew of the old commandments with a new emphasis on 'love'. Allied to that was a specific forecast of imminent apocalypse, from which only the faithful would be saved. The huddle around his pulpit grew into a cluster, then a big crowd. Attendance at his lunchtime lectures snowballed, until the authorities were forced to cordon off sections of Tiaska Square for traffic. In due course, he was prevailed upon to take his mission on tour.

Over the next few years Eliphaz criss-crossed every province along the River Jordan, from Acre to Galilee.

When his followers numbered several thousand, the governor of Judea finally stirred and had the sect infiltrated by spies. They reported that the hidden hand behind the scenes was Joe's. It was he who wrote the scripts. The governor awaited further developments . . .

'If only Eliphaz had listened to you, Joe!' Mary said in a sing-song voice. 'Why don't you tell me again for the twenty-ninth time?'

'That's right, beautiful,' said Joe, ignoring her sarcasm. 'He started believing his own publicity, the fool. As donations from the faithful poured in, we were doing very nicely. I had a hundred denarii! I could easily afford ten trips to Rome.'

'But then —' said Mary, smiling at her husband's frustration and air of wounded pride when on his familiar hobbyhorse.

Joe continued as he always did: 'Eliphaz thought he was untouchable and started throwing in his own unscripted lines about how the earthly empire was sucking us dry, how we had to have an independent Jewish state. I kept reminding him of the wisdom in keeping things vague, but oh, no, he was too big to take advice from the man who'd got him there.'

But Eliphaz wouldn't listen to Joe . . .

The Roman governor panicked at the hint of tangible insurrection. Eliphaz the Eloquent and his core group were rounded up. After a show trial Eliphaz was transported to the capital and wound up as tiger meat in the Circus Maximus. Some months later, his followers were released as part of an amnesty. Joe, though, had been identified as the mastermind.

He was politely warned, with a dagger to his throat, not to set foot in Jerusalem ever again.

'Poor, poor Joe,' said Mary, and this time it was she who hugged him and tried to smooth away his grimace.

'Well, I'll tell you this, Mary,' he said with a scowl meant to convey determination, 'about poor, poor Joe. If I ever get back to civilization – and I will, when the heat dies down – I'm going to find me a brand-new Eliphaz. I know that my crooked face would prevent anyone listening to me. But give me some pliable good-looking youngster with nice warm eyes. I will supply the words. Then my beautiful girl, you and I will get our palace all right . . . Oh, yes! And riches beyond your dreams.'

'Yeah, right, can't wait,' said Mary, but she wasn't so angry any more. 'In the meantime, darling husband, while we wait for our riches to be delivered, I was thinking that you might get back into doing a bit of carpentry.'

'What? And abandon my writing? Surely you wouldn't ask that of me?' said Joe.

'No, never,' said Mary, 'I only mean part time, say, five mornings a week; you could still spend the afternoons at your desk.'

'I suppose . . .' said Joe, doubtfully.

'I suppose "yes" or I suppose "no"?' said Mary.

Joe took a deep breath and whispered, 'Yes.'

Mary took him back into her arms and within moments he was undoing the clasp on her gown. She responded by pulling loose his top and her hand reached down to his loins. They stripped each other naked and in two clumsy steps fell together on the bed.

Joe rolled on top of Mary.

'Aren't you forgetting something?' she asked before he went further. Joe sighed and reached above the head of the bed to a piece of sheep gut that he'd hung on a nail. It was six inches long and one end had been sewn shut with thirty small stitches. He went about the tricky business of pulling it onto his erect penis while Mary closed her eyes and awaited his entry. When it didn't slip on first time, Joe decided not to bother . . .

31

Really asking for it

Halstatt, Germany, 550 BC

Freda had been married to Eber for only a few weeks when they had a row about his staying out late and returning home drunk. Eber slapped her in the face.

Freda would endure many things but not this. As was her right under the law, she took her husband to the local court and charged him with having slapped her. As she laid the charge under oath, Freda noticed that the judge was winking at Eber. Stepping closer, Freda smelled alcohol on his breath and guessed that this judge was in fact her husband's drinking companion.

The case proceeded before a small gallery and Eber's testimony was an honest admission that he had indeed slapped her. 'But,' said he, 'she was really asking for it.'

'I can well believe it,' said the judge. 'Which of us can bear the shrewish nagging of a vexatious wife?' This played well with the crowd of mostly male spectators, who nodded and grinned.

323

'And after all,' continued Eber, 'it was just a slap.'

'For what is a slap anyway?' interrupted the judge again, 'if not the most inconsequential of assaults, a mere trifle, a bagatelle? Only a very silly plaintiff could make such a fuss over so little.

'I hereby pronounce,' said the judge, 'that the defendant is guilty. His fine shall be one obol, to be paid to the plaintiff.'

Only one obol! Freda gasped at the leniency of the fine.

'Oh,' said Eber, pulling out the lining of his pocket, 'but I seem to be wearing the wrong trousers. I have no money on me.'

'Then go and get it for me,' said Freda through gritted teeth.

Eber went off, jogging for the first few yards, then slowing to a stroll. The crowd trickled from the court-room, satisfied that justice had been served. Freda and the judge, however, had to remain until the fine was paid. They sat waiting.

And waiting.

And waiting.

All the while, the judge played with the ends of his moustache and smirked at Freda.

'I'm still wondering about your verdict,' she said finally. 'Am I to understand that one obol is always considered sufficient payment for even a very hard slap on the face?'

'Yes,' said the judge smugly. 'Always.'

Hearing this, Freda strode up to the judge. She slapped him across the mouth with all the strength she could muster. He fell sideways. Streaks of blood trickled from his nostrils. He even spat out a tooth.

'Right,' said Freda, turning towards the door, 'you may keep the obol when my husband returns with it.'

32

The fate of all romance?

He used to be so romantic but not any more. I used to come home to find him sitting on the steps outside my bedsit on Moyne Road with daisies he'd picked for me down by the canal, for no particular reason. Now he barely manages to organize a credit card delivery of clichéd red roses from a florist on Valentine's Day.

Which is true.
There was indeed a time when I was always doing wonderful things for her. But even my most generous gestures never actually cost me any effort at all. They seemed so natural and right and true.
That was love.

Once he had spark and spontaneity; every morning was the promise of a stroll hand in hand to a park or a pier where anything might happen. Now I open my eyes knowing far too much of the future for absolute certain. And the No. 1 certainty is that my chances of being whisked away to Paris for a surprise this weekend are ... nil.

Now years later I'd have to force myself to do such things. They no longer just naturally occur to me. Apparently I should do romantic things anyway. I hear it's called 'working at the relationship'. But if I replace joyful instinct with effort, is that still love? And how exactly is 'working at love' different from pretending?

33

Wrong

T he wrong reason.
    . . . Because Marjorie fell pregnant. That simple. There was no need for debate back in those days. Unless you wanted the business end of a screwdriver in your back.

The wrong person.
    . . . Not particularly compatible, Marjorie and I. More like opposites repel. She's just a very highly strung emotional person, is Marjorie. Whenever we'd get into an argument she'd screech and cry, never ever just stick to the facts of the matter in hand. I used to try to reason it for her but it never worked. Next time I'd try harder, hone the logic even tighter. Nope, still no better. Which I suppose meant that eventually I did give up. Most evenings after I came back from work we'd eat in silence. Then she stayed indoors with the kids giving them hell while I went out in the garage. Wonderful things, car engines. No matter how broke they are, they can always be fixed. Unlike wives.

The wrong solution.

. . . The garage did get a little lonely. I cut it down to every second night. I began to spend alternate nights down at Buck's Tavern. That's where I met Cindy. We saw each other for ten years.

The wrong impression.

. . . Silly bitch got it into her head that I'd leave my wife and family for her. Not a chance!

The wrong motivation.

. . . Yeah, things kinda came to a head: Cindy's ultimatum and then my little trip to the oncologist. Thankfully the cancer had been detected early but it was apparent I was going to need a lot of nursing. That's something only a wife can really give. So I split with Cindy and I have to say that Marjorie really came up trumps. She can still be an annoying old bat, but she's a good cook and looks after me and I could do a lot worse. I've been a hundred per cent faithful ever since.

The wrong year.

. . . When our first boy began showing an interest in such things we pretended our wedding took place a year earlier, so he wouldn't twig that he himself had kinda popped the question. Actually, if anybody went to the trouble of checking certificates, they'd find that today is not our thirtieth anniversary but our twenty-ninth.

He walks away from the urinal, pulling up his zipper, not troubling to visit the sink. He walks out into a hotel function room full of smiling faces: children, grandchildren, friends and neighbours. He sits down at the head of the table, takes his wife's hand and begins the speech he has prepared.

'Today marks the thirtieth anniversary of the luck-iest day of my life. That blessed day long ago when I wed Marjorie, my best friend and soul-mate, the love of my life.'

34

Some kind of creature was scratching in the attic

The first time I heard it, I was standing at the sink: just inches above my head, some kind of creature was scratching the other side of the ceiling. Hardly able to breathe, I backed away slowly, eyes glued to the spot. The vibration was so strong I expected a large rat to break through. Then, as abruptly as it had started, it stopped and the house returned to silence. It was twenty minutes before I could persuade myself to make a mug of cappuccino.

'Matt,' I said to my husband when he came home from work, 'you must go up to the attic to investigate. I nearly lost my life with the fright.'

'Oh, yes, certainly,' he said. 'Directly after supper – what's it tonight?'

After eating, the old codger headed straight for his armchair and started watching a programme about Hillary and Obama and the US primaries. By the time I'd cleared the table, he'd dozed off.

The man I married had a full head of hair, his own

teeth and more energy than a crèche full of toddlers. That was thirty years ago and lately the age gap between us is beginning to show. At fifty-seven, I'm in my prime, but at sixty-four Matt is definitely past his. Hair and teeth thinning out is one thing, but the most worrying change is his loss of get-up-and-go.

I got him up and made him go. Half asleep and grumbling, he made a big deal out of fetching the stepladder. Then he couldn't find a torch. Then he had to put his shoes back on and get a coat because it's cold up there in winter. Then he armed himself with a carving knife.

I handed him a saucer of poisoned corn. Which he spilled. Of course it was muggins who had to sweep it up for him. Finally, he pushed open the trapdoor and climbed in. As his stumpy legs disappeared, I winced and waited.

'All clear,' he shouted, rather too quickly for my liking. Three minutes later he was back down and nestling in his armchair. I doubted he'd searched properly, gone through all the nooks and crannies.

Next day I spent my morning at a meeting of the Kenmare Social Development Community Initiative. It's a local voluntary group of which I'm chairperson. We run various training and information schemes to help the long-term unemployed. And the old folks. And the foreign nationals. And the unmarried mothers. And people like that.

Anyway, when I came home and started making our bed, there were sinister noises overhead. This time it was a rustling: it sounded like some old newspapers were being torn, gnawed upon, chewed up and swallowed. Of course, the little beast wouldn't oblige and just eat its poison. As I stood frozen in horror, I could make out a slight quivering in the ceiling where the creature was sitting. It must have knocked something over, perhaps with its tail. Suddenly there was a loud bang and I ran from the bedroom with a shriek. Outside in the safety of the car, I rang Sheila on my mobile. We decided to go for half a round of golf.

By the time I came home Matt was already back from work and half asleep under his newspaper. But I had devised a plan.

'Are you wondering what's for supper?' I asked.

He didn't reply. He just looked at me with that dazed expression I'm so familiar with from my voluntary group. The foreign nationals especially – you have to ask them every question twice.

'Nothing!' I continued. 'You'll get nothing to eat until you go up to that attic and find the creature. And drive it out or trap it or kill it.'

'Come on now, dear,' he said, 'be reasonable. It's probably just birds landing on the roof or something.'

'IT'S NOT BIRDS LANDING ON THE ROOF!' I said.

'Okay, dear, have it your way,' he said quietly. 'But I'm not in a fit state to go up again. If there's going to be no supper, I'd just as soon go to bed.'

And that's what he did. So much for my clever ploy. I started to make him a sandwich and thought about where and when it all went wrong.

Matt's decline was sudden, dating back three months to an incident at Lynch's Haulage, where he coordinates trucks and freight. One morning he collapsed out in the trailer yard. They thought he was dead but the doctor brought him back to consciousness and then moved him to Tralee for tests and scans. Which revealed nothing: apparently his heart, reflexes and blood were all fine. But something was no longer quite right. Something inside his skull. He went from thinking he would never die, to worrying that death was just around the corner.

Since then he's lost his energy. He does his day's work but no more. I ask him to do simple chores – say, put out the wheelie bin and bring in a bucket of coal – but he doesn't bother and leaves it all up to me. I recently suggested we visit our daughter and grand-children in Ballymahon. No, he couldn't face the trip. Another evening I asked him to fix a curtain rail – a man's job if ever there was one. He began the task. Then I pointed out that it wasn't quite level and started helping. Next thing, he put the screwdriver into my hand and strolled off. To the toilet, I assumed. Eventually I found him doodling the face of a cowboy (in profile, wearing a stetson) on the back page of the TV guide. He looked up and asked, 'Did you get it fixed yet?'

And no, it's not the onset of Alzheimer's. I thought of that. He forgets nothing. And he's not shaking, so it's not Parkinson's either. We got broadband recently, and I've searched all over the internet and found nothing that matches his behaviour. Nothing medical anyway: truth be told, Matt has always had a tendency towards laziness.

Through the early hours of the morning I lay wide awake while Matt snored beside me. Overhead there were sounds – something creaking, something tapping – but no sound I could definitively say was the creature. No doubt it slept by night and would be foraging around on the morrow.

I got up and retrieved the yellow phone book from the hall. There were numerous options under 'Pest Control'. How wonderful it would be to just get the professionals in and have done with the matter. But I couldn't take the risk that my neighbours would find out. Maura Coyle, in particular, is like a ferret. If she saw a strange vehicle parked in our driveway, she'd be straight over to find out what for. Within hours the whole of Kenmare would have the story of my rat infestation. No, I realized that muggins would just have to go up in the attic herself.

As the morning was so nice, Matt decided to walk the mile to Lynch's yard, so I had the car for the day. I went to Killarney to buy a wedding present for Sheila's nephew. There was a great sale on in Quills so I picked up a nice pleated skirt for myself and a casual jacket for Matt. Then I did some business at the bank. Then I paid a quick visit to my sister Angela. On the way back I stopped for groceries in SuperValu. When I got home I gave each room a quick tidy and started peeling the potatoes for dinner. But I was just putting off the inevitable.

There was scratching overhead again, louder than before and in two distinct places. Perhaps the creature had spawned some progeny. Sickened though I was, I knew I could avoid my mission no longer. I must go up and find out the exact nature of the beast.

I got the torch. The stepladder was not where it should have been in the press; no doubt Matt had put it back somewhere stupid. Inch by inch, I pushed a sideboard across the hall to just underneath the trapdoor. Then I placed a stool on top and, risking life and limb, scrambled aloft.

It had been more than twenty years since I'd been in the attic. If anything ever needed to be got down, that was Matt's job. So I was not surprised at how messily all the boxes of accoutrements were arranged. As for the creature or creatures, there was no sign. The poisoned corn lay untouched.

There was, however, a horrible sickly smell and I distinctly felt some kind of presence. I surmised that if I disturbed it, the thing might make a dash through the hole and down into my living area, so I closed the trapdoor. Then I turned the torch up to strong beam and began the search. Under the apex of the roof I could stand up full height, so I walked down the length of the house. At every pace I shone the torch left, then right, trying to discern traces of rat in the shadows: maybe a glimpse of a tail, or, worse, a small pile of its black bean-like excrement, or, worst of all, a pair of sparkling red eyes.

When my initial sweep failed to unearth anything, I began again, this time crouching down and swinging the torch into the furthest corners of the eaves. Distracted by a cobweb in my hair, I missed my footing and tumbled over one of the boxes. In the crash my torch went off and would not come back on. The attic was now pitch dark.

I crawled towards the trapdoor but succeeded only in banging my head off a crossbeam. Amid my un-ladylike curses I thought I heard something moving and fell silent. Yes, there was the old familiar scratching and it was just three or four yards away.

It was between me and where I thought the trapdoor was located. I held my breath.

A newspaper rustled not four feet from where I knelt. Frantically, I groped around for something to beat off the attack that was coming. My hand alighted on a rounded stick. Perfect, I thought, but then I couldn't lift it up. After more groping, I realized it was a rung from the stepladder, left here, of all the stupid places.

While I was fumbling with the ladder, the thing had come closer. It was now inches away. I screamed.

'Ssshhik!' came the sound of a match being struck.

'I'm so sorry, dear. I never meant to scare you,' said Matt, and put a consoling hand on my shoulder.

Startled by his touch, and by the shock of seeing him there, I shrieked again.

The match burned out into darkness and he lit another. I could see that he was still dressed in his blue work suit and tie.

'Matt, what the hell are you doing up here? Why aren't you at work?' I said.

Then, for the first time in our long lives together, Matt began to cry.

35

Cross word

ACROSS

5 Horticulturalist ... capacity in which I employed that blasted Matty Kimball (8)

6 More than just friends ... relationship which 'blossomed' between Kimball and my wife, Lady Stowcroft (6)

7 Men's lower garment ... Kimball's was hanging from an apple tree branch while he bloody well xxxxxed my wife in the lower meadow (8)

9 My reaction on learning of this odious deceit (4)

11 Reprisal ... that which I swore would be mine (9)

12 Cunning plot ... by which I planned their comeuppance (6)

DOWN

1 Repeat performance ... that which occupied them next afternoon when I made my first move (6)

2 Jewellery for the finger ... several of which the constabulary later discovered stuffed in Kimball's trouser pocket upon his arrest (4)

3 Tool for trimming bushes ... that which the constabulary found stabbed through Lady Stowcroft's heart when her body was located (fully clothed!) behind the gazebo (13)

4 Disbelief ... look on my face (demonstrating my incomprehension of evil in this cruel world) at the trial where Kimball was tried for theft and murder (5)

8 Female progeny ... of Kimball, aged 19, who was most sincere in her apologies and sympathies at my wife's funeral (8)

10 Divan ... that which I now share with said girl (a delightful little filly too!) (3)

36

While driving to the
Pre-Marriage course

Offaly, Ireland, April 2008

'Slow down, sweetheart. You're driving too fast,' said the woman.

'Okay, honey,' replied the man, and squeezed down gently on the brake.

There was a brief moment of tranquillity. Then from the backseat came the sound of whining. It was the baby they were minding for Clodagh. She was teething.

'Oh, no,' said the woman. 'I can't stand seeing her in pain. She badly needs a cuddle. I wish we were there already so I could pick her up.'

The whining turned to howling and the speedometer started to climb.

'SLOW DOWN!' said the woman. 'You're going to make us crash. Don't you realize you've a tiny precious baby to think of as well?'

How could he not realize? Her shrieks were piercing his eardrums.

'But, honey,' he said, 'I was just trying to get us there sooner so you could pick her up. Like you said . . .'

353

'I knew I should have driven,' said the woman.

After dropping the baby off at Clodagh's they continued on to the Pre-Marriage course. The man (still driving) reached down and across to the glove compartment and flicked it open.

'What are you doing, sweetheart?' asked the woman.

'Getting a CD to put on,' he replied.

'While you're driving?' she said.

'You're right,' he said. He turned his eyes back onto the road just in time to avoid a cyclist. 'That was dangerous. Do it for me, will you?'

'No problem, sweetheart,' she said. 'Which one do you want put on?'

'Bob Dylan,' he said.

'No bloody way,' said the woman. 'You made me listen to more than enough of him last week. I'll see if there's anything on the radio.'

So they listened to a current affairs programme.

'Left or right? Left or right?' the man bellowed.

'Left . . . I think,' said the woman. 'Yes, it's probably left.'

'But that's back the way we bloody came. For Jesus' sake, give me the map. We're definitely going to be late now. That's the last time I rely on you to navigate.'

They found the hall eventually, parked and went to the door. Sister Agnes, who was running the Pre-Marriage course, greeted them warmly and took herself back into the hall.

'Now then, folks, if you'll all just take your seats once more,' she said in her loud schoolteacher tone.

The participating couples (about a dozen) finished up their tea and biscuits and did as they were told.

'So,' said Sister Agnes, 'having learned earlier about Communication and Conflict Management, the next segment of the evening is where we look at how these are implemented in practice. To that end, I've invited along an exemplary couple of my acquaintance to talk to you. Married now for thirty-three years, and having recently had their first grandchild, they'll offer tips on how they have managed to maintain a loving commitment for so long. Ladies and gentlemen, please welcome Brendan and Maureen.'

And she beckoned them in.

37

Rage and reconciliation fifteen miles from Chelyabinsk

'No,' I said.

Mrs Pesotskaya turned and shrieked at me but this time I was determined not to yield.

'Mr Pesotskaya! You blaggard!' she shouted, her cheeks inflamed at having to tell me twice. 'By the saints and Blessed Virgin, by the blood of Tsar Anatole himself, I'll not give you a moment's peace till you do.'

'Excuse me, Mrs Pesotskaya,' I said, determined to remain well mannered, 'but I think you'll find that I've already done my share of the washing up.'

It was true. Sitting on the draining board, still dripping, lay my plate, my spoon and the black saucepan.

'I've done my share too,' she said, and pointed at the ware on the other side of the basin: her plate, her spoon and the grey saucepan. 'But it was I who cooked the meal,' she added, as if that were going to settle it.

'Yes,' I said, 'thank you, it was lovely.' But then I pushed on, 'However, it was I who grew the vegetables and corn. It was I who shot the rabbit.'

For a minute she made no reply but glared as she pondered her next move. The big blue vein near her temple bulged a little bit more. It could go either way now: more shouting, possibly some throwing of objects, or else a silent sulk. In the event, she stormed off into our bedchamber and slammed the door.

Still in my chair, I shook my head and wondered what had possessed me not to just comply as usual. Now I was knee-deep in the kind of conflict that thirty-one years of a difficult marriage had taught me to avoid. I filled and then lit my pipe. I reached for my shotgun and loaded a cartridge. Then I called the dog and we went outside for a ramble in the woods.

It was dusk when we returned, but there was enough light to see that the cause of the falling out remained. In the basin of cold grey water it stood: a shiny new silver pot. Inside it were the leftovers of a sweet porridge that had been delicious in the eating. Now all that remained was a sticky lumpy mess clinging to the sides and at the bottom a layer of solid brown paste, burned in when my wife got distracted while cooking.

'Mrs Pesotskaya probably thinks I'll give in as always and scrub it before nightfall,' I said to the dog.

But I didn't. I hung up the shotgun, removed my boots and went to join her in bed. Moving in the dark without a candle, steering by the sound of her snores, I bashed my small toe against the dresser. It throbbed for an hour.

*

Next day, I was up and out early with the dog. It was time to move the goats from the mountainside to the five-acre field. Three stragglers caused us an amount of trouble, and I was famished by the time we arrived home for lunch. The aroma of a piping hot meal was conspicuous by its absence, however, and my wife wasn't in the house. I went to the back door and noticed the pot still unwashed in the basin. Mrs Pesotskaya was across the yard, scattering food to the hens. Their portion looked twice as big as usual. Sighting me, she turned away and gave those hens a big smile. The big smile she reserves when angry for any person or creature that is not me.

'So this is how it's to be,' I said to the dog. 'I'll be starved into submission.'

I put my cap back on and set off immediately for the lakeside, hoping it was lunchtime there too. I called on our neighbours Nikolay and Rosa Razumikhin, who insisted I come in for a big bowl of soup.

When I returned in the evening, the hens were all huddled together on the porch. Squatting with their heads tucked down into their feathers, their bellies were big and bloated. I went back indoors to Mrs Pesotskaya's brooding tranquillity. And an empty larder.

The shape of the conflict had been set, and the next few days followed a similar pattern. My breakfasts and suppers were cobbled together from whatever few bits Mrs Pesotskaya had forgotten to hide: wrinkled apples and slices of a stale sweetcake. At lunchtimes I didn't bother to go home, only called on each of our neighbours. But by the fifth morning of the quarrel my options were thinning out. The

361

only neighbours left to visit were two bachelor brothers and a flirty old spinster called Eva, who might get the wrong notion. Watching as Mrs Pesotskaya swept the floor in silence, I began to think maybe the time had come to reopen negotiations. Perhaps I could explain that I was tired of having my compliance with her every request taken entirely for granted. Maybe we could set up a roster for washing this new silver pot, which was still standing in black week-old water. Maybe whoever washed it this time wouldn't have to do it for the next two times. Or maybe we could halve the job, both have a go at it with some boiling water and a scrubbing brush for five minutes apiece . . .

I was still lost in thought when the dog started barking outside. I put on my cap and went out.

He was in the yard standing guard over one of the hens. I picked it up. There was no sign of the dog having interfered, yet it was dead. Its belly was grotesquely swollen and I slit it open with my penknife. Onto the ground spilled entrails and their contents: undigested bread, carrot, scraps of meat. The sight of it made my teeth grind.

Then the dog began licking it all up. I realized that he too was on a starvation diet, so I dropped him the carcass to eat. When lunchtime came I visited Eva.

The next day, I was in the shed fixing a blade of the plough when my wife strolled in and spoke her first words in a week. 'Hello,' she said, 'I just wanted to remind you that lunch will be at noon today.'

I didn't know what to make of this development. I turned up as appointed anyway, on guard for disappointment. Instead she had indeed laid on an excellent lunch and was talkative, asking me what news I'd heard from the neighbours. The silver pot still sat in the basin but she'd managed with the other pans. As is my custom after a big meal, I settled down in my chair and got out my pipe. My tobacco was not on the shelf.

'Oh, chicky, that's a shame,' said Mrs Pesotskaya. 'Perhaps I could find some for you, if you'd only do me the little favour of scrubbing a pot. And I might even be able to find you a bottle of vodka.'

God, it was tempting. I was dying for a smoke. A drink would be fair heaven.

I weighed it up. Just as well. Who should wander in from the yard but the dog. In his mouth he carried my little pouch of tobacco and a naggin of vodka. He dropped them at my feet and got a kick in the ribs from Mrs Pesotskaya for his trouble. She looked quite vexed but did not go back into her sulk. Nor did I wash the pot.

The next day brought torrential rain and I felt the time had come to make a gesture. Straight after breakfast I went over to the silver pot and noted that the interior was now matted with fuzzy grey mould. I took it from the basin, darted outside and placed it in the middle of the yard.

'Perhaps,' I explained to Mrs Pesotskaya, 'that heavy shower will wash it for us.'

She looked sceptical.

Later, when the sky had cleared, we wandered out together and surveyed the outcome. It was not impressive. The lumps of porridge had proved far too solid, the burned brown bottom impervious. At least the fuzzy mould was badly damaged. It would, said Mrs Pesotskaya, take several days to grow back.

Strolling back to the house, I risked putting an arm around her shoulder. She did not shrug me off. In fact, she had another idea. Why not simply use the pot for feeding the dog, instead of just pelting his leftovers on the mud? I agreed.

That evening Mrs Pesotskaya went to bed first and she was humming a tune that went *la li la li la*. I smiled smugly, knowing that hostilities were now completely over. 'Dog,' I said to the dog, 'I have survived her shouting, sulking, starving and bribing. For once I haven't given in.'

One evening, a month later, Mrs Pesotskaya and I were sitting out on the porch with our hands in a clasp. Suddenly a voice hailed us from a distance. With her sharp eyesight my wife immediately recognized the approaching lady on the mule as our daughter, Sonya. 'Oh, isn't it wonderful, Mr Pesotskaya?' she exclaimed, and withdrew her hand from mine.

It was. Unmistakably, it was. For a moment I too basked in delight at the prospect of this unexpected visit from our only precious girl. She visited rarely due to the strenuous fifteen-mile trek from Chelyabinsk town. But, as she grew closer, something else struck me and I hurried out into the yard to fetch the silver pot. Frantically, I stumbled left, then right, searching for a hiding place, before stuffing it into a bush. The pot, you see, was a gift from this same precious Sonya. She'd given it to us on her last visit and wouldn't be impressed to see it relegated so soon to holding dog food. Just as the mule trotted into the yard, I turned to my wife, expecting some kind of grateful expression, perhaps a wry smile to praise my discretion. Instead she was shaking her head grimly and her eyes were lit up in a way I'd come to dread. From the village church a mile away came the faint tolling of evening prayer. I realized I had shown weakness.

When supper was ready, we sat down to the table and my beautiful smiling daughter regaled us with exciting tales from Chelyabinsk. Still, there were pauses in the gossip occasionally, and I got the distinct impression that Sonya was peering over my shoulder. In that direction lay the kitchen. Perhaps she was straining for a glimpse of the new silver pot she'd bought us. Perhaps she was wondering why there was neither sight nor sign. When I looked over to Mrs Pesotskaya, I saw her cheeks getting a shade redder. When I looked back at my daughter, I felt sure her smile had drained just a touch.

The poor girl was exhausted after her long journey, so directly after supper Mrs Pesotskaya suggested it was time for bed.

'You poor chicky,' she said. 'You can come into the comfortable bed along with me. Your father doesn't mind sleeping out here on his chair.'

It would have been nice to be consulted.

And then she pushed me even further. 'Oh, and for breakfast,' she said to Sonya as they retired into the bedroom, 'I think we'll have a brew of sweet porridge. You and I can cook it together in that nice new silver pot you bought us.'

There was just time for her to give me a menacing look before she closed the door.

*

So again I was under pressure. Now there was absolutely no avoiding it: on the morrow my sweet precious daughter would be searching for that pot. If I didn't have it washed and ready, she'd be desperately disappointed. How could I make her understand? Should I explain to my priceless little princess the cost of living with a bully like her mother? That I do not like to be shouted out, nor sulked at? That the apparent peace is a false one, in which tending our farm has only ever been half my occupation, because keeping Mrs Pesotskaya happy has proved at least as time-consuming? A life of being ordered to trim the hedge now, lockspit the path now, sweep the chimney now, paint the door now and still hear 'Oh, Mr Pesotskaya, you've missed a bit!' And so on and on, until I learned to stay a step ahead in anticipation of each morning, whence would come her next mountainous dissatisfaction. Yes, I learned well, under control without a word needing to be said, but daughter, dear daughter, sometimes, just sometimes, I get an urge! Well, I got that urge and I said no – but it would be much more expedient to wash the silver pot.

I went outside and retrieved it from the bush. Then I took some hot water off the stove and poured it into what was now a blackened interior. I pulled up my sleeves and raised the scrubbing brush in readiness. But then I felt a presence behind me. Holding my breath, I squinted into the gloom and made out two eyes glinting from the bedroom door.

'Good,' hissed Mrs Pesotskaya. 'I see you finally faced up to your fate.' Then she withdrew and closed the door.

Breathing out slowly, I laid down the scrubbing

brush. I poured out the hot water. I went back out into the yard and replaced the pot in the bush. When I came in, I took my shotgun down and loaded a cartridge. Then I sat down in my chair and fondled the gun for a long time. Finally I closed my eyes.

'Wake up, you blaggard, in the name of the Blessed Virgin and Tsar Anatole himself,' said Mrs Pesotskaya just after dawn. 'Sonya is putting her clothes on. Soon she'll be out and looking for that silver pot. Have you washed it in readiness for her?'

'No,' I said, opening one eye.

'What kind of a father are you, to break his daughter's heart so?' she said. 'Wash it this minute or I'll go in and tell her the truth of the matter.'

'Yes,' I said, caressing the hammer of the gun, very discreetly pulling it back. 'Tell her the FULL truth of the matter.'

So off she went, and from within I heard urgent whispering. Sonya emerged looking very upset. I put down the shotgun.

'Daddy,' she said, not looking at my face, concentrating on my boots. 'Mammy said that you didn't like the silver pot so you gave it to your dog to eat his food from. Is that so?'

'No, Sonya,' I said, swallowing hard. 'I think, though, that the time has come when I must explain some things to you.'

She looked up into my face, hopeful that I would fix everything, the girl who I will always feel is aged four and a half.

'The terrible truth,' I continued, 'is that . . . well, the pot is gone. I didn't give it to the dog, but, yes, it was he who carried it off to who knows where.'

She began to cry.

'I'm sorry,' I said weakly.

My beautiful daughter continued to cry. I looked towards Mrs Pesotskaya. Her cheeks were not red; the big blue vein in her temple was not bulging. There was no need: she was winning again. As my teeth began to grind, I had a moment of decision.

'I'm disgusted, Sonya,' I said, 'with what that dog did to upset you. I've been far too lenient with him recently. I think the time has come to punish him.'

'What?' said Sonya uncertainly.

'Yes! Do punish him,' said Mrs Pesotskaya, animated again.

I picked up the shotgun once more.

'What?' said Sonya in disbelief. 'You're going to shoot him?'

'Yes, chicky,' I said solemnly, 'for what he's done to your silver pot.'

'No,' said Sonya softly, 'no, no, no!'

'Yes, go on,' said Mrs Pesotskaya, 'do shoot him. It's the only punishment he'll understand.' Her eyes were sparkling; perhaps she was still bitter over that time he'd retrieved my tobacco and vodka.

As I left, Sonya tried to grab at the shotgun but was restrained by her mother. They collapsed together on the floor.

On my way across the yard I paused briefly to get a length of rope from the shed and I collected the silver pot from its hiding place in the bush. Then I whistled for the dog and we walked down to the lakeside. Once there, I chose a suitable spot near an ancient willow tree. I laid down the silver pot and made a good knot in the rope. The dog was as trusting and loyal as ever while I tied him to the tree. Then I picked up the shotgun and took careful aim. In the last moments of stillness I heard the rusty cry of a single old corncrake while a scattering of quails called plaintively across the lake to one another. I pulled the trigger and silenced them all.

One shot was plenty: it blew a huge hole in the bottom of the silver pot. I then threw that cursed vessel as far as I could out into the lake.

To the dog I said, 'Don't fret. I'll set you free again tomorrow afternoon when Sonya has gone back to Chelyabinsk.'

When I returned home, my two women confirmed that they'd heard the gunshot. We didn't talk about it any more. Nor did we ever again refer to the silver pot.

When Sonya next visited, it was nearly a year later. I told her that the dog at my side was actually a puppy of the original dog, now fully grown. She seemed happy enough to believe me.

38

What exactly does it mean, 'to clean'?

Olten, Switzerland, 1911

Towards the end of his distinguished career, Swiss linguist Ferdinand de Saussure made a series of disastrous business investments. As a consequence his final years were spent in a state of financial embarrassment. With the modest pension provided by Leipzig University, he could rent only a small town house. Employing a valet, servant or maid was out of the question. For the first time in their lives, Ferdinand and his wife, Madeline, had to look after themselves. Considering their cosseted past, their friends were none too optimistic that the elderly couple would manage.

Yet manage they did, and remarkably well at that. Largely this was due to the formidable Madeline, who pared back some of their previous extravagances.

'Now that I am doing all the cooking and laundry,' she told Ferdinand on the first day, 'you will receive just one hot meal daily. Also, I'll provide you with a newly pressed shirt every second day instead of every day. So make it last!' Ferdinand was perfectly satisfied with the new regime, retiring to his study and his stack of unopened letters.

'You seem agitated, darling. What's the matter?' asked Ferdinand one day. His wife was seated at the dinner table, head in hands, rubbing at some flaky skin on her forehead.

'Tonight's the night the Tronchins are coming over for dinner. Remember?'

'So?' said Ferdinand, placing a hand on her shoulder. 'I thought you liked them. Won't we four have a jolly old time of it?'

'Perhaps,' said Madeline, 'but in the meantime I've a hundred things to do to get ready.'

'Oh dear,' said Ferdinand, moving away towards the pantry to see if he might scavenge something to eat. 'I hate to see you so fretful. I wish I could help.'

He began to root around for some biscuits he remembered seeing.

'Well, actually you can!' said Madeline.

Ferdinand froze in mid-bite. This was unexpected.

'I have to go out to the market for some fresh vegetables and a leg of lamb,' continued Madeline. 'You could clean the bathroom while I'm gone.'

'Damn!' whispered Ferdinand. And the biscuit was stale.

Before she left, Madeline took Ferdinand to the broom cupboard and pointed out various useful items that he might use: mop, bucket, bottle of bleach, tin of soap powder, gloves, hard bristle brush, floor cloth. After seeing her out the door, Ferdinand returned to the cupboard and took another long hard look at its contents. With a big sigh he pulled out a single broom. Then he closed the door.

Once in the bathroom, Ferdinand decided to time himself, just out of interest. He moved with impressive speed. First, he picked up various scraps of tissue and a faded copy of the *Zurich Herald*. Then he used the broom to destroy cobwebs located in each corner of the ceiling. Then he brushed the floor tiles, gathering a sizeable collection of hairs, fluff and dead spiders. The whole lot went into the little rubbish bin, which he duly emptied downstairs. On his return he decided to go the extra mile and used a piece of tissue to give the mirror a wipe. He was finished. He checked his watch and clocked the whole operation at six and a half minutes. He was proud. He hung around the hall waiting for his wife's return, rather excited about sharing his methodology.

'No, no, no!' said Madeline. 'It's not even half done. I thought you said you were going to help me.'

'But I did,' protested Ferdinand. 'I swept every bit. Look!'

'Perhaps,' said Madeline, 'but how long could that possibly have taken you? Five minutes?'

'Six and a half, actually!' said Ferdinand, an element of sulkiness creeping into his tone.

'What you have done,' explained Madeline, 'is "tidy", not "clean". In order to clean you must use hot water. You have to scrub. All "tidying" achieves is a surface impression of good order, but in reality the room is still filthy.'

'Where exactly?' challenged Ferdinand.

'There, for instance,' she said, 'and there and there and there . . .' as her accusing finger pointed out, in sequence, dust on top of the skirting board, ground-in stains on the tiles, spatters of soap scum on the walls around the sink and indeterminate discolorations under the toilet seat.

'Pshaw!' said Ferdinand. 'None of that stuff is really noticeable.'

'I notice it,' said Madeline.

'Pshaw!' said Ferdinand again.

'And more to the point,' said Madeline, 'Mrs Tronchin will be certain to notice it. Now I must go to prepare the joint of lamb. Please, Ferdinand, complete this task correctly, as you promised you'd do.'

An hour later, Ferdinand strutted into the kitchen carrying a thick heavy book. He had not spent the intervening period scrubbing the bathroom with bleach and hot water. Rather, he had been in his study, flexing his linguistic muscles, poring over his vast collection of dictionaries from around the world.

'*Nettoyer*,' he said to Madeline, who was peeling carrots at the table. '*Kempenn, putzen, glan, kirei ni suru, pulire* and *stada*. I have researched the verb "to clean" in every language from Irish to Japanese, Italian to Swedish.'

'And proved what exactly?' said Madeline with a sigh, laying down the knife.

'Proved, darling, that in not so much as a single language does the verb "to clean" necessarily entail scrubbing. Nowhere is it mentioned that hot water is essential. The Dutch, the Danes, not even your people, the French, insist on it. So why should you?'

'Because Mrs Tronchin is coming,' said Madeline, her eyes beginning to sparkle with annoyance. 'Now please go and clean as I've asked you.'

'No,' said Ferdinand, laying his book propped open

376

on the carrots in front of her. 'Instead I will leave you this most comprehensive of my thesauri so that you may peruse it at your leisure and see that I am right.'

He strutted away again.

When Ferdinand returned to the kitchen two minutes later, he was not strutting but running in panic. Madeline, he had realized, never took these things lying down. She might well be concocting revenge. She was still seated at the table, and her knife and the carrots were still there. As he'd feared, however, the book was gone.

'What have you done with my thesaurus?' he said. 'My precious thesaurus. It's the only one of its kind in all Switzerland. Really, Madeline, you must give it back at once.'

His wife smiled at him sweetly, but her mouth remained closed.

'Where is it? Somewhere in this room? You couldn't have had time to put it elsewhere.'

Ferdinand's gaze swept the room and then alighted on Madeline's face. He attempted to sense which way she was trying not to look. Then for the first time he took account of what his nose was telling him. In the air hung the familiar smell of roasting lamb but there was a hint of something else. Something else was baking along with the lamb.

In a way that belied his years, Ferdinand pounced on the large wrought-iron pot in the fireplace. It was surrounded by red-hot embers, and meat (and a book) were cooking inside at 200 degrees. When Ferdinand attempted to remove the lid, he was lucky to singe only three fingertips.

'Aaaargh!' he shouted and wedged the fingers into his mouth for relief.

'Perhaps you should use oven gloves,' said Madeline, 'or at least a tea towel.'

'Aaaargh!' was all Ferdinand could reply.

'But then again, you don't know where such things are kept, do you?' said Madeline. 'Meanwhile your precious book probably won't survive in there much longer ... Maybe you should think about what I asked you to do earlier?'

Clutching the sink for support, Ferdinand knelt down on the floor of his bathroom. Having already mopped, he went at it with a hard brush to remove some stubborn stains. His wife came upon him just as he was using his thumbnail to dig out black sticky matter from between two tiles.

'You've done a good job,' she said.

He did not reply or look up to face her.

'As you can see,' she continued, 'it really is an endless struggle. An endless struggle that is always without a final, permanent victory.'

Ferdinand still did not reply, though he did take a break from cleaning for a moment. He pushed his wedding ring up against his knuckle, scratching at some irritation beneath.

'You know ... the struggle against dirt,' she said.

'Yes, darling,' said Ferdinand, looking up into his wife's face. 'That too. That too ...'

39

A Hug will be permitted

Here, Now

If you are particularly fortunate, you will finally find
A spouse to both Like and Lust.
Not a brother or a sister.
Nor a bloody best friend!

Driven mad at regular intervals.
In blazing rows burn a hundred words.
And Like loves logic. Scalded it turns away.
While Lust stays under its quilt for a week.

But there is a thing more basic
Than speech, or even sex.
It's to touch.
It's being touched.

A Hug is what is called for.
When all else fails, the solution is
To press your animal skin
Against the skin of the other.

Sooner or later
A Hug will be permitted.
Sooner than later
Hug.

40

My first full day of married life

I try to be quiet, slipping back into bed, but the toilet is still flushing loudly. Her left eye flicks open.

'God!' she whispers. 'Wasn't that the best wedding ever in the history of the world?'

'Yes!' I say, laughing. 'In the history of the world. Ever.'

It is 9 a.m., on 6 January, the morning after this gorgeous young woman became my wife. We are in the bridal suite at Dromoland Castle Hotel.

'Every single person said it to me,' she says. 'That it was absolutely the best one they were ever at.'

'Yes,' I say again. I do agree. Even if we're a bit biased, it was a fantastic wedding, definitely top ten material. So much stress went into planning every detail, from the handmade heart-shaped invites, to the bagpipes-player outside on arrival at the reception, to the dozen dancing lessons we took for the first waltz. But it was worth it. Every little thing came off just as intended except –

I don't know – my head feels muzzy so I can't think clearly – yet I sense there was one fairly major thing that didn't quite pan out . . .

I decide to ask my wife if she knows what it was, but she's sitting up in bed, engrossed in reading the Dromoland Castle wedding brochure.

'I'm going over the whole thing again,' she laughs. 'I just want to savour every detail. I don't want to forget a single thing.'

I close my eyes and focus on the disturbance inside my skull.

My brain, I now begin to appreciate, is not happy. I felt fine on waking but a hangover is beginning to kick in and it's getting more intense by the minute. How many pints did I have? It's impossible to say. First, there were the two I drank during the meal. They were essential in order to calm the nerves for my speech. And before that maybe two glasses or three of mulled wine on arrival. But it was after dinner that the confusion really started. I never went near the bar but, as I circulated around the party, people were buying me pints left, right and centre. I must have started at least a dozen of them. After a few slurps I'd put down the pint and be dragged over to chat with cousins at a different table, where a creamy new pint would materialize in my hand.

I open my eyes and notice a pint glass of water on the bedside locker. That was a good idea. It would have been even better if I'd drunk it.

'These sheets,' says my wife with a big smile, 'it says in the brochure, are the finest oatmeal-coloured Egyptian cotton. And they are! Just feel them.'

'Huh?' I say.

She places my palm against the sheet and I feel the texture of embroidered leaves. Yes, that's nice. It does nothing to improve my hangover, though.

'Totally and absolutely perfect!' says my wife again, but this time I close my eyes and do not reply.

No, not totally perfect, I think, but I can't figure out why. It's not just the headache. There is something else. Something that went wrong . . .

'I bet,' says my wife, 'that the towels will just be to die for.'

A memory floats to the surface. Last night at 3.30 a.m., when my brand-new wife and I had eventually said goodnight to everyone, when they'd all had a chance to thank us for having them, and we'd thanked them all for coming, and finally it was just the two of us in the privacy of the bridal suite, we jumped on this king-sized bed to have sex. But I couldn't. It simply would not come up.

Though my gorgeous wife practically tore off her wedding dress . . .

Though she stripped most provocatively out of bra, stockings and panties . . . Though she played with the little fella . . .

I was too drunk and too exhausted. I didn't even have the energy to be properly embarrassed. I passed out in mid-session, slipping away to the sound of her laughing. Not at me! But not exactly with me either, I suppose. And saying, 'Maybe he just doesn't like me any more.'

So I was right. Something has indeed gone very much amiss. I resolve that I must rectify it immediately. I turn towards my wife but I'm too late. The brochure has fallen to the floor and she's drifting back to sleep. I reach out and touch her nipple but she burrows further down into the quilt. As I watch, a faint snoring begins. Well, not snoring exactly, more little snorty noises that are quite endearing. Between breaths she murmurs '. . . a splendid array of bath and shower accoutrements . . .'

'No, no, no, no, no,' I growl to myself in the shower. 'That cannot be the way our married sex life begins. On such an auspicious occasion, it sets completely the wrong tone.'

But there is still time. This is our first full day of married life.

'Right!' I say, glowering up at the showerhead, 'we are not leaving this room until we've had sex. Proper full sex.'

When I emerge from the bathroom, my girl is still asleep. Deciding I'll give her another twenty minutes, I pick up the TV remote and press to see if there's anything half decent on.

'Hello again,' says my wife when I poke her gently. We embrace and without the need for words one thing leads to another. I caress her hair; hands alight on my bum. I kiss her nipples; thighs wrap around mine. We pull closer. The temperature rises to such an extent that she throws the lovely Egyptian sheets to the floor. Everything is moving smoothly. My little fella is strong and seems almost ready to do his bit; even my hangover is in suspension.

Out of the corner of my eye, I sense the door handle twisting. Then someone is knocking loudly on our bedroom door.

'Hey, young lovers. Wakey, wakey!'

I continue rocking, caressing and kissing. My wife, however, has slowed slightly.

'Hey girl, hey John. C'mon, c'mon. It's time to get up.'

It's Karen, our chief bridesmaid, my wife's best friend. My wife has stopped moving completely.

'Thank you, Karen. Now go away,' I manage to gasp.

'Everybody else, just like you, John, is very much "up" already,' says Karen. 'They're all down at breakfast and going mad looking for ye. Especially your mother, John.'

I too stop moving.

'She said to tell you, John, that you never had a proper chat yesterday with your aunt who made the effort to come over from England.'

Will she just go away?

'So now,' says Karen, enjoying this far too much, 'she wants you to come down and say goodbye to the English aunt before she heads for the ferry. And have a photo taken with her. She specifically asked if you could manage to wear something other than your horrible stripy jeans. Byeeeee.'

With that Karen is gone. As is my erection. As is my wife. Not even pausing to catch her breath, she levers herself out of bed. She looks serious, she looks beautifully naked, she looks bewildered.

'Searching for your bra?' I inquire.

She nods.

'I noticed it earlier. You flung it over onto the coffee-making facilities,' I say.

She laughs and retrieves it, then puts on fresh panties from her case. I stay where I am.

'C'mon,' she says. 'You coming?'

'No,' I reply, 'I'm staying here.'

'Don't you want to go down for breakfast and to meet everyone?'

'No, actually. I was thinking it would be more romantic to have breakfast in bed alone together.'

Using the word 'romantic' is tactical: how can she resist something romantic?

'Oh, sweetheart,' she says, 'that's a lovely idea. Yeah! Feck Karen and feck your mother! It's the morning after *our* wedding. I want some time alone with my new husband. Let them wait a while longer.'

And so, mind made up, my wife does not hang about. First, she picks up the phone and orders our breakfast. Second, she tears off her bra and panties. Yes! I reach out for her.

'Down boy,' she laughs. 'I reckon while we're waiting for brekkie is an ideal time to try out the jacuzzi. There's no point in having this beautiful bridal suite unless we make the fullest use of it, is there?'

She turns on her heel, leaving me with arms still outstretched.

I grind my teeth.

'Tell me,' I ask, when I join her in the jacuzzi, 'have you a hangover?'

Mine has returned with a vengeance.

'Only slightly,' she says while turning the bubble jets up to max. 'But then I drank several pints of water after you passed out.'

'Yes, about that . . .' I start to say but thankfully she changes the subject.

'I think,' she says, 'that last night was an insight into what it would be like to be famous.'

'How do you mean?' I ask, sinking beneath the blanket of suds.

'Well, when you're the girl in the big white dress everyone knows your name. Even all the hotel staff, even all the distant relatives from your side whom I'd never met before. Strangers were just strolling up to me, calling me by my Christian name and saying nice things. That's what fame must be like, mustn't it?'

While my wife continues to muse about the fame game, I notice that I can no longer see her face over the swelling mound of suds. Maybe she put in too much bubble bath, but the foam is reaching epic proportions. No longer confined by the jacuzzi, it starts to spill over onto the floor.

'And whenever I went to the bar counter, there was no queuing, the staff always rushed to take my order immediately —' she says and then jumps upright shouting, 'Jesus! We're going to flood the place.'

So my girl, who just last night was a celebrity, has to hop out of the jacuzzi and pick up an armful of suds. She puts them into the sink. Then she scoops up another big load, but the sink is already full so she has to stuff them into the toilet. As she tries to flush them away, we nearly choke ourselves laughing.

Room service has left us two full Irish breakfasts. I'm feeling a lot stronger after the jacuzzi but I stick to tea and toast. The bedside phone rings. It's Mum.

'John! It's after eleven o'clock! Why haven't you come down yet to say goodbye to your aunt?'

'I'm having breakfast in bed,' I tell her. 'My gorgeous new wife insisted.'

'Yes, well . . .' says Mum, plainly fuming, but knowing she can't really pull rank on this one occasion.

'Don't worry,' I add to placate her, 'when I do finally appear I won't be wearing the stripy jeans.'

'Good! I should hope not. Anyway the thing is, after we check out at noon, Dad and I are going out on the hotel golf course with the McMahons. We're hoping to squeeze in the full eighteen but in these conditions it might not happen. At least I had the foresight to pack our orange balls.'

'Okay, Mum,' I say, 'have a nice round.'

When I put down the receiver I realize that I am not feeling that strong. Pausing just long enough to push my breakfast tray aside, I run to the toilet and throw up.

'Poor baby,' says my wife. 'Here,' she says, handing me a toothbrush pre-loaded with a big slug of paste.

I feel much better now. In fact, now I'm ready to rumba. But when I emerge from the bathroom my wife is over in the corner where we stacked all the wedding gifts.

'Look!' she says. 'The Hazlitts gave us Arnotts vouchers for €300.'

'Nice,' I say. 'I wonder what it'll all add up to, in the end?'

'Well, if it runs along the lines of Fiona's,' says my wife, 'then we can expect gifts to the value of maybe €20,000 with a breakdown of roughly a third in cash/cheques, a third in vouchers and a third in actual gifts.'

'And what's that candlestick-shaped parcel there?' I ask.

392

'That,' she says, tearing the paper so I can see, 'is a candlestick.'

'Hmmm, I don't like that shade of grey.'

'Fear not, dear sir,' she says laughing and scrambles to open another parcel. 'We have the exact same model in charcoal as well.'

The two candlesticks look the same to me.

'God!' she says. 'All this money, all those vouchers, all these lovely gifts. Isn't this just the most perfect wedding?'

I say nothing.

She turns from the presents and peers at me. 'Okay, what's the problem?'

I hesitate.

'It's because you want to have sex, isn't it? Isn't it? You won't be quite satisfied until you've done the deed. Fine! Though it wasn't my fault that Karen interrupted. If you're going to keep sulking until you get laid, c'mon!'

She throws off her dressing-gown, bounces onto the bed and lies in a mock crucifixion pose. She closes her eyes and opens her legs, saying, 'I'm ready, take me.'

Yes, I do want sex but this is not ideal. She is too angry and maybe I am still too weak. What if I fail again? Shudder! But I cannot back out now. I simply must perform. I drop my dressing-gown and clench my teeth.

And it goes well. Before long her anger has melted and I am on top and inside. We are moving in sync, rocking in and out, starting to freewheel downhill at an increasing speed. A cloud of euphoria begins to crystallize in my skull. Then there's a loud cracking sound from behind the curtains. There's another bang.

It must be a pebble or something hitting our window. Damn! I am losing concentration, losing velocity. From the hotel car park below comes the sound of girls' squealing laughter. There is a further clatter on the window-pane, this time perhaps a volley of gravel.

'Hey, randy lovebirds,' shouts Karen, 'we're all going home now. Byeeeee!'

I try to keep going with the task in hand, but it's already obvious that I'm losing altitude. I'm not going to make it. My cloud of euphoria is dispersing once more. With one last forlorn thrust, I give up. Head buried in the pillow, I lie still for a minute, catching my breath. When I catch my wife's eye, I laugh. As does she. Weakly.

She gets up and goes over to the window. We hadn't opened the curtains, so she does so now.

'I think,' she says, 'that you'd better come and see this.'

I follow her over to the window. It's a pleasant surprise. Outside the world has been covered in a heavy fall of snow. Despite the hangover, the vomiting and the failed sex, we smile.

'Should we go out for a stroll?' she asks.

It's nearly three o'clock by the time we eventually get out for our walk. We both needed another shower and then the packing took ages, what with all the clothes and gifts. Full to the gills with valuables, our car is now parked right in front of reception.

Also there was an unforeseen delay when I went down to check out. There was a misunderstanding about the bill, but thankfully I was able to sort it out with the duty manager. I don't tell my wife about that; I don't want to ruin her buzz. She's still chirpy as we

394

finally crunch into the snow down past the frozen fountain pool. 'Even the woman from housekeeping just said it to me,' she says as she grabs my hand, 'that it was the best wedding ever in Dromoland Castle!'

The scene is almost magical. Only almost, because the snow's pristine loveliness has been spoiled by golfers and their pursuit of orange golf balls. In addition to their unlovely footprints and trolley-wheel tracks, the golfers are also a health hazard. Though we keep to the path, a ball whizzes closely by us at head height.

'Evasive action is called for,' says my wife pulling me sideways. 'C'mon!'

So to escape we scurry across the sixteenth fairway, laughing, while golfers shout curses and call out, 'Where the hell do you think you're going?'

Then we cut straight in at ninety degrees to the path, up a steep craggy slope, under cover of evergreen trees. Within a minute we are faraway from the bellowing of short stout men with three-irons.

By four o'clock the early night of winter is almost upon us. The darkness is exacerbated by our walking in a dense part of the woods. No sky is visible above, only branches. Without any path to follow, we've spent an hour just wandering in twists and turns, losing all sense of direction. My wife has announced that we're now officially lost. But it doesn't matter; we've spent most of the stroll (or hike, considering the terrain) chewing over everything that happened yesterday and laughing.

'I just hope,' says my wife as we scramble up another slope, 'that the camcording man will have captured some of it. Or at least the photographer. I can't wait to see how they come out.'

'D'y'know what?' I am moved to say.

'What?'

'I love you.'

'And I love you too,' she says, just as we crest the hill and find ourselves at last out in the open again. It's a small clearing in the woods and must be the highest point for miles around. Before us we can see a patchwork of pale fields and yellow lights just coming on at a faraway farmhouse. And in all our meandering we haven't actually gone too far; behind us, Dromoland Castle is clearly visible, as is the lake and several parts of the golf course. From here the world is silent, looking beautiful in white. The only blemishes are the tiny figures of four straggling golfers crawling up the eighteenth fairway.

'Look at this view!' says my wife, stepping closer. I slip my arm around her waist. 'Is this not the perfect ending to our first full day of being married? I mean, after this we have some hassles ahead. We have to drive back tonight, which will take at least three hours, probably longer with the holiday traffic. Then we have to unpack the wedding gear and pack the honeymoon stuff ready for going to the airport in the morning. So, effectively, this is the end of our wedding and our first full day together. But it really is a perfect ending, isn't it?'

No. It is not, in my mind, *the* perfect ending. What would constitute the perfect ending would be much like this, but instead of having my arm around my wife's waist, I would lower it onto her bum, and she would reciprocate. I would unbutton her as she unzipped me. Jackets, jeans and woolly hats would be frantically cast aside as we got down to having sex right here, right now, al fresco, in this cold white twilight. And we would be wrapped around one another, trembling with desire, peals of pleasure piercing our loins, until at last it grew unbearable. And we would howl and scream news of our mutual orgasms so that the sound penetrated the heavy silence. And in the surrounding trees, owls would take flight, foxes would creep closer to watch, and faraway on the eighteenth green a golfer would be distracted and miss his putt for par.

But no: based on how things have gone so far today, it probably wouldn't work out like that. Either my wife wouldn't agree, or if she did then we'd both freeze to death in the attempt. Or if all else went smoothly, then good old Karen would jump out of the trees, flinging snowballs.

I am arm in arm with my gorgeous new wife, on a mountaintop, looking down on a beautiful snow-covered landscape. And we are in love. And we are laughing. Another failed attempt at sex would just leave a bitter aftertaste to what has been a pretty good first day of married life. I don't want to throw that away. (Anyway we'll probably be back in Dublin before midnight, so there will be a chance of a quickie then.)

I keep my hand around her waist, above her hips, and because complete honesty is overrated, and because it's not always helpful to tell your spouse exactly what you're thinking, I say: 'Yes, it is a perfect ending.'

But this is *not* the perfect ending. It's just a pretty good ending.

Acknowledgements

Thank you to all those without whom this
book would not exist (which would be a dreadful
thing obviously!)
Martin and Brigid Liddy, Mazo Meehan, Séan
Fennell, Niamh Liddy, particularly Declan Meade
and most especially Patricia Deevy